QUEST *for*
REDEMPTION

Other Books by Jessie Chandler

Shay O'Hanlon Caper Series
Bingo Barge Murder
Hide and Snake Murder
Pickle in the Middle Murder
Chip Off the Ice Block Murder
Blood Money Murder

About the Author

Jessie Chandler is the author of six mysteries, one (so far) stand-alone novel, and five crime capers in the Shay O'Hanlon Caper Series. Her crime fiction short stories have been featured in the anthologies *Blood Work, Down to the River, Learning Curve, Cooked to Death, The Law Game, Lesbians on the Loose: Crime Writers on the Lam, Happily Every After, Conference Call, Women in Sports, Writes of Spring, Women in Uniform,* and *Why Did Santa Leave a Body*.

As a kid, Jessie honed an interest in crime and punishment by avidly reading Nancy Drew, the Hardy Boys, Encyclopedia Brown, and Alfred Hitchcock's The Three Investigators series under the covers with a flashlight.

She currently lives in central Minnesota with wife, Betty; partner in crime, Angel; mini-partner in crime, Kayla; three mutts (Fozzy Bear, Ollie, and Nato the Potato); and three deviously cute cats. Fall and winter finds Jessie feverishly writing, and she spends springtime knee-deep in edits and revisions. Summers are spent selling T-shirts, books, and other assorted trinkets to unsuspecting conference and festivalgoers. Find out more at www.jessiechandler.com

QUEST *for* REDEMPTION

JESSIE CHANDLER

BELLA
B O O K S

2020

Bella Books, Inc.
P.O. Box 10543
Tallahassee, FL 32302

First Bella Books Edition 2020

Editor: Medora MacDougall
Cover Designer: Sandy Knowles

ISBN: 978-1-59493-569-5

Acknowledgment

The first thing I need to do is thank my publisher, Bella and Linda Hill, for their incredible patience in waiting for this manuscript. This book has been over three years in the making, and I was never sure if I would actually ever finish it or not. I cannot express the extent of my appreciation. I humbly say, "Thank you."

The book you hold in your hands has been a journey, sometimes painful, sometimes fun, and always from the heart. I have to give a shout out to my crazy family, to Betty, Angel, and Kayla who cajoled, ordered, and begged me to write. They have been cheerleaders who believed when all I wanted to do was hang up my laptop. I lost belief in myself as a writer through this endeavor, and they were always there to give me the kick in the ass I needed.

Lori L. Lake, MB Panichi, and Judy Kerr, you three have been my writing backbone. From brainstorming to edits, I cannot express enough appreciation to the three of you. Judy, thank you for driving forty-five minutes one-way to meet me at a coffee shop and write. Some days you were the only reason I kept at it.

Medora MacD, I'm so thrilled you're the poor editor who wound up with this "hot mess." Thank you for cooling it off and understanding where I was going even when I didn't. Your words were a lifeline.

Finally, to anyone who has struggled with depression, battled the grip of alcohol, tried to deal with love lost, this book is for you.

Dedication

Auntie Pearl, I didn't finish this before you left us. But you'll live on in the heart of Tubs forever. Thank you for loving me no matter what.

CHAPTER ONE

Summer 2001

"Mikala Ana Flynn, get your caboose in gear. It's almost five thirty."

"Coming, Tubs." I pasted a reluctant smile on my face even though she couldn't see me through the wall dividing the living room from my bedroom in her apartment.

My grandmother—Tubs to me, Tubby to family, Leah to friends, and Leahlabel Flynn to the rest of the world—was a clock hawk. We were due in an hour to the 2001 Goldsmith Foundation dinner at the Museum of Jewish Heritage near Battery Park. Even if we were Johnny-on-the-spot we were late in her book.

Probably where my father had gotten his sense of punctuality.

Ah, crap. Why did my mind have to go there now? The thought of him dropped me right back into a boatload of morose memories, exactly the state my grandmother was trying to shake me out of. I knew she meant well. And I knew she struggled too. Today was the one-year anniversary of my father's death. Her son's death. Death? No. It wasn't just a death. Call it what it was.

Murder, plain and simple. Cold-blooded homicide. And, as yet, unsolved.

Three hundred and sixty-five days ago my fourteen-year-old self walked into the house my father and I had shared in Key West, Florida—the same place we'd lived since I was six.

It looked like a World Wrestling Federation cage match had rolled through the joint. Broken glass. Trashed furniture. And blood. So much blood.

I admit I freaked the hell out when I found my strong, tall, capable father—an Army officer—sprawled on the kitchen floor, bleeding from a gash in his neck. He'd been a West Point grad, then an airman. After that he transferred into Special Forces.

Special Forces, dammit! He trained people to kick ass. How could anyone have gotten the better of him?

Terror had chased itself from the back of my neck down my spine, made my legs weak. Even now, a year later, when I thought too hard about it, that exact feeling shot like liquid lightning through my body, leaving me shaking and spacy.

I'd pulled myself together and called for help, then attempted to stop the unstoppable with a dish towel. I begged my dad to hold on, pleaded with him over and over and over again, until emergency responders dragged me away.

Military police came to the conclusion it'd been a burglary gone bad. The place had been tossed, but only one item had been taken. My secure world was blitzed—demolished. I was confused and pissed. I hurt so much I couldn't think straight.

My grandmother—my dad's mom—came to Florida from New York and helped sort everything out. She brought me back home to Brooklyn—to the house in which I'd spent my "formative years" as my dad used to say—from the time I was eighteen months until I turned six. But that history's another story.

Three hundred sixty-five days is an eon. Yet it's the blink of an eye. What a paradox. Boy, would my English Lit teacher appreciate that word.

I sighed, rolled off my bed, and tucked a white button-down shirt into a pair of jeans. Under the shirt I wore a white tank top so as soon as this fiasco was over I could lose a layer. Thanks to years in the tropics in not much more than shorts and a T-shirt, I hated constricting clothes. Summers in New York City were almost always hot, but the daylong drizzle that had been falling from battleship gray skies upped the humidity and reminded me of what I'd lost in the Conch Republic.

I trudged into the living room.

Tubs waited by the front door, arms crossed.

She looked me over. "You're damn lucky this isn't a black tie affair. Jeans? Honestly. Kids these days. At least your shirt is clean."

At five-eight and still growing, I could now look her in the eye. With a one-sided smile that took some effort, I said, "And I buttoned my shirt. Besides, it's not like you're all dressed up."

She wore faded black Dockers, a blue blouse with a bunch of flowers on it, and what folks down south might call shit kickers. A pair of reading glasses rested like a permanent growth on top of her head, ready to be whipped off and put to use at a moment's notice. She devoured three newspapers every morning and read like a bookworm on steroids.

"Is this a Western-themed thing?" I asked.

"What?"

"The boots."

"No. Figured if the rain came again I could stomp through the puddles with you."

I laughed. Tubs possessed a great sense of humor, and her mind was always busy calculating this or that. Romani ancestry had bestowed upon her dark skin, deep-chocolate eyes, and salt-and-pepper hair that she always wore in a braided ponytail.

While I'd inherited Tubs' russet color and bone structure, the added olive tinge beneath my skin came from my Italian mother. Thanks to the two of them, I didn't burn—a good thing when I'd lived in Florida. The nod my genetics gave to my dad's half-Irish heritage were his green eyes and a mess of dark-brown hair that glinted red in the sun.

When I looked back, I realized how amazing Tubs was. A child of the Holocaust, she was lucky to have made it out alive.

A survivor in so many ways. Before I was born, my granddad was killed in a construction accident while helping to build the World Trade Center's Twin Towers. Tubs had rallied and worked multiple jobs to take care of her only kid. She managed to put herself through college and then grad school. She was nothing if not stubborn, a trait I'd been told numerous times we shared in spades.

All that crazy perseverance of hers led to an appointment to the President's Commission on the Holocaust back in the 1970s. The commission came to the conclusion that it was high time the US did something to honor victims of the Third Reich. Eventually the United States Holocaust Memorial Museum in Washington, DC, was built, and when I was a little kid, we visited every year.

After that, she helped get the ball rolling on Manhattan's Museum of Jewish Heritage. She still worked there as one of the exhibition coordinators, and that's where we were headed today.

"Come on then." She grabbed my arm and manhandled me out the door. "Time's a-wasting."

* * *

We exited the subway at Bowling Green. Battery Park was soggy and quiet as we scurried through the rain toward the Museum of Jewish Heritage. The building was ablaze with amber light, sharp edges softened by mist that hung heavy in the air. Clouds pressed low, bringing twilight early, and threatened to dump even more rain on our parade.

I smelled the damp in the air, mixed with scents uniquely New York—an unsettling combo of bus exhaust, food aromas wafting through open café doors, and garbage rotting in the gutter—a world away from the sun and salt water of Key West. Once in a while I had to remind myself that this was my new reality.

"Thank you," Tubs called to a man who held one of the museum's huge glass doors open for us.

We scooted into the lobby, better known as the Grand Foyer. This was where Tubs would mingle and I would be bored as hell until we were dispatched up to the Events Hall for dinner. Then I would have to listen to gossip about the Goldsmiths, their foundation, and whatever fancy-schmancy award was being given out.

While she wasn't Jewish, Tubs' family name was Lautari. She was Romani—Gypsy, for the ignorant—and her family had made the mistake of settling in Poland near Lodz, about seventy-five miles from Warsaw.

The family was rounded up by Hitler's war machine, and Tubs had been born in the Lodz ghetto. She was the only one in her family of six to make it out alive. Her father bought off a couple of guards and somehow managed to smuggle Tubs out just before mass deportations to the Chelmno concentration camp began.

Whenever I thought about that, I felt physically sick at how close Tubs came to death and how lucky I was to be able to escort her to these pain-in-my-ass events. My father sure would have gotten a kick out of the fact that his impatient, moody, restless, and sometimes reckless kid would do something so civilized. That thought brought me full circle and I sighed.

Tubs tightened her hand on my arm. "Mikala, would you please find me a beverage?"

"Sure," I said. "What do you want?"

A woman I recognized from another city museum said, "They're wandering around with those cute little pink drinks with Hawaiian umbrellas."

"Music to my ears," Tubs said. "Mikala, will you please find me a glass of that pink concoction?" She patted my arm, and I put my hand over hers. We'd been through a lot together, and there wasn't much I wouldn't do for her, no matter my mood.

I meandered through the sea of overdressed humanity, and the roar of voices grew louder as more people arrived. This was so not my style. It wasn't Tubs' style either, but she got a kick out of taking highbrow society down a couple of notches by simply being in attendance.

She always told me never to underestimate the power of place and presentation, and she was right. Thanks to her association with the museum, someone she knew had pulled strings that allowed me to take the entrance exam to Stuyvesant High School late last summer after we'd gotten back from settling my dad's affairs in Florida. I'd scored okay and the school accepted me. Later I found out how hard the place was to get into. I didn't understand what the big deal was, but my acceptance made Tubs happy, and that mattered.

Tuxedoed waiters dodged through the crowd with trays of appetizers and flutes filled with champagne. I didn't see anyone carting around little pink drinks, though.

My stomach rumbled. I snagged a couple apps from a passing attendant and popped one in my mouth. The bite-sized turnover tasted good. I eyed the other, a tiny triangle of bread with a white smear of cream cheese topped by some gelatinous mess that looked like black beads.

I popped it in my mouth, chewed, then swallowed in a hurry. Fish guts on the dock was the first thing that popped into my mind.

So gross.

I grabbed a glass of bubbly off a waiter's tray and downed it before he could stop me.

Halfway across the space, I zeroed in on a tray of pink drinks with multicolored paper umbrellas. Bingo. Now I needed to get from here to there before the server's tray was emptied. I zigzagged around people, weaved through groups of Goldsmith Foundation donors and groups of groupies who liked to hang around groups of Goldsmith Foundation donors.

I was so homed in on the prize that I didn't see a blond girl in a black dress step backward.

It was too late for me to sidestep and I plowed right into her. She was shorter than me, but solid, which was a good thing or our impact would've sent her flying right out of her black high heels.

"I'm so sorry!" I grabbed her arms to steady her. The pink beverages and their umbrellas disappear from view.

"Shit," I muttered under my breath and refocused on my near-victim. It took a second to realize that I knew this person in the fancy dress. Embarrassment bubbled up from the bottom of my stomach. My cheeks flamed and my ears burned. I'd nearly flattened the daughter of the head of the Goldsmith Foundation. "Kate! Oh, my god. I'm so sorry."

The corner of her mouth lifted and two dimples creased her cheek.

My stomach did a weird flip-flop, a cross between horror and something else. Kate Goldsmith went to Stuyvesant, too, and was what I wasn't: one of the popular girls who came from wealthy families. When I first arrived at Stuy, depressed and aching for my dad, I somehow wound up on the radar of an asshat senior and his asshat friends who didn't like their school tainted by a lowlife military brat. For weeks I tried to be cool about it, put up with being shoved into lockers, having my books knocked out of my hands, ice cold stares, and biting, belittling comments.

Until the day I completely lost it.

I was already pissed at myself for screwing up a midterm in geometry when one of the dickheads hip checked me into a drinking fountain. Thirty seconds later my antagonizer lay sprawled on the brown-and-black-flecked hallway floor, blood oozing from a fat lip and one eye rapidly swelling shut. Kids cheered or jeered, depending on whose side they were on.

Not a good idea to mess with the daughter of a Special Forces soldier. My dad made sure I knew how to fight and how to defend myself when I was a tyke. The moves he taught me worked pretty damn good.

I'd been suspended for a couple days, he transferred somewhere else. However, the endless ridicule had already done its damage. Hateful words had seeped into my blood. I wasn't one of "them." My family didn't jet to Cabo for vacation or run up to Martha's Vineyard for the weekend. I was only in Stuy because someone took pity on me and my sad situation.

Winter semester trudged into spring. Kate and I wound up in the same Intro to Bio class. She'd sat a desk ahead of me but had a different lab partner, and we hadn't shared more than a periodic hello and goodbye. Though she wasn't overly snooty considering her upbringing, she ran with one of the many crowds I steered clear from.

It was all very black and white. She was born into money and I worked for mine. That drew a pretty clear delineation in our social strata.

And now, here she was, peering at me with a sideways look, half-grin still in place. "Mikala, right? From Bio. You ought to slow down. I think the speed limit is thirty in here."

I laughed. I was so out of my element. Why hadn't I stayed home in the solitude of my bedroom, safe with my books and Walkman, where it didn't matter what embarrassing comments might escape my lips? I said, "Call me Flynn. Otherwise you'll sound like my grandmother." I glanced around again. "Speaking of whom, she sent me on a mission for one of those obnoxious pink beverages, and I was hot on the trail when I just about took you out. Gotta run."

She grabbed my elbow. "The ones with the umbrellas?"

"Exactly."

"Come on." She grabbed my hand, gave it a tug. "Let's go."

* * *

Fifteen minutes and much giggling later, we'd chased three different wait staff through the crowded Grand Foyer and caught up with one before she'd run out of cocktails. We each nabbed a Jersey Girl—stupidest drink name ever—and found Tubs. She had drifted away from where I'd left her and was chatting with another couple.

Tubs lit up when I handed her the glasses. "Why, it's a twofer. Thank you, Mikala." She looked Kate up and down. "Who's this pretty lady?"

"Kate Goldsmith, meet my grandmother, Leahlabel Flynn. We go to Stuy together."

"Call me Tubs," my grandmother said.

Kate shot me a weird look, then said, "Nice to meet you. Tubs."

"And you." Tubs beamed. "It's nice to see Mikala with a friend. It's a rare occurrence."

I loved Tubs, but sometimes I wished she'd keep her mouth shut. My ears got hot again.

Kate said, "You've got a sweet, smart granddaughter."

It was my turn to give *her* a weird look. An entire semester of casual greetings and in fifteen minutes she thought she knew me well enough to call me sweet and smart? Wow.

"I certainly do." Tubs said. "Since I can't check my watch without dumping my beverages, Mikala, can you stop gaping long enough to see the time?"

I closed my mouth and did the deed. "A little after seven."

"Okay. We've still got forty-five minutes before they'll begin seating. Would you mind running down to my office for the *Faustian*? If it's not on my desk it should be on the bookshelf under Petropoulous."

"Yeah, sure." Perfect excuse to get the hell out of Dodge and enjoy some peace and quiet for three seconds.

Tubs handed me her key card and dove back into whatever she and her friends had been discussing.

I gave Kate a quick shrug and rueful grin. "Sorry to run, but..."

She took my arm again and steered me away from Tubs and company. "What's the *Faustian*?"

"It's about art the Nazis looted in World War II."

"I'd love to see it. Can I come with you?"

Come with me? *The* Kate Goldsmith wanted to go somewhere with me? Was the world about to end?

Kate gave my arm a squeeze. "Has anyone ever told you you're cute when you frown?"

What was happening? "Sure," popped out before my brain had a chance to catch up to my mouth. "I mean no." Jesus Christ, Flynn. "Sure, you can come, and no, no one's ever told me that."

"They should've. Come on, let's go."

I'd learned in the last fifteen minutes that Kate not only had a good sense of humor but that she was bossy. Her dad was the head of a multimillion-dollar foundation. Probably had to be bossy to make that work.

Man, I was so out of my league. What was I doing hitching my wagon to a shooting star? I plowed our way through the foyer. As my mind raced, I realized it was more like Kate hitched her shooting star to my wagon. She clung to my belt, plastered against my back so we didn't get separated. Five hundred people had to be packed in this foyer. The more the space filled, the hotter it became, and the more I wanted out.

The security door at the rear of the Grand Foyer lead to a warren of business offices. By the time I passed Tubs' card over the black security box, I was sweating. The box beeped and the red light turned green. I wrenched the door open and we slipped inside. The door shut behind us with a thud and I paused to let the cool air and silence swirl over me.

"Whew." Kate fanned her flushed face with a hand. "I hate these events. We all know Dad appreciates the support, but I'd sure rather be doing anything else."

"Who's we all?"

"My brother Will, my mom, and me."

"Won't they wonder where you are?"

She lifted a shoulder. "I don't care. They won't notice unless I'm not at the table when they seat everyone for dinner. Wily Will snitched a whole bunch of those Jersey Girls and is probably puking in the bathroom, and my mom is probably still talking to the award coordinators. Too many 'probablys' for me. I was trying to escape from the awards people when you ran into me."

"Uh…" I was such an idiot. "Sorry about that."

"Are you kidding?" Her ice gray eyes bored into me. They reminded me of the storm clouds outside. "You saved me from a slow, painful death. Now, where's that book?"

I led the way through a maze of hallways and found my grandmother's office door open. Sure enough, the book she wanted was on her desk. I grabbed it and turned around.

Kate stood at the floor-to-ceiling bookcase that filled one wall and was running a finger along the shelf, reading titles aloud. "*Salt Mines and Castles: The Discovery and Restitution of Looted European Art. Nazi Looted Art. Art Treasures and War. Hitler's Art Thief: Hildebrand Gurlitt, The Nazis, and the Looting of Europe's Treasures.* Wow. What does your grandmother do?"

I had a general idea but no clue about the particulars. "She researches art provenance and coordinates exhibitions."

"Provenance?" Kate echoed. She slid the *Faustian* from my hands and turned it around so she could read the cover. "*The Faustian Bargain: The Art World in Nazi Germany.* I knew the Nazis looted art but didn't realize an entire library on the subject existed."

I'd been surrounded by the topic my entire life so it wasn't as foreign to me as it might be to others. "Provenance is the history of a piece of art. Ownership traced back to its origins."

"Who knew I'd actually learn something tonight." Kate looked up from the book. Her eyes were so intense I felt like they scorched a hole right through me.

My stomach flipped again. I blinked in an effort to buffer the connection and occupied myself by retrieving the book from her. "Come on, we better get this to Tubs."

Kate trailed me out of the office. "Why do you call your grandmother that?"

Boy, she asked a lot of questions. "Don't know. Always have."

The rest of the short trip back to the Grand Foyer was taken up deliberating nicknames. Once we exited the offices, Kate took off to find her parents and I hunted Tubs down and delivered the book. Before too long, dinner seating began. Hopefully that meant we were at least half done with this fiasco.

* * *

"Thank you," I said to the server who'd removed my plate amid the clatter of silverware. The chicken hadn't been too bad, but the mixed vegetables were mushy. Yuck.

I laid my napkin on the table in front of me and wished I could fast-forward time. Although I had to admit, thinking about the time I'd spent with Kate Goldsmith was a pleasant distraction.

Now, dessert still needed to be delivered, and somewhere along the way the awards ceremony would begin with the inevitable speeches by too many people, most of whom thought they were a lot more entertaining than they were.

I blew out a bored sigh.

Tubs paused in her conversation with an art donor to give my leg a pat.

We were seated toward the back of the second floor Events Hall, and that made me happy because when this was over we could make a quick and easy escape. The time it took for five hundred people to filter out after the presentation ended was no fun. I swirled the almost melted ice in my water goblet and willed the freak show to get on the road.

Someone startled me out of my attempted mental telepathy with a poke in the back. The poker poked again, and I twisted in my seat to see if I was somehow in the way.

"There's that frown I like," Kate said with a smirk. She settled her hands on my shoulders.

Smack me dead with a feather. Kate Goldsmith was touching me. My brain exploded again. "Hey," I managed.

"Come on," she said, "let's blow this overblown Popsicle stand for awhile. I know just the place we can go."

"I, uh—"

Tubs elbowed me. In addition to all of her other tricks, she had a weird ability to hear two conversations at the same time and keep track of both. "Go on," she said. "Come back before nine thirty so you can escort me home."

I grinned. "Okay. Thanks, Tubs." Before I thought too much about it and balked, I followed Kate out of the hall to a set of fire stairs. We descended and went outside to the Garden of Stones, which was my very favorite place in the entire museum.

The garden was finished last year—a memorial to those who perished in the Holocaust and a place of reverence for those who survived. The garden's creator, Andy Goldsworthy, was a British dude who specialized in combining sculpture with living stuff.

Eighteen boulders were placed in a rectangular area maybe half the size of a basketball court facing the Hudson River. Dwarf oak saplings were planted in holes that had been drilled out of the rocks. The trees were still little, but as time went on, they'd grow tall and strong. They were supposed to merge with the rock. It was a cool idea, a reflection of how life could survive in the most unlivable of places.

I trailed Kate down a series of steps to the crushed gravel that made up the base of the memorial. The rain had stopped. Concrete benches installed along one side of the garden were still puddled with water. A waist-high plexiglass wall hemmed in the far end.

Kate pulled me through the stones and stopped at the wall. "I love this place."

"Me too. It's…peaceful, I guess."

She shifted to lean a hip against the plexi. "You're interesting."

Good interesting or bad interesting? "What did you expect?"

She looked across the black expanse of river. The lights of Liberty State Park and Jersey City, with its jagged landscape of skyscrapers, apartment buildings, and row houses, were softened by fog, kind of like an impressionist painting.

"You're different than the kids I usually hang out with."

Probably because I didn't have dollar signs after my name. "How so?" My fingers curled around the drippy handrail attached to the wall.

"You're not trying to one-up anyone, and you obviously don't care how you look."

Ouch.

She caught my expression. "Wait, that didn't come out right." She released a frustrated-sounding breath. "What I meant was, you…you do what you want. You don't follow the crowd. I respect that."

Well, jeez. That wasn't so bad. I figured she'd say the difference between her friends and me was that with me she was living on the edge by hanging out with trash from the other side of the river.

"And," she said, "You're kinda…cute."

What the hell? I ripped my gaze from the blurry reflection of lights on the water to peer at her again. My mouth opened, but I couldn't make anything come out.

"For a girl. You're cute for a girl, I mean."

My heart double-timed. Was she coming on to me? Didn't I remember her dating one of the jock lacrosse players last year? I wasn't sure myself about which team I batted for, but I knew kissing a guy did nothing except make me want to hurl. Self-conscious, I tucked behind an ear a few strands of hair that had come loose from my ponytail. "Thanks, I think. You're not so bad yourself in that skimpy dress."

The darkness muted the power of her eyes, but I felt their weight anyway. Kate released me from her devastating gaze and mirrored my stance, hands resting on the railing. "I suppose we should go."

We backtracked in silence through the garden and up to the Events Hall. At the entrance, Kate stopped.

Inside someone droned on in the midst of a speech. She said, "You made this night bearable. Thank you."

I gave her a roguish grin. "Anything for a damsel in distress. Although I think I was the one in distress trying to get my hands on those Jersey Girls. Thank *you*."

"Anytime."

I inhaled, thought about asking for her phone or pager number. Just to touch base. Before I could open my mouth, she pressed her finger in the divot in my chin, smiled, and spun around to thread her way between tables to her seat.

Tubs glanced at me as I sat and scooted the chair closer to the table. "Have a good time with your girlfriend?"

My stomach flopped again. "She's not my girlfriend."

A delighted smile lit Tubs' face. "Relax. It's a turn of phrase. That's how we referred to friends of the same gender back in the last century." Differentiating between Tubs' teasing side and her serious side sometimes took more work than I was prepared to deal with.

I bared my teeth in a faux grin and prayed for the night to come to an end.

CHAPTER TWO

"Hey, Flynn!" A familiar but unexpected voice startled the crap out of me. The pizza dough I'd been tossing hit the edge of the counter and dropped to the floor with a heavy thud.

"Bombs away!" Joey of Joey's Pizzeria hollered. "Dough is money, ya know." He scrunched his red-cheeked, sweaty face up to let me know he was mostly kidding.

Joey was a family friend, a beefy guy, jovial and always shiny from the heat of the huge oven that dominated the tiny boxcar-shaped store. The pizzeria might be small, but we produced some mighty tasty pies when the dough didn't land on the laminate.

Kate Goldsmith stood by the cash register at the end of a chipped red counter that divided the minute kitchen from the even more minute waiting area.

I'd died when she'd said my name, and now as she looked around at the aged interior of my part-time job, I died again. A black choker was wrapped around her throat, and she was wearing a rhinestone tank top and designer jeans with artful frays that cost more than I made in a whole month. I had 501s that were ripped, but I'd worn them out and didn't feel the need to buy replacements until school was back in session. A flour-dusted, sauce-speckled apron covered my T-shirt and thighs, and I knew there had to be white smudges of flour on my face. Just the way I wanted someone like Kate to see me.

"Joey," I said, "can I take five?"

"Yeah, sure, kid."

I peeled the dough off the floor, tossed it into a garbage can, and approached the girl whose name I hadn't been able to get out of my mind for the last week. On the way I grabbed a damp rag and wiped my hands off, then rubbed them dry on the inside of my apron.

"What are you doing here?" I asked.

"Good question. I meant to ask you for your number last Saturday. So here I am."

I leaned against the counter and crossed my arms. Might as well be direct. What's the worst that could happen? "I was thinking the same thing." A long, giddy beat hovered between us until I asked, "How'd you find me?"

I wondered if I was being chick-stalked and didn't even know it. Where was the fun in that?

"My mom talks to your—Tubs, and Tubs talks about you all the time."

"Awesome." Oh, brother. "So…"

"So," she echoed, and for the first time looked somewhat uneasy. "I was um…wondering…if you might be interested in a date—" She slapped a hand over her mouth and I raised my brows. Her next words came out in a rush. "Not exactly a date, I mean…er…wanna hang out sometime?"

Don't overthink, go with it, Flynn. "I'd like that."

"When do you get off?"

"Off?" My voice squeaked. "As in today?"

"Why not? I have nothing but time to waste."

A not-exactly-a-date sounded great after I'd had some time to panic and sweat and worry about what to wear, and in even a less-than-perfect world it wouldn't be my work duds. But then how often is the world perfect?

I shot a look over my shoulder at Joey, who was working a new batch of dough to replace what I'd fumbled. "Hey, Joe."

"Yeah?"

"I'm done in an hour. You care if I bail early?"

"Nah. Go ahead."

"Thanks, man." I untied my apron, still stunned Kate stood in front of me. "Give me five and I'll meet you out front."

* * *

I'd snagged two slices of pepperoni pizza as we left the shop. We munched as we meandered up Henry Street toward the Brooklyn Bridge. It was a good thing I thought to grab the pizza because it allowed me to keep my mouth busy so I didn't have to speak. I had no idea what to say. In fact, it was surreal to be strolling anywhere alongside one of the most popular girls in school.

As I chewed, I thought it was even more unbelievable that Kate had taken the initiative to seek me out.

Me.

The aloof kid, who hung on the fringe, who stayed as far away from the drama and bullshit that came from running with the "in" crowd as she could. I'd never been a follower. I was content to do my own thing, and the change of residence from a laid-back scene to an uptight horde hadn't altered that worldview.

Kate finished eating before I did, most likely because she wasn't trying to delay the inevitable. She said, "I hope you don't mind me showing up like this."

I stuffed the last of the crust in my mouth and shook my head. Once I swallowed, I said, "No. Not at all. Bit of a shock, but a good one."

Her dimples dimpled again. "Whew. I debated for three days on whether or not this was a good idea."

"Good idea. Definitely a good idea."

We stopped at the corner of Henry and Cranberry. Ruffino's, one of the many corner stores populating the city and one of my personal favorites, had its door propped open to let in the fresh air. It'd been a nice day, all blue skies and puffy white clouds, mid-seventies. At half past seven, the sidewalk cafes, bars, and eateries were in full swing. The pace of the neighborhood ebbed and flowed—unlike Key West, where things started slow, wound up through the day, and stayed crazy long into the night.

"Hey," I said, "want something to drink?"

Five minutes later, we exited the store with a bottle of Surge for me and a Diet Coke with Lemon for Kate. As we wandered down Cranberry toward the waterfront, she twisted the lid off her soda and took a swallow.

"How's that furniture polish?" I asked.

She nudged me. "Smart ass. I like my furniture polish just fine, thank you."

I downplayed the thrill I felt at her touch and wracked my noggin for something more to say.

Thankfully, Kate did a better job of small talk. "So I hear you're from Key West."

I shot her a sideways look and downed some of the green stuff. "You've been busy, haven't you?"

"You're…intriguing. All tall, dark, and moody."

I laughed. "Okay, then."

Kate's presence made my thoughts scatter and I struggled to pull them together. "Let's see. I lived here, in Brooklyn, with Tubs from when I was a squirt 'til I was six. My dad was in the military, and his position moved him around a lot. He sent me to stay with Tubs because he couldn't do the toddler thing and keep up with his military responsibilities. Once it was time for me to start school, Tubs convinced him he needed to settle down and be a real dad. He found a permanent post at the Naval Air Station in Key West and brought me down there."

"He hauled you from here all the way to Florida? That must've been hard."

I shrugged. "I didn't think about the transition as either easy or hard. It just was. I adapted. Sure missed Tubs a lot, though.

My dad was good about bringing me home to visit." I went silent for a minute, thinking about that last trip back I'd made here with my father. School had let out for the year, and it was a couple of weeks before that shit-ass day when my life blew up. When all our lives blew up.

Kate's eyes were glued to me, and I wondered what more she'd found out playing private eye.

"Can I ask you another question?"

"Maybe." Please don't let it be about my dad, I thought, but felt myself nod anyway.

"Where's your mom?"

Whew. Easy one. "Early in my father's first deployment he'd been stationed in western Italy. As the story goes, a pretty Italian girl from the town of Terracina worked in a café near the base. He fell for her long black hair and kind eyes. She fell for his charm. Nine months later I came along. According to my father, life was great until Mom drowned swimming in the ocean when I was about eighteen months old."

Kate's eyes went so wide it was almost comical. "Flynn. Oh my God. I'm so sorry. I never would've asked—"

I held up a hand. "It's okay. I don't remember her, and it's a little like she was never there in the first place because I don't have any memories of her anyway." Deep breath. "All right. Enough about me." I let that hang for a second. "There's an ice cream place off Water Street, near the piers. Then it's your turn for the inquisition."

Those gray eyes searched mine. Once she realized I was good, she lit up like a sparkler. God, she was adorable.

She said, "Lead the way, my shiny knight in chocolate syrup. I'll tell you anything for a hot fudge sundae."

Fifteen minutes later we were seated at a table on the patio of Dumbo Creamery with a bowl filled with enough ice cream, fudge, whipped topping, and cherries to choke an elephant, as my dad used to say every time he brought me here. When I was a lot younger, I thought Dumbo the Disney elephant made all the ice cream in the world. Not until later did I learn that Brooklyn's DUMBO meant Down Under the Manhattan

Bridge Overpass and regular old humans churned the frozen stuff. This had been our special place and frankly I was a little amazed I had shared it with Kate.

Across the East River the lights of Manhattan were beginning to twinkle, and the sight always sent a thrill down my back. "Your turn, Miss Goldsmith."

Kate licked ice cream off her lip. "What do you want to know?"

I tilted my head and regarded her. "It's Friday night. Why on earth are you slumming with me when you could be out with your friends? I'm sure they'd provide a lot more excitement."

Her eyes softened. "I've been watching you. In school, I mean. Not in a weird way."

"You have?" News to me. Interesting news. She was almost always bubbly and cheerful and could change the tone of a classroom by strolling through the door.

"You're not like the kids from here." She spooned up some chocolate. "You're intense. You're unfailingly polite, even when others aren't nice."

"Tubs and Dad drilled that into me." I corralled one of the two cherries the server had dropped onto the ice cream and popped it in my mouth.

"I saw you not long before the end of the year helping that homeless person after a couple stupid football dickheads knocked her down in front of the school."

I remembered that incident. We'd had a freak spring blizzard. Fat, heavy flakes deluged the city. It was icy cold. Those two asshole jocks rampaged down the entire block before lumbering without a care through the front doors of Stuyvesant.

A tiny, elderly homeless lady had been shuffling down the sidewalk through the snow, pulling a rolling wire cart filled with her worldly possessions. One of them shoved her out of his way as they'd steamrolled past.

She toppled in slow motion, like a bowling pin nicked by the ball. Her cart tipped over with her, scattering her meager belongings into the gutter. I helped round up her stuff and gave her the ten bucks Tubs had given me for lunch. She needed the money way worse than I did.

Then, over the course of the next couple days, I hunted those two idiots down and made sure they paid for their thoughtlessness. One showed up to school with a bruised face and the other a splint on his nose. Neither talked about how they wound up that way, and I knew it was because they didn't want it to get out that a girl had kicked their sorry asses.

I lifted a shoulder, self-conscious. "Anyone would do that."

Kate leaned toward me, her eyes intense. "No. It's not what anyone would do. Nobody stopped to help but you." She looked away. "I walked right by and did nothing."

How did this conversation become so serious?

"Hey." I reached over and put a hand on her clenched fist. Her skin was warm. My stomach did its anticipatory flip-flop thing that I was beginning to associate with her. "Next time I bet you'll be the one giving the assist."

"My friends laughed. Laughed at her and laughed at you for helping her. I told them to fuck off."

Holy shit. Kate Goldsmith told someone to fuck off? That made me feel...good? I scooped up a blob of whipped cream and swiped it on the end of her nose.

She laughed and picked up a napkin.

Time for a redirect. "What about you?" I asked and took another bite. The coolness of the ice cream soothed the not entirely unpleasant sensation that ping-ponged around my insides. "Hopes? Dreams? Big plans for the future?"

The smile that had tugged up the corners of her mouth vanished, and the playful twinkle in her eyes faded. Maybe I shouldn't have asked after all.

I opened my mouth to retract my words, but she said, "Hopes and dreams, yes. But not so much big plans." She fixated on the napkin in her hands, twisted it, and huffed a sigh. "There's the great divide between what's assumed I'll do and what I want to."

"What do you mean?" The look on Kate's face was dead serious.

She flipped her twisted napkin aside. "My father expects both my brother and me to follow him into the family business. The Goldsmith Foundation." She deepened her voice. "The Goldsmiths always do what's expected of them."

I raised a brow. "You channeling your dad?"

"Yes." Her tone was flat.

"So if you could do what you wanted, what would it be?"

In a heartbeat her expression shifted from almost sullen to animated. She leaned toward me. "I'd join up with International Volunteer HQ."

I'd never heard of it before. "Is that like the Peace Corps?"

"Kind of, but better. Check this out. It's based in New Zealand, but they do stuff all over the world. You can get involved in some crazy cool things. What I really, really want to do is go to Sri Lanka and help with wild elephant conservation. Or, if I can't get into that, they have another group working on Buddhist temple renovation and restoration."

She bounced in her seat. "Animals and buildings. Two of my favorite things. Once I'm done volunteering, I want to come home and study green architecture. My mother's a tree hugger and she passed me that gene. You can do lots of environmental good with concrete and rebar and wood and glass and grass. Maybe I'll find a way to incorporate our four-legged friends into it somehow too. Or not."

I didn't exactly follow her concrete, rebar, wood, glass, and grass plans, but I got the gist. Watching her talk about her passion was like watching a moss rose open in the summer sun. Somewhere along the line, Tubs had mentioned Kate's mom and the work she'd done for the environment, but I hadn't paid much attention. Now, I was on high alert. "Your mom's a real inspiration, isn't she? That all sounds really cool."

"She totally is. A family friend did the volunteer thing last year and had the most amazing experience. She went to Costa Rica and helped with a turtle conservation project. She said it changed her life."

"So why don't you do it?"

Her voice dropped. "My dad would never okay it. He practically forced Will into school for a business degree. That's the same route he expects me to take."

I scooped a swallow of puddled ice cream and pushed the bowl toward her. "You finish."

She picked it up. "I think that might be why Will parties as hard as he does. To block out reality."

Total suckage. To know exactly what you wanted to do with your life and instead feel like you had to accept some preplanned destiny had to bite big time. "Can't you explain to him how you feel?"

Kate scraped the bowl clean, licked off her spoon, and sat back with her arms crossed, gazing at a ferry on the river for a few beats. Then she locked those gray eyes on mine. Her intensity made the flutter in my gut ramp up again.

She said, "I've tried. Mom's on my side, but he doesn't want to listen to her either."

I'd grown up under both Tubs and my father's expectation that I give my all to whatever I chose to do, but it was always clear that the actual choices were mine to make. Maybe that's why I felt so adrift now—lack of expectation? If anyone thought they could force me onto a path I didn't want to travel, I'd fight tooth and nail. Too much stubborn in me, too much need for independence. The thought of being told how to run my life made me feel antsy. And from watching Kate's personality shift now, the prospect of filling her dad's shoes drained the life right out of her.

"Can't you just say no?" I asked. "Tell him you're not going to do it? What's the worst that would happen?"

She ran a hand through those golden locks, pulling her hair away from her face. "I don't think he'd pay for architecture school. And I can't fund it myself."

"What about loans?"

"I don't even want to ask. I can't stand the thought of another lecture about the importance of our Jewish heritage and the foundation."

"Couldn't someone else take over?"

"Not in my dad's eyes. It's Will and me." She thumped a fist against the table, making the empty bowl jump. "Enough about me. What about you? What's your future look like?"

My own prospects paled in comparison to either Kate's probable reality with the foundation or her wishful future in architecture and animals. Yeah, Flynn. You're the one with choices. What are you going to do with *your* life?

* * *

"That you, Mikala?"

I closed the front door and bolted it before tossing my backpack onto the recliner. "Who else would it be?"

"You hush." She turned from the sink and fired a wet dishrag at me. It sailed over the dining room table, past the recliner, and I caught it with a wet splat. Advantages to living in a five-hundred square-foot apartment were few, but a living room/dining room/kitchen all mashed together was handy if you were going to throw something at someone.

I didn't pause very often to think about it, but the apartment was certainly close and cozy.

The living room portion of the space held a TV, a worn green recliner, and a threadbare but amazingly comfortable couch with an ancient quilt folded over the back. Baby Tubs had been swaddled in it when she'd been sneaked out of Lodz.

The dining room table was four feet beyond the couch, across from a tall hutch filled with a collection of World War II memorabilia. In contrast to the heavy history behind some of Tubs' keepsakes, she'd decorated the walls with colorful 50s' pop artwork, making the place a lot less dark and museum-esque.

A couple feet past the "dining room" was an RV-sized, one-counter kitchen with chipped green and yellow tiles. A hallway off the kitchen led to our two bedrooms and ended at the bathroom.

I grabbed a handful of peanut M&Ms from a bowl on the table and popped a couple, crunching loudly as I dropped the dishrag back in the sink.

"Hungry?" Tubs asked as she pulled a casserole pan from the oven and set it on the stovetop. "I made sarmi."

"I am now." Ice cream or not, I'd eat her sarmi—a Romani recipe for stuffed cabbage rolls—any time. After Tubs'd been smuggled out of the ghetto, she'd lived with her aunt and uncle and their kids. The clan fled to Ireland, and although the Irish weren't exactly friendly to the Romani people, the government wasn't out to snuff them, either. That's where she'd met my grandfather, Harlan, and left the wanderer life when she was seventeen.

Ten minutes later, we sat at the table snarfing the cabbage rolls and sopping up sauce with thick slices of homemade bread.

"So," Tubs said after she swallowed a bite, "you're home late tonight."

I was supposed to have been off at eight, and it was now a quarter past nine. "A friend showed up at the pizzeria, and Joey let me leave a little early. We went to Dumbo's."

Tubs surveyed my now almost empty plate. "You're full of ice cream and you still managed to fit three cabbage rolls in that belly?"

I grinned.

"You." She gave my cheek a love tap. "Was this friend the same one you ran into at the Goldsmith ordeal last week?"

My ears flamed so fast I could feel heat radiate from them.

"It's about time you found someone your own age to hang around with."

"But I love you and the Art Squad."

Tubs had an inner circle of six close friends, and they called themselves the Art Squad. They got together every other week or so for coffee and gossip. When that crew of history-buff museum geeks got going, you never knew what stories might come out of their mouths. The Squad was dorky and fun and just my speed.

Each specialized in an interesting aspect of art. Rich was an artwork conservationist who stuttered when he got nervous.

Beni Higuchi was a police sketch artist—what a totally cool job, plus she told great stories.

Anton was a walrus-mustachioed gallery director—super nice and super boring.

Elizabet was a special effects makeup artist at the Jewish Theatre of New York. She could transform anyone into anything. I'd seen her do it.

Then there was Char, a crackerjack art historian and one of the kindest people I'd ever met.

Last but not least was Sahl Hadad, an Arab estate appraiser who could've doubled as a comedian.

Tubs lifted her coffee cup to her lips and took a sip while she eyed me. "I know you like the gang, Mikala, but one of these days you'll appreciate a more youthful outlook on life."

I stuck my tongue out. She grabbed her fork and whapped my knuckles. We finished eating and I cleared the table while Tubs squirted some Dawn into the hot water filling the sink.

"Thank you." She nudged me out of the kitchen. "Wipe the table and go relax. I'll finish up."

"Thanks, Tubs. I'll take care of cleanup tomorrow night."

"Deal." She wrung out the dishrag and tossed it to me, more gently this time. I snagged it and watched for a moment while she hefted the dishes I'd left on the counter into the soapy water and began humming while she worked.

I headed for the table but paused, as I often did, at the hutch. On the top, all by itself, rested a wooden puzzle box made in the shape of a house, maybe five inches tall and three inches wide. Various pieces of the box slid back and forth. If you did it in the right order, the house opened up. When Tubs left the ghetto, this and another puzzle box, both made by her father, were smuggled out with her.

I picked it up and felt the worn, smooth wood, darkened with age and oils from investigating fingertips. Once, years ago, Tubs' aunt broke the code. Inside were three family photos, a locket, and a letter written by Tubs' father outlining the horrors they'd had to deal with in Lodz.

Tubs had given my father the second, unsolved, unopened box. It was very different from hers, about the size and exactly the shape of a hardcover book. Three sides were concave, maybe two or three inches high. The top and bottom hung over those sides by about a quarter inch. The fourth side bowed out like the spine of a book. Inlaid on the top, or cover, was a brown, upside down triangle surrounded by four diamonds, and between the diamonds, four spades. Six hearts surrounded the diamonds and spades.

We'd surmised the hearts represented Tubs' mom, dad, and siblings. And the rest? Who knew.

Dad had always kept the box on a dresser in his bedroom. Every so often we'd mess around and try to figure out the puzzle. The box rattled when we shook it, so we knew something was inside. As much as I wanted to smash it open when I was a little kid, even then I understood it held a lot of emotional value and that wasn't anything we would do.

I could still see that box in my mind's eye and its loss speared me in the gut. Whoever stole my father's life had also taken that puzzle box and, along with it, whatever secrets were hidden inside.

"Honey," Tubs said, snapping me out of my thoughts, "let it go. Wipe the table and get a good night's sleep. You work tomorrow at eleven?"

"I do." I abandoned the box, took care of the table, then swung back into the kitchen and tossed the rag into the suds.

Tubs rinsed a handful of silverware under running water and set it in the drainer. "I'm working tomorrow, so if you need me, you know where I'll be."

"Okay." I gave her a squeeze. "Love you."

"Love you too, sweetie."

Once I was settled in bed, memories of Kate and the time we'd shared made me thrum. I was still in shock she'd come all that way to see me. To see *me*.

My head sunk into the pillow. I was exhausted and wound up all at the same time. I closed my eyes and replayed the exact moment I'd heard Kate's voice in the pizzeria. The thrill that'd shot through me zipped down my spine again. It was a feeling that would be all too easy to become accustomed to. And that was a problem. What would happen when school was back in session and all her snooty friends surrounded her? Did I think for one minute that her summer distraction with me would mean anything then?

Fat chance.

Fat chance or not, I drifted to sleep with the vision of Kate sitting across from me at the ice cream shop with that dollop of whipped cream on the end of her nose and a giddy grin as wide as the East River plastered across her face.

CHAPTER THREE

Since Kate had been brave enough to cross the river and visit me at work, I figured I could be brave enough to call her and see if she wanted to get together to watch the Fourth of July fireworks.

We agreed to meet at the corner of Waters and Pearl at six the evening of the Fourth and bum around South Street Seaport until the rocket's red glare burst off the barges in the river.

I was stuck working at Joey's until five and then I hauled ass over the Brooklyn Bridge into Manhattan. The sidewalks were crammed with people. Native New Yorkers walked fast, heads down, trying to get from point A to point B as rapidly as they could. Tourists wandered along at half-speed, taking pictures, mouths agape at the wonders of Gotham.

I worked my way over to Fulton, then trekked the four or so blocks down to Pearl Street. The temperature was in the mid-eighties, and sweat dampened my shirt by the time I reached the Titanic Memorial in front of the South Street Seaport Museum.

We'd agreed to meet at the base of the relocated sixty-foot lighthouse that had been built in honor of those who perished on the Titanic on that icy night in 1912. I didn't see Kate, but a number of our classmates milled around the area.

Great. Maybe if I didn't look at them they'd ignore me.

The lighthouse had been built on the tip of a triangular area the size of a three-sided racquetball court if there was such a thing. A sea of pavement hemmed in three sets of trees, and a number of benches were scattered around. Most of the benches were occupied, some by kids I recognized and many more by people doing the same thing we were, biding their time until the fireworks started.

Boulders of varying sizes, knee-high to hip-high, had been placed around the base of the lighthouse. One of them was unoccupied, so I claimed it and climbed aboard.

From my perch on the rock, I watched the ebb and flow of humanity scurry past. Too many people. So different from Key West. Even through the winter, when snowbirds flocked like hungry pelicans to the southernmost point in the US, I could find places on the island where I could be alone, or mostly alone, anyway.

Here, no matter where I turned, it always felt like someone was breathing down my neck. Didn't bother me most of the time, but right now, surrounded by my uppity peers, it did.

My watch read 6:16. I wondered if I'd gotten the time wrong or if Kate forgot. Or maybe she was standing me up. Why would Kate want to spend Fourth of July with me anyway? She was probably on some fancy rooftop with her friends, maybe even staring down at me. Me—who was stupid enough to have believed someone like her would want anything to do with the kid from the wrong side of a lot of things.

"Hey!" a voice called, ripping me out of my malaise.

I turned around so fast I almost fell off my boulder.

"Whoa." Kate grabbed my arm. At the touch of her hand, my breath caught. I slid off the rock and she let go once she was sure I wouldn't get up close and personal with the flagstone. My stomach dropped at the loss of contact. Cripes. Get yourself under control. Jeez.

"Thanks," I said, and it was then I realized Kate had someone with her I didn't recognize. The girl was shorter than me, with long black hair pulled back in a ponytail. Sparkling brown eyes caught mine, and she had a big smile filled with good humor. I couldn't help return her smile.

"Flynn, Ursula Thiebaux, Urs, this is Mikala Flynn, but don't call her Mikala. She might bop you."

If it was possible, Ursula's grin grew even wider. "I think I'm gonna like this one." She wore shorts and a yellow and black T-shirt. The logo on the front of the shirt was a bird with widespread wings. Above it read CENTRAL PARK, and below, HAWKS.

I said, "You go to Stuy?"

"Yup, I'm a year behind you and Miss Poke-a-long here."

"Hey," Kate said. "Not my fault I couldn't decide what to wear."

It was then I registered Kate's attire. She had blue jean short-shorts and a purple one-shoulder stretch top that didn't entirely cover her chest. The exposed skin was tanned and toned. I swallowed hard. Then I remembered I should look at Kate's face instead of her cleavage. God, what an idiot.

"You look great, Kate," I muttered and got caught in those gray eyes, losing myself for a second until Ursula cleared her throat.

I blinked and cleared my own throat. "Okay. What's the plan?"

Kate bit her bottom lip and scrunched her nose. Could she be any cuter? Gah.

She said, "How about we walk around awhile and then grab a snack." She grabbed a pager out of a miniscule pocket and pressed the button to light it up. "6:45. Urs, who's on the Fulton stage next?"

Ursula pulled out a piece of paper and unfolded it. "Moldy Peaches at 7:00. The big boom's at 9:20." She stuffed the paper away and rubbed her hands together. "I love fireworks. Can't wait."

"Come on." Kate slid an arm through mine and one through Ursula's. "Let's wander."

For the next forty-five minutes, we explored the seaport. I learned Kate had met Ursula a couple of years earlier when Will, Kate's brother, played hockey at Central Park's Lasker Arena. Urs, as Kate called her, was a hockey ace, a left-winger who was talented and smart enough that she'd likely score a full ride to Boston College, Wisconsin, or Minnesota.

"Wow," I said. "You sure have your future planned out."

Ursula lifted a shoulder. "Have to. I was born in Michigan, but I'm First Nations. My mom moved home to Nova Scotia when I was two, and that's where I grew up. She sent me to Manhattan to live with my aunt when I began outplaying the boys in my age group back home. They have a lot of hopes pinned on my hockey success. I'll do whatever I can to honor them."

I walked along the edge of the sidewalk next to the street. A group of kids approached from the opposite direction, so I stepped closer to Kate to get out of their way. My arm bumped into hers, and for a second I thought I felt her fingertips against my palm. Then the whisper of her fingers disappeared, and I wondered if it'd been wishful thinking. What was wrong with me?

I said, "From the sound of it, Urs, you're taking care of business. That's a lot of pressure. One day maybe I'll get my own life in order."

Ursula leaned around Kate to look at me, pushing her into me again—not that I minded—and said, "Don't know what you want to do when you're done with school?"

I was silent a couple of beats. "No. I don't. I—" My words were cut off when someone slammed into me. I stumbled backward.

"Hey," an unfamiliar voice said. "Kate! Lookin' good, babe." I narrowed my eyes. He went to Stuyvesant. Now I locked on. He was a football player, a teammate of the two jerk-ass jocks

I'd taken to task over that incident with the homeless lady. With him was a girl I recognized as one of the pack Kate often ran with—blonde, made up, and oozing arrogance. She was all over Mr. Muscles. Had her claws embedded in his steroid-infused biceps. I knew I shouldn't jump to conclusions, but sometimes I couldn't help it.

Beside me, Kate stiffened, and the hairs on the back of my neck jumped to attention. She said, "Hey, Nate. Stella Ann."

Stella Ann? Who'd name a kid that? No wonder she was wound so tight.

Stella Ann looked at me, then sized up Ursula before turning her attention back to Kate. "I thought you told me you had other plans tonight." Huge hoop earrings dangled from her earlobes and they jiggled when she spoke. She was dressed in a super low-cut halter and jeans so tight she must've had to grease herself to get into them.

Kate inhaled and held it a second. "I did have other plans, Stella Ann. Right here with these two."

Stella Ann laughed, a high-pitched sound that I imagined might burst from a squealing hyena. Made me want to clap my hands over her mouth. It took her three squawking breaths to get herself under control. "You're with," she pointed at me and Ursula, "these dumbass losers?"

My blood began a slow boil. I took a step forward and felt Kate's hand on my forearm. "They're not losers, Stell. They're my friends."

Stella Ann whooped again. This time I shook off Kate's hand. "Listen, Little Miss Hypocrite." I stepped closer. "Leave Kate alone. Leave us all alone and back the hell off." At this point I was nose to nose with the little snot.

Ursula took a long step and came even with me, pushing Kate behind us, which was exactly where I wanted her, out of harm's way.

"Wait a minute," Kate said. She attempted to wedge her way between Ursula and me. I had to admit we made a fantastic wall.

"Words are nothing more than words," Ursula said. Her voice was calm, and in contrast to my tense body, she appeared almost relaxed. "Words cannot hurt unless we let them. If Kate wants to hang with us for the evening, then that's what she's gonna do. Call us whatever names you want, but remember, what you fling at others tends to come back and smack you where it counts. Now, why don't you two continue your little date and walk."

Nate frowned. Looked like he was either trying to figure out what Ursula had said or was hit with a sudden case of indigestion.

Stella Ann humphed. "Kate, we'll talk about this later. I'll call you." She pulled Nate into the crowd.

"You might call, but I'm not answering," Kate muttered under her breath.

I let my own out and looked at Ursula. "Damn, you've got wicked skills."

She smiled, her teeth white against her dusky skin. "*Verbal Judo*. It's a great book." She prodded Kate's shoulder. "If all your friends are like that you need to start hanging out with some new ones."

Kate shook her head once. "You're right, Urs. I think I've reached my limit of entitled, pigheaded bitches. Come on. Let's go watch some fireworks."

CHAPTER FOUR

The summer of 2001 was the best summer I'd ever had. After that Fourth of July, Kate, Ursula, and I became the Three Musketeers of the Big Apple.

On the days Ursula and I didn't work—she stocked shelves at a bodega in the Bronx not far from where she lived and I kept Joey on his toes at the pizzeria—we'd all get together and roam the city like a pack of curious wolves.

We caroused through Central Park, the New York Public Library, the Museum of Modern Art, Battery Park, and even found time to make two trips to the Statue of Liberty and Ellis Island.

The 354 narrow metal steps up to Liberty's crown were magical and meant different things to each of us.

To me the journey represented everything my father had stood for: strength of character and the belief that the impossible could be overcome with persistence and determination.

Kate viewed Lady Liberty as a symbol of the freedom she wanted but didn't believe she could have.

To Ursula, the statue was an emblem of purpose and courage—a talisman of sorts that she drew on when the going got tough.

Each of us learned about our personal histories. We spent hours running names through genealogical computers. I found Tubs when she and Harlan emigrated to the US.

Urs was First Nations, the Canadian equivalent of Native American. In our research efforts, she managed to find a few far-flung relatives who'd brought their families into the country. She was of the Mi'kmaq, or, as it was better known, the Micmac band.

One of the coolest things Kate found out was that in the mid-nineteenth century, the Micmac created the world's first hockey stick. Ursula had followed in her puck-chasing ancestors' footsteps with her biscuit-in-the-basket touch. I had a sneaking suspicion Ursula already knew all that but didn't want to burst Kate's bubble as she filled us in. Ursula possessed a patient gentleness that I admired.

During both Liberty trips, Kate made detailed drawings and notations about the statue in a notebook. I could see her designing buildings that went beyond four walls and a roof.

All too soon, summer came screeching to a halt, and we found ourselves back at school. Nothing had changed and everything had changed. I was a junior, still adrift, although maybe not as wounded as I had been. For the first time I had two good friends my own age, and what a huge change. Needless to say, Tubs approved.

The other realization I came to was the reason for the funny feeling in the pit of my stomach every time Kate was near. Why it felt like sparks flew each time our hands brushed. Why I felt both thrilled and breathless whenever she rested her palm on my shoulder.

I wasn't allergic to the girl. I was attracted to her.

Her touch sent shivers down my spine. I liked Ursula, too, but in a different way. No fires were kindled when she put a hand on me, no charged flashovers happened when she slung her arm around my neck. She was my sister from another mother, and I'd do anything for her. For either of them, for that matter. These two, with such different backgrounds from my own, had somehow become my best friends.

I'd never had a real boyfriend—never wanted one—although on a dare I had kissed the son of my dad's Army buddy. That experience had left me wondering what the hell the big deal was.

Now, based on my physical reaction to Kate's presence, I'd bet that kissing her would blow that experience sky high. In fact, I had to admit that a favorite distraction while I pounded pizza dough at Joey's was daydreaming about what Kate's lips might feel like against my own.

Up until I met Kate, I'd never questioned my sexuality. Was I gay? Straight? Bi? Was it nothing more than an oddity that Kate brought these strange but amazing feelings out in me? I just didn't know.

Tubs wouldn't care either way. She was cool like that—had a few gay friends of her own, both male and female. She'd love me no matter what. I realized I was lucky. Not everyone's family was so understanding.

I didn't know where Kate ranked on the rainbow scale. She was a flirt, and she flirted with everyone, boy and girl alike. In all the talking the three of us had done, our sexuality had never come up. If I was wrong, I could destroy our friendship. I wasn't about to take that chance.

Kate still hadn't found the courage to talk to her dad about what she wanted to do with her life. Most of the time she didn't bring it up with me, and when she did, she said she didn't want to think about it.

But this was her junior year, and she needed to make some big decisions soon. I didn't want to add my complicated emotional mess to her burden so I became good at boxing my feelings up when we were together.

The three of us wouldn't get much of a chance to hang around together, and that sucked. Ursula, entering her sophomore year, was laser-focused on the upcoming hockey season, scheduled to start in mid-October.

The one class Kate and I wound up in together was Environmental Science. The topic wasn't exciting, but the opportunity to be with her the last period of each day was. We didn't have any classes with Ursula, but we all shared lunch, so at least we'd see each other then.

Before summer had ended, we'd promised to stick together no matter what, but who knew how that would go. Kids always promised friendship for life, especially in yearbook autographs, but I knew better. Nothing lasts forever.

* * *

The first week of school, all three days, whipped by like a hurricane. I was relieved Kate hadn't fallen back in with her old clique. She'd grown into a stronger, kinder person over the summer. I hadn't wanted to pry her head out of her ass, but I would've if I had to. She was so much better than they were in so many ways.

I straggled into Enviro-Sci, dumped my books on the lab table, and collapsed onto a stool next to Kate. Kids filed in, chattering about who had what plans for the weekend.

Kate's textbook lay open in front of her, but she studied me instead. "You look like hell."

"Thanks." I was too tired to flip her the bird. "Pre-Calc is already kicking my ass and I have no idea why I decided to take Early British Lit. I'm already behind and it's only been three days. I'm drowning in words." I closed my eyes and frowned. "And numbers." I dropped my head in my hands.

"Poor thing."

I felt her fingers on my hair. My synapses snapped to attention. Then she began massaging my neck. I might've skipped dying and shot straight to heaven.

"I might haul you home and never let you go."

"I'd be fine with that. As long as Tubs cooks."

"Mmm," I groaned as her thumb found a knot. "That means I can keep you 'til Monday."

She laughed. "Why 'til Monday?"

"Tubs leaves then for a four-day seminar in DC. I'd have to cook for you then, and we both know how that would end up."

Her hand stilled on my neck. "She's gone until Thursday?"

Her tone of voice made me sit up. She gave my neck a final squeeze, and her thumb might've traced my jaw before it fell away. Had my imagination gotten the better of me? Then I realized she had a calculating expression on her face.

"Uh huh." My stomach did its Patented Kate Flip. Could she be thinking what I was? In a light voice, I said, "What's rolling around in that brain of yours?"

Her eyes sparkled like they did when she planned something devious. "You should stay over while she's gone. I have a queen bed. There'd be plenty of room."

I wanted to leap into her lap. I restrained myself.

Kate had visited my apartment numerous times, and we'd been to Ursula's once. But never to Kate's place. I knew she lived in the Financial District in some posh condo complete with a doorman to keep out the riffraff. I was intimidated as hell at the idea of going home with her.

And then, the thought of a night in her bed? Even more awesome would be for her to stay at my place while Tubs was gone, but my grandmother made it clear I was to have no one over in her absence. And how could I keep my hands off her?

I cleared my throat. "What would your parents think?"

"They wouldn't care. I've talked about you and Urs all summer. They want to meet you. Up close and personal, not like at the foundation fundraiser where they only caught a glimpse of you."

I opened my mouth to answer, but the teacher shut the door with a bang. The room quieted. He said, "Don't forget about our field trip to Battery Park Tuesday. I need those permission slips back in by Monday, people."

Kate elbowed me and whispered, "See? We can leave from my place together and you won't have to get up so early."

She had a good point. I was not a morning person. "Okay," I said under my breath, wondering if I'd lost my marbles.

Nothing like leaping into the gaping maw of my unfulfilled desires. "Check with your parents and I'll talk to Tubs."

* * *

Monday after school found us hoofing it toward Kate's.

"Are you sure they don't mind?" I asked for the tenth time as we neared 90 Williams, a silver-sided, multi-windowed, fifteen-story building.

"No! Let me say it again. No, no, no, they don't mind. Now shut up and come on."

The feeling low in my belly wasn't excitement or the Patented Kate Flip. It was terror. I was about to enter a world far removed from my own. I shaded my eyes and looked up. The sun and puffy white clouds reflected off the shiny exterior. The main floor was taken up by businesses: a dry cleaner, coffee joint, nail salon, and a barbershop. I followed Kate to a corner entrance and a doorman opened the door for us. Just like I'd anticipated.

"Thanks, Hans," Kate said, and we slipped into the foyer, all dazzling white marble from floor to ceiling. I almost needed sunglasses. To one side was a security desk, and straight ahead were three banks of elevators.

Kate led me to the elevators and pushed the up button.

The elevator dinged and the doors slid open without a squeak. No surprise they were silent. I imagined any problem was dealt with lickety-split, not in a matter of weeks or months as sometimes happened at home.

We climbed aboard and floated toward the fifteenth floor.

"You okay?" Kate asked.

"Yeah," I said, ignoring my queasy stomach. I was about to meet the high-society, rich-as-God Goldsmiths of the prestigious Goldsmith Foundation. The parents of a girl I was afraid I might be falling in love with.

A wry smile tugged up a corner of her mouth. "No, you're not okay." She grabbed my hand and squeezed it. I was so nervous I didn't feel the usual blast of heat from her touch.

"But you will be just fine. Trust me. They'll love you. They already know you through Tubs, anyway."

It took me a moment to realize that the elevator had stopped and the doors had opened. Kate pulled me down a hall that zigged one way and zagged another, past one apartment labeled 15A. We stopped at 15B.

Kate unlocked the door and swung it open to reveal an octagon-shaped, tiled entry. "We're home, Mom," she called.

"Hi, honey. I'm about to leave for a meeting." Mrs. Goldsmith, decked out in a teal pantsuit and black heels, carried a matching teal purse. She strolled down the hall toward us, all elegant and self-assured. "Mikala, hello, sweetheart."

"Hey, Mrs. Goldsmith." I'd spoken to her on the phone occasionally when she called Tubs and I answered, but I hadn't seen her until the Goldsmith fundraiser at the Museum of Jewish Heritage last June. Where this whole...thing...began.

"Make yourselves at home. Dinner's in the fridge. Pop the casserole in the oven at three-fifty for forty-five minutes." With that she slid past us and crossed the threshold into the outer hallway. "I'll be back about nine and your father won't be home 'til late. See you two later." With that she wiggled manicured fingers goodbye and disappeared around the corner.

Kate shut the door and locked it. "She's on too many boards. Come on, I'll give you the grand tour."

I followed her into a room immediately off the foyer.

"This is Dad's office." She stopped next to the desk and I almost rear-ended her. I put a hand against her back to steady myself, her skin warm beneath the cotton of her Moldy Peaches T-shirt. I let my hand linger as I looked around.

It could've been an office anywhere. The requisite desk was a behemoth, all glossy dark wood. Files were piled askew on one side with a computer monitor in the middle. In front of the monitor were sheaves of papers and Post-its and other bits of scribbling on scratch paper. A phone and a small lamp took up the rest of the space on the desktop.

Who knew? The rich and famous could be messy too.

A black leather love seat sat at an angle on one side of the room, and behind it an entire wall of shelves was full of what looked like war-related relics. Which made sense considering the foundation the Goldsmiths owned had risen like a phoenix from the rubble of *Kristallnacht*—the Night of Broken Glass—when Mr. Goldsmith's father's jewelry store had been looted and burned by the Nazis.

I stepped closer. So many objects: an old black shoe, a cracked pocket watch, various pieces of jewelry in clear boxes.

Kate said, "Most of those were recovered by my grandfather and my dad after the store was destroyed. Dad says we can look all we want, but if we touch he'll find out and chop our fingers off."

"Unbelievable." I felt like I was in someone's personal museum, which I supposed I was. "What horror people inflict on each other." An object on a lower shelf caught my eye, and I took a step closer.

What was that? I skirted the couch, put my hands behind my back, and leaned forward, trying to get a better look.

Plain as day, a carved puzzle box sat between what looked like an old cigar box and a tarnished silver beer stein engraved with German writing. The box looked like the one that had been taken from my father's house in Key West the day he'd been killed.

Could it be? No way. Right? I itched to reach out and pick it up, to take a good look. My dad's box had a crack on one corner, not big enough to make it unusable, but enough to make it memorable. The corners on the front of this box looked intact, but I couldn't see the back. It killed me to not turn it around and check it out.

What were the chances that my puzzle box could've made its way to Kate's father's collection? "All this stuff," I said as I stood, "did it come from the store after it'd been ransacked?"

"Most. Not all. For years my dad has hunted for items that could be traced back to my grandfather's shop. I think in the last couple years he's found two or three pieces. It's so weird. He has to buy them—buy them back, I guess."

Was it possible Kate's dad bought my kin's ghetto heirloom? Could he have had something to do with the attack on my father?

No. Ridiculous thought. I needed to stop this train before it derailed me.

I spun around and almost knocked Kate into the couch. I grabbed her and yanked her into me, wrapped my arms around her. My frontal lobe told me it was to keep her from tipping over while my lizard brain started cheering wildly. God, she felt good. Too good.

Kate laughed and I stepped away. "I'm sorry." My ears burned. "For almost leveling you, I mean."

"Feel free to do that again. Come on." With that she flounced out of the room. It took me a second to realize I needed to follow her as I tried to process whether she meant feel free to body check her or feel free to wrap my arms around her.

Jesus. I was discombobulated and we'd been alone in her house for less than five minutes. Unaware of my inner turmoil, she pointed out the bathroom next to the office and moved on.

We followed the L-shaped hall past her room on the left, kitty-corner from the kitchen on the right. Next came Kate's brother Will's bedroom. Since he'd left for college and lived in an apartment close to campus, Kate told me Mrs. Goldsmith had threatened to turn his room into a study. But for now it still displayed the posters and paraphernalia of an adolescent boy.

Mr. and Mrs. Goldsmith's room was at the end of the hall.

We backtracked to the kitchen, which was as big as Tubs' living room and dining room combined.

"Want some soda?" Kate asked.

"Sure."

She opened the fridge. "Root beer or Pepsi?"

"Root beer's good."

While she rummaged through the fridge, I checked out the rest of the kitchen. Black countertops with white speckles gleamed. Shiny pots and pans hung from a grid suspended above a butcher-block-topped center island. Did anyone actually cook in here?

A bowl of fruit like you might see in a watercolor painting sat in the middle of the island. Real or fake? It all looked too perfect to be edible. Curiosity overcame propriety and I was in the midst of inching a finger toward a brilliant red apple when Kate closed the refrigerator door. I snatched my hand back and stuffed it in my pocket before she turned around to hand me a can of A&W.

I cracked the top, took a slurp, then followed her through the dining room, past a gigantic oak table that seated eight, and into the living room.

The living room was dominated by a picture window the size of a movie-screen that looked west across the city. I could almost see the Jersey shore past the Twin Towers and the other skyscrapers standing like spires above the world. They must've paid a pretty penny for that view.

A black leather U-shaped sectional sofa surrounded a humungous projection TV. I sure wouldn't have minded settling in with a bowl of popcorn and doing some heavy-duty TV time in front of that monstrosity.

The framed works of art hanging on the walls weren't prints. They were the real deal. At least this room was much brighter and lighter than Kate's dad's office with its dark wood, dark furniture, and dark memories. That thought brought me back to that damn puzzle box.

Kate said, "Let's bring your stuff to my bedroom and do some homework."

Her suggestion pulled me out of my confused musings. "Okay. Lead the way."

Twenty minutes later, we lay side by side on Kate's bed, textbooks forgotten as she showed me brochures for her volunteer program. Her arm was pressed against mine, and my skin felt supersensitive to her every move. I ached for more. I wanted to caress her cheek, kiss her pouty lips.

"...and then if I can't—Flynn! Where are you?"

I ripped my eyes from her incredible mouth. "What?"

She threw the brochure over her shoulder, rolled toward me, and shifted onto her side.

"Kate, what are you doing—"

She kissed me. The lips that I'd coveted for so long were finally on mine. Any words I'd considered saying died in my throat.

She was kissing me. Kate Goldsmith was actually kissing me!

Once I recovered enough to realize this wasn't another daydream, I parried enthusiastically, pulling her body tight against mine.

God, she felt good. As my lips memorized hers, I ran my hands down her back and palmed her gorgeous butt. The movement made her groan and that may have been the sexiest sound I'd ever heard.

Minutes later we broke apart, breathless and wide-eyed. Kate propped herself on an elbow above me, a half-amazed, half-amused look on her face. Our legs were entwined, and one of my hands had found its way beneath her shirt. The skin on her back was so incredibly smooth, so incredibly hot.

I was burning alive.

She dipped her head and nibbled my bottom lip, then soothed it with her tongue before pulling away.

My brain was mush. "I…what? Wow."

"I've wanted to do that since June."

"Buh—" Jeez, Flynn, I thought. Pull yourself together. If you were a boy you would've already shot off like a bottle rocket.

I slid a hand up into her glorious hair and pulled her to me again. This time I took the lead, investigating every inch of her mouth, her tongue, her lips. I'd always been better at showing than I was at telling anyway.

This time when we broke the kiss we weren't a frenzied, gasping mess. She'd calmed down, I'd calmed down, and in that moment I understood what fireworks between two people meant. And neither of us had gone beyond PG-13.

"All I can ask," I said as I trailed my knuckles over her cheek, "is what took you so long?"

* * *

After a lengthy make-out session interspersed with a lot of "why didn't we come to this sooner" talk that left me hot and hungry and happy, we heated the enchilada casserole Kate's mom had left us and chowed down like we hadn't eaten in days.

We laughed about the surprise of that first kiss and the longing gazes we both thought we'd hidden from each other. Kate told me she caught me checking her ass out more than once, and I admitted that somewhere along the line my feelings for her had shifted from friendship into something much deeper, but I'd been too afraid to tell her.

"You're a chicken." She gave me a smirk. "But a tasty chicken. I wonder if other parts of you taste like chicken, too."

And there was deadly, flirty Kate. A bolt shot straight to my chicken parts and I shuddered. "You're a dope and you're going to kill me." I paused, wondering if I even dared to ask the question that loomed in my head. At this point, why not? "Have you ever, uh…"

Kate waited a couple of beats. When I didn't continue, she said, "Done the dirty deed?"

"You dated that lacrosse player last year." I hoped I didn't sound accusatory. But the thought of that ape-like boy-man touching her…I shoved that thought out of my head fast.

"Jack the Jock?" She rolled her eyes. "He would've loved if I'd said yes. No, it never went that far, but far enough to know that he did nothing for me." Her brow crinkled. "If fact, none of the boys I've ever dated came close to making me feel a fraction of what you do. And no, I've never gone all the way with anyone."

She drilled me with those killer eyes, filled with lust and longing and maybe something else.

My breath caught in my chest. This was crazy. What were we doing? Was I a lesbian? Was she? Was this some experiment destined to blow up in our faces? Did I care?

No. What I cared about was this person who was looking at me like she wanted to consume me. The feeling was entirely mutual.

Unaware of my inner turmoil, Kate polished off the last of her enchilada and took a sip of water. "What about you?"

I burst into flustered laughter. This was crazy. Discussing our sex lives or lack thereof over enchiladas was insane.

"What?" Kate looked like she wondered if she needed to throw her ice water on me to startle me out of my hysterics.

I explained my train of thought, and when I was done, waited for Kate to speak.

All humor had drained from her face. "I don't know that I've considered being with a girl before you came along, but this," she put a hand on top of mine, "feels right to me. Way more right than I've felt with any of the boyfriends I've had. I'm willing to play this out, see where it'll go. I like you. I like you a whole lot."

I thought my heart might burst. "Me either."

"Me either what?"

"I haven't, ah, slept with anyone, either."

"Then we're two-of-a-kind, aren't we?" She leaned toward me and I met her halfway, cupped her cheek as I caught her lips with mine. She tasted of cheese and red sauce and I couldn't get enough.

"Girls," Mrs. Goldsmith's voice floated into the dining room from the foyer along with the sound of the front door slamming shut. "I'm home!" We broke apart and scrambled to rearrange the guilty expressions on our faces.

Kate grabbed our dishes as her mom rounded the corner into the kitchen.

"There you two are." Mrs. Goldsmith set her purse on the counter. "You're just eating now?" She didn't wait for a response, because she followed that up with, "Anything left?"

"More than enough," I said and helped finish clearing the table. "Kate left the casserole in the oven to keep it warm. The enchiladas were great. Thank you."

"Yeah, Mom, thanks." Kate scooped up the cups I'd set on the breakfast bar and stuck them in the dishwasher.

"You're both welcome. Glad you liked it."

Her food was great, but I liked her daughter a whole lot more. Wasn't about to announce that, though. "How was your meeting, Mrs. Goldsmith?"

Mrs. G gave me the kind of look an adult gives a kid when they've done something right. "Thank you for asking, Mikala. I've spent the last three months working with four different organizations to join together to change city code. We want to encourage a shift to sustainable development. I have one last meeting tomorrow and I think everything's coming together."

"What's sustainable development?" I asked.

"It's a great idea," Kate said. "It's one of the reasons I want to get into architecture."

I followed Mrs. G and her enchilada-laden plate to the table and settled into a chair beside Kate. I made a conscious effort not to touch her, and boy, was that hard. It was like once we let that genie out of the bottle, it was next to impossible to shove it back in.

While Mrs. G ate, we talked about green buildings and how they were good for the city. I'd never heard about environmentally responsible construction or how these kinds of green structures helped use less fossil fuels. By the time Mrs. G finished, I thought the entire concept was amazing.

"It can be quite complicated." Mrs. G pushed her plate away. "Coordinating things between the client and the design teams, the engineers, architects, landscapers, electricians, and all the pieces of the puzzle that go into it is a real challenge."

Puzzles. Puzzle boxes. Damn, would every little thing remind me of that box no more than twenty-five feet away?

I shoved mystery boxes out of my mind while we chatted. By the time we said our good nights I'd gained a new appreciation for Kate's mom. She was one cool lady.

Once Kate shut her bedroom door, I asked, "Does your mom knock before she comes in?"

"What?" She took one look at my face and knew exactly where I was going with my question. "Oh, yes. She does."

I hoped she was right as I backed her up to the bed. She wound her arms around my neck, and I whispered against her lips, "This sleepover business was the best idea you've ever had."

* * *

My lids felt glued to my eyeballs. Where the hell was I? Why couldn't I move? Then memory slammed home. I was flat on my back in Kate's bed. She was half-sprawled on top of me, with an arm across my middle and a leg over mine. Her head rested inches away and I could feel her exhale against my cheek.

The room was pitch black, and I wondered about the time. Trying not to wake her, I rolled my head toward her nightstand. 2:34.

We'd made out for a long time before we crashed under a fuzzy blue blanket, tangled together, still fully clothed.

I needed to pee but was reluctant to lose the blissful connection we had. I wanted to fall back to sleep, but the urge only grew stronger. If I didn't want to leave a puddle in Kate's bed, I'd better do something about it.

Careful not to wake her, I sat up.

She mumbled, rolled onto her back, then quieted. Once her breathing evened out again, I slid off the bed and stumbled out the door and into the bathroom.

As I took care of biz, the thought of that damn box—right next door—flared hard. My fingers itched to touch it, to see if it felt as familiar as it looked.

I stood in the bathroom doorway and contemplated my options. I could go back to bed. I could walk into that office and take a peek. I could get busted taking a peek and find myself kicked out of the Goldsmiths' house with orders to never return, which might happen anyway if Kate's mom and dad found out what we'd been doing in her room.

I listened hard for thirty seconds.

Silence.

Man, this place had to have some serious insulation to drown out the sounds of the city even this late at night. The pull I felt to solve this mystery was as irresistible as Kate herself. If there was even the slightest chance that box could be the one, I needed to know. And then find out how it came into Mr. Goldsmith's possession.

I felt my way down the dark hall and into the office.

Ambient light seeped through the uncovered window and illuminated the room enough that I was able to find the lamp and switch it on without running into anything. The bulb was dim, illuminating a much smaller area than I'd expected. That meant I was going to have to pick up the box and bring it to the light.

No time like the present. I'd come this far.

With a deep breath, I crept over to the wall of shelves and held my breath as I slid the box off the shelf. It felt familiar in my hands and the weight seemed about right.

My heart thumped harder as I held it under the light. It had the same wood inlay. I slid my fingertips to the sections that I knew moved, and felt the pieces slide.

My hands began to shake. I turned it around, looking for the cracked corner.

This box held no damage. Disappointment and confusion warred within me. This wasn't my father's puzzle box. But it was identical in every other way. Did Tubs' dad make this one too?

A skritching sound coming from the front door scared the shit out of me. I almost dropped the box.

A key rattled in the lock.

Heart lodged in my throat, I doused the light, but in my panicked groping almost knocked it over.

The click and snick as the deadbolt retracted was so loud. No way was I going to be able to replace the box, much less escape.

Where to hide? Behind the couch or under the desk were my two options.

I axed the couch. Too exposed.

Through the study door I watched a beam of light widen across the foyer floor as the door swung open. In a split second, I'd be visible to whoever was coming in.

I scrambled around the desk, shoved the chair out of the way, and slid under it. Thank God the desk was huge or I never would've fit. I hugged the puzzle box tight against my chest and held my breath.

What a cliché. Hiding under a stinking desk.

The door closed with a thump, cutting off the hallway light. Another second and the deadbolt reengaged.

I remembered then that Kate's mom mentioned Mr. Goldsmith was coming home late. Why hadn't I remembered that?

With any luck, he'd bypass the office and head straight for bed.

The sound of a heavy sigh and a thump on the desk above my head nearly made me scream.

He was *right* fricking there.

Then came the familiar click of the lamp and light spilled on the carpet outside the desk.

Shit, shit, shit.

I pressed the back of my head against the side of the desk. I was dead meat. So stupid. Why hadn't I gone back to Kate's room, snuggled up to her, and drifted off to sleep? Because I was too goddamn nosy, that's why.

Seconds dragged by like hours. Inches from the top of my head, I heard a couple latches pop.

Paper rustled, as if he were sorting through a stack of sheets. Then he yawned, loud and long, and mumbled, "Enough for tonight."

The light clicked off, and his footsteps faded away.

CHAPTER FIVE

The next morning, I stood in front of Kate's enormous living room window, looking out at a perfect September day while shoveling Froot Loops into my mouth. I'd already dressed and was waiting for Kate to finish up.

I was very relieved both Kate's parents had already left for work. I still couldn't believe I hadn't been nailed last night.

While I'd found out the puzzle box wasn't my father's, I now had more questions than answers. Why did Mr. Goldsmith have a box identical to ours? Did his father know my great-grandfather? I didn't dare ask because then it would come out that I'd been in the no-go zone touching the forbidden relics. Nothing like alienating the parents of my brand-new girlfriend right out of the gate.

Girlfriend. Was Kate really my girlfriend? We hadn't gotten that far in discussing our relationship last night. We were too busy getting busy.

I spooned a heaping mound of Loops into my mouth. People on the ground looked like ants. The Twin Towers were enormous. It felt like I could reach out and touch them even though they were five blocks away.

"Hey, you," Kate said. She wrapped her arms around me from behind and nestled her chin in my neck.

Sparks shot through my body. I still couldn't believe we were here. I swallowed and pressed my cheek against hers. "What time is it?"

She checked her watch. "8:45. We have plenty of time."

Sweet. The more alone time I had with Kate the better I liked it. For once the world looked bright and shiny, full of hope and possibility. I hadn't even realized until that moment I hadn't felt like that in a long time.

I scooped up more cereal and twisted around to offer it to her. I aimed the spoon toward her mouth and jerked my hand to a stop when she gasped, her eyes locked on the picture window.

"What?" I dumped the spoon back in the bowl and followed her gaze. A huge, bright red ball of fire spewed out of two sides of one of the Twin Towers. Debris sailed from the building and pieces of the façade peeled away to fall in huge chunks to the ground. "Oh my God!" I yelped. "What the hell?"

Kate stepped from behind to beside me.

I grabbed her hand. She threaded her fingers through mine. Her other hand clamped over her mouth. Between her fingers she croaked, "I don't know. I thought I saw...no. No way."

I glanced back at the horrifying sight. "Saw what?"

"A plane."

"An airplane?"

"Yeah. No. I don't know. All those people..."

The worst thought ever blossomed in my mind. "Kate," I said, "where are your mom and dad?"

She whispered, "I don't know." She put a hand to her forehead and squeezed her eyes shut. "Dad. Today's Tuesday. He has a foundation meeting every Tuesday at the museum..." She trailed off.

"At the museum. He's at the Museum of Jewish Heritage?"

"Yes."

"That's about ten blocks from the Trade Center. That's good. What about your mom? Where was she going for that meeting?"

I glanced away from the sickening sight at Kate. She pulled away and began pacing in front of the window.

"Shit." She cupped her forehead again, pivoted, and charged through the dining room into the kitchen.

I followed.

She raced to the refrigerator and ripped off a paper affixed to the metal surface with four apple-shaped magnets.

"Every week Mom leaves a list of appointments and phone numbers where she'll be, just in case." She slapped the sheet on the counter and ran her finger down it. "Here. She's here. At the National Development and Research Institute."

"Where is that?"

"I don't know." She yanked a drawer open and rummaged through it. "Her addresses—maybe the…here." She yanked out a pale green book held shut with a gold band. She ripped it off and flipped through the pages. "2 World Trade Center. Thirty-ninth floor." She looked up at me and I can testify that when they say the blood drains from someone's face, it's true. "Jesus fucking Christ. Which tower was hit?"

We dashed back to the window. I had no idea which tower was which. Flames licked out between the columns, but now thick black smoke billowed from the impact site, or the bomb site, or whatever it was. Plumes of smoke were so dense it was hard to see the top of the structure.

Kate dragged her fingers through her hair. "Okay, okay, okay. Dad always says the tower on the left is number two and the tower on the right is number one. All right. That means she's in the other one. She's okay—"

The ringing of the phone startled us both. Kate dove for the cordless sitting on an end table next to the couch.

"Hello!" Kate shouted, her voice up about sixteen octaves. "Tubs. We're fine. Hang on, she's right here."

She thrust the phone at me.

I bobbled it, then got hold of it and pressed it against my ear.

"Mikala, you're both okay?" She sounded winded and worried.

"Yes. We haven't left for the field trip yet."

"Are Kate's parents home?"

"No."

"Okay. Listen to me, honey. You two need to get out. Now. You're not safe. Go home. No subway, no cab. On foot. Okay?"

"But—"

"No buts. Leave the second we're off the phone. I'll be in touch as soon as I can. There's a cell phone in the bottom drawer of my dresser under my granny panties. Grab it and turn it on. Keep it on you and keep it charged at all times, okay?"

My brain whirled. "No subways and find the cell phone."

"Yes. I love you, Mikala. You'll both be fine."

Before I could get another word in, the line went dead. I hung up. "Kate, we need to leave. Now. Grab your backpack and get your shoes on."

The lobby was empty when we emerged from the elevator and tore out of the building. The tense silence we'd been suspended in was shattered as soon as we hit the sidewalk. Multitudes of sirens screamed, echoing through the streets. So many people faced the same direction, watching the black plumes of smoke pour out of the wounded skyscraper. Chills raced down my spine. We hustled toward the entrance to the Brooklyn Bridge. Before us was a picture perfect day—cloudless and bright blue. Behind us, charcoal clouds of death discolored the heavens.

We made it about a quarter of the way across the bridge, jogging around a horde of terrified individuals intent on getting their own asses out of Manhattan, when a tremendous explosion shook the bridge.

Every single person on the walkway spun around en masse.

A fireball shot out of the middle of the second tower.

"NO!" Kate screamed. "Mom!"

A tall Asian guy with muscles and tattoos said, "Shit, man. It was a plane. I saw it. Maybe a 747. We're under attack."

I grabbed Kate's shirt and took off, dragging her behind me. I weaved through the stunned mob as fast as I could. Any moment they'd bolt, and I didn't want to be trampled.

Thirty hard-won minutes later I was never so happy to see the familiar red and cream-colored entrance to our apartment.

Sirens still screamed, both from afar and nearby. The shrieking helped propel us the last few hundred feet to what I prayed was at least temporary safety. We leaped up the four steps to the entrance and charged to the bank of two elevators.

I pressed the call button while Kate chanted, "Come, on, come on, come on," under her breath.

The doors squeaked open and then we were on a slow, grinding ride to the ninth floor. My hand trembled as I keyed the door to the apartment open and we dashed inside.

"I'll be right back," I told Kate and bolted for my grandmother's room.

Sure enough, hidden under her bloomers was a Motorola flip phone and a charging cord. What the hell was Tubs doing with a cell phone in her unmentionables drawer?

I keyed it on. Fully charged. I grabbed the cord and stuffed it in a pocket along with the phone.

Next stop, my bedroom. A mini boom box sat on my desk. I snatched it up, switched it on to make sure the batteries still worked, and hoofed it back to Kate.

She handed me a glass of water, which I downed in three huge swallows. "Thanks," I gasped and dragged my forearm over my lips. My mouth tasted like burned cardboard. "Let's head up to the roof."

Kate nodded, her expression stoic. "Thank you."

"Haven't done anything to be thanked for. Come here." I pulled her into my arms.

She held on for dear life.

I buried my face in her hair and hung on to this blip of normalcy.

She pulled back and gave me a quick, solemn peck on the forehead. "You're my guardian angel."

"No angel here." I gave her a grim smile. "Come on."

The roof had fewer people milling about than I expected. We all lined up along the west side of the building, mesmerized by the thick blue-black smoke pouring from each of the towers. The smoke from the two buildings merged as it drifted at an angle toward us, caught on a current of wind.

I balanced the radio on the edge of the wall against a rusted metal safety bar of questionable integrity and turned it on to New York's news station, 1010 WINS.

In a tone of hushed horror, the announcer described what we were seeing. He speculated that two airplanes had been hijacked and used as massive bombs. The Pentagon had also been hit, and another plane had crashed somewhere in Pennsylvania.

It felt like we were caught in the middle of the worst imaginable nightmare. My entire body trembled.

"Hey." Kate pressed herself against my back and pressed her chin into my shoulder. It felt like we were back at her place, looking out the picture window before the world blew up right before our eyes. I wasn't sure I'd ever be able to look out that window again.

I whispered, "Aren't you worried about people seeing?"

She pressed her lips to my skin. "Seeing what?"

"Us. This." I pressed my back into her.

"Fuck 'em. If someone wants to bitch about this public demonstration of affection in light of that," she nodded toward the burning buildings, "I don't give a shit. You're all that's holding me together right now."

If she didn't care, I wasn't going to either.

For long minutes no one looked away from the impossible.

Without a speck of warning, it was as if the south tower had turned into sugar and someone poured water on it. The building dissolved in on itself. With an incredible whoosh, it disappeared from view. In its place, an immense, roiling, dark gray cloud of dust and debris rose, a mass of darkness filled with the detritus of death.

"No!" Kate howled in my ear.

"Shit! Oh, shit. Look at that," another person shouted.

I whipped around to face Kate and pivoted her away from the gruesome sight. She pressed her face against my neck. Her tears burned my skin. I held her tight and watched unimaginably huge debris clouds roll toward us through the city streets.

Were we far enough away? Was that horrifying, roiling mass from hell going to reach us? So many thoughts raced through my mind amid the chaos and destruction and terror. Was Kate's mom dead or alive? Was her dad okay? How would New York ever recover?

Numerous times I tried to call Ursula on Tubs' cell phone. The circuits were busy.

We held onto each other and witnessed tragic history in the making. I was hyper-aware of Kate's fragility, her strength, her desperate fear, and her love.

With each second that ticked by, the feeling of fury inside me grew, solidified, filled me with a purpose I'd never before had. The aimlessness that'd overwhelmed me ever since my dad's murder evaporated.

It was as if a blindfold had been ripped off.

My mind cleared.

One plane could have been an accident. Two planes was a planned assault intended to kill as many innocent people as possible.

I now knew without a doubt what I had to do with my life. My grandfather gave his own life building what had just been taken down by absolute evil.

I wasn't going to let the reason for his death be forgotten. Two more years of high school, and I was going to march in my father's footsteps directly to West Point.

After that, I'd do whatever I had to do to help hunt down the lunatics who did this. Then I'd find the bastard who killed my father.

And I'd get our stolen puzzle box back and unlock whatever secrets it held.

From the moment that first plane hit, all of our lives had been changed. The path ahead wouldn't be easy, but like Tubs had always told me, I was stubborn and willful. My dad often said that once I made my mind up, no force of nature could stop me.

It was time to prove them both right.

It was time to prove to myself that I was capable of more than existing, that I could make decisions and follow through. That I could make a difference.

The time to begin that path was now.

CHAPTER SIX

Summer 2007

Sometimes, no matter how hard you try, life refuses to cooperate with your carefully crafted plans. That little gem swirled through my mind as Kate and I hauled ass up the packed Hudson Yards subway station escalator.

"Excuse me," I said for the thirty-fifth time in the last hundred feet and skirted two women not much interested in accommodating my rising desperation. Why couldn't people who wanted to stand still on the escalator move to the right like the posted signs asked?

At the top, we leaped off the moving staircase and charged outside. The incredibly bright May sun reflected off Manhattan's skyscrapers and shined through the circular, gridded dome that hovered over the subway stop like a lost UFO. My retinas sizzled and the pounding in my head increased tenfold.

"Come on," Kate called.

We streaked down 34th toward the Javits Center. I would've loved to take time to enjoy the mild weather and smell the almost-bloomed roses, but I was too preoccupied with being late to my own commencement ceremony to notice. If we made it in time, I'd become a full-fledged graduate with a major in criminology and minor in art, a rather sad consolation to what I'd envisioned for myself after college.

Yeah, that was another instance my carefully laid plans hadn't gone as expected. Senior year of high school was the proverbial kiss of death. I'd blown any chance I'd had of attending West Point because my stubborn drive for what I thought was right got in the way of common sense. I'd been arrested along with my grandmother Tubs and half the student body at Stuyvesant protesting the US invasion of Iraq. While I was desperate to be a part of the hunt for Osama Bin Laden and his henchmen, I couldn't justify the invasion of a country I didn't believe had a hand in destroying the Twin Towers and murdering Kate's mom on the day that time would never forget.

As noble as my intentions may have been, my actions were enough to prompt West Point's admissions board to eighty-six my app.

That was then. Now, my fingers desperately clenched the paper bag containing my gown lest I lose it in the rush to graduation, and I glanced down to make sure my mortarboard was still stuffed under my arm. I vividly and completely understood now why it was a good idea to wait for the real graduation party until *after* the actual event.

Kate slowed to a walk and put a hand to her abdomen. "Almost there," she sucked in a breath and made a face.

"You're not going to throw up again are you?"

"I hope not."

So did I.

The sidewalk widened as we neared the convention center doors. We stopped to let some people enter ahead of us and Kate blew out a steadying breath. "In three weeks remind me of this moment."

"You got it, babe."

We'd be doing this graduation thing all over again when Kate's turn came to don the fancy robe and hat as she bid farewell to the Cooper Union School of Architecture.

Once we made it inside, the lobby was hot and crowded. I pulled her out of the incoming stream of humanity and wrapped her in a tight hug. "Love you so much."

She leaned back in my arms and gave me the crooked grin I adored. "And I love you, Mikala Flynn."

I bit back a smile of my own, kissed her goodbye, and lost myself in the crush of fellow John Jay College about-to-be graduates.

* * *

Six hours later, Kate and I gratefully pulled out chairs and sat on either side of Ursula in the back room at Joey's Pizzeria. I had succeeded in moving my tassel from the right side to the left after all, and Tubs, Urs, Beni, her boyfriend Gary, and Sahl had all witnessed the miraculous event. When it was over, they'd left before Kate and I did and beat us back to Joey's.

Everyone chatted and were stuffing their faces with yeasty, garlicky, melty cheese bread. Joey's familiar, off-key humming floated from the kitchen into the party room as he worked on our pies. Surrounded by family and friends, in a place that felt like a second home, I felt my whirlwind day and the accompanying stress dissipate like low-hanging fog in a stiff breeze.

I closed my eyes, imprinting the chaotic, joyful sounds in my mind. Hang onto this moment, I told myself, because big changes were afoot. I wasn't fond of change, but understood it was inevitable. I shoved that train wreck of depressing thoughts out of my mind, determined to live in the here and now and not get caught up in melancholy memories.

Hunger finally beat out what was left of the hangover. "Want some?" I asked Kate.

She licked her bottom lip as she considered it. "Yup."

I snagged a couple of plates and loaded them up. My fingers brushed hers as I handed over the goods. Her love-filled eyes caught mine, and my insides warmed as they did every time she graced me with her gaze. God, we were hokey, love-struck idiots. Even after six years together, I couldn't believe someone like her (grace, beauty, brains, and lots of dough) would want to be with someone like me (not so graceful, no beauty, average smarts, blah blah blah).

She glommed a huge bite, cheeks rounded like a chipmunk's, and managed to squeak out, "So hungry. Could probably eat an entire pie myself."

I caught a flicker of amusement cross Ursula's features. She said, "Tubs and I took bets on whether or not you were going to make your own graduation, Flynn."

Tubs stabbed a piece of pizza she'd cut up and pointed her loaded fork at me. "That'll teach you not overdo it the night before a very important date."

Urs pushed her empty plate away. "You're right as always, Tubs. Have to admit I barely made it in time to meet you guys myself."

Tubs said, "That's because you were moving with the speed of a sloth. It's a good thing their cuteness makes up for their lack of urgency, just as yours does, young lady."

Laughter rang out.

My memory was a bit holey, but I recalled Ursula finishing up our celebration by talking Kate and me into some sort of three-shot challenge. I wasn't clear on what exactly transpired after that.

I took a sip of water to wash down the bread. "It's all a learning experience, as you like to say, Tubs."

She dramatically threw a hand over her heart. "You've finally got it, Mikala. Maybe that expensive education was good for something after all."

No matter how much a pain in the ass my grandmother could be, she always had my best interests at heart.

"Flynn…" Gary, perched between Tubs and Beni, paused to wipe cheese off his goatee. "What comes now that you've completed your degree?"

"I'm headed to the National Protection and Investigation Unit's training academy in July."

He looked at me curiously. "That's a mouthful I've never heard before."

"Yeah," I said, "I'd never heard of it before either. Two NPIU agents showed up one day at John Jay to do some recruiting. One thing led to another." I waved a hand in dismissal. "Long story. Anyway, the NPIU's a branch of Homeland Security."

"Like the FBI?" he asked.

"Not exactly. The FBI's with the Justice Department. The NPIU's Homeland. The focus is specifically on combating homegrown terror. The unit's available to any agency that requests their help, much like the FBI, as long as a danger to the public's established."

Joey interrupted me by dropping two "Congrats on Your Graduation" pies on the table. "Kid," he said, "never thought I'd live ta see this day. Proud of ya." He thumped my back and disappeared into the kitchen. He was a man of few words, but what words he uttered he meant, and that meant a lot to me.

"Here, Flynn." Kate handed me two slices of buffalo chicken.

"Thanks." I folded a piece and refocused on Gary. "Anyway, I'm sure you've heard all about the issues law enforcement agencies have communicating with each other, especially within different levels of government."

Beni slapped the table and I jumped reflexively.

"Sorry," she said. "He's heard all about it. I've complained long and loud for the last couple weeks about exactly that. A victim'd been assaulted by a gang member and I was called in to do a sketch. Somehow the ATF got involved. For reasons they refused to share, they steamrolled the investigation. Essentially booted us off of our own case." She jabbed a finger in the air. "And their focus isn't the vic. It's a mess."

Sahl rumbled, "That is terrible. Just terrible."

"It is," I said. "That's why the NPIU's focusing on finding a way to bring positive cooperation and communication between all agencies."

Tubs literally snorted. "Such a novel idea. Over the years I've listened to Beni tell too many stories of multi-agency buffoonery. I, for one, am glad you're heading into that battle, Mikala. You have an innate sense of justice and fairness, and you play well with others."

"Ninety percent of the time she does," Ursula said. "The other ten she bops you over the head if she doesn't get her way."

Everyone at the table laughed, including me. Couldn't argue with the truth.

Conversation drifted on to other topics. As I ate, I thought about Tubs' comment, about how she was glad I was going into a job that had the potential to make a real change in a very flawed system. That was one of the big reasons I'd pursued the NPIU over the FBI. I was under no illusion that my piece of the puzzle would make any real difference, but I could always hope.

* * *

Two months flew by like an open-throttled crotch rocket on a deserted highway. The day before A-Day, or Academy Day, had finally arrived. In less than twenty-four hours I'd be treading the hallowed halls of the FBI Academy in Quantico because the FBI was kind enough—or was forced, who knew—to share space with the NPIU.

While the FBI wasn't steeped in nearly as long a history and tradition as the US Military Academy at West Point, it was sometimes called the West Point of Law Enforcement, and I thought that was ironic. Comparatively, the NPIU was in its infancy, but with that came more of an ability to leave one's mark, and that's what I intended to do.

Kate and I stood in the bedroom of the Brooklyn apartment we'd rented our freshman year of college, peering at one of Tubs' half-filled suitcases laying open on the unmade bed. The NPIU provided agent trainees a packing list for the academy, and I'd already gathered most of the items on it. The attire was a little business, a little casual, and a lot athletic.

I was ready to end this interminable wait. The path I'd chosen wouldn't be easy, but I knew, with every cell in my body, I'd conquer whatever the NPIU trainers threw my way.

The actual academic part didn't worry me. School might've been a chore but had never been a real problem. I'd upped my physical workouts from once to twice a day in the name of passing the NPIU's redundantly named fitness assessment test, called The FAT, an ironic acronym if there ever was one. The FAT was comprised of sit-ups, push-ups, a timed obstacle course, a two hundred-meter sprint, and a two-mile run. The test fell in the academy's first week, and if you didn't pass you found your ass on the next flight home.

My ass was staying as far away from anything that flew as I could keep it.

I dropped the last of the seven required pairs of white, no logo socks into the suitcase and double-checked my list. "That's it. We'll throw my pillow in tomorrow morning and that'll be that."

Kate huffed. "I really am excited for you." Her flat tone defied her words.

"I know, baby. But you'll be heading for Belize in a week, and then you'll forget all about me as you scuba dive the reefs."

She thwapped my shoulder. "Not true. Though, now that I think about it, there might be a special Honeycomb Cowfish that could take your place."

I gave her a rakish grin. "I guarantee you that fish won't have the special skills I do."

"God." She sighed dramatically. "I'm going to miss those special skills."

"Absence makes—"

"Uh-uh. Don't even."

"Whatever you say, volunteer girl."

Not long after she started college, Kate finally worked up the nerve to talk to her dad about her interest in International Volunteer HQ. She also told him that when she was done volunteering she wanted to continue her mom's work in sustainable architecture instead of stepping into a position in the Goldsmith Foundation.

He didn't even blink. After he lost his wife in the 9/11 attack, his attitude had fundamentally shifted. He gave more quality time to Kate and Will and actually listened to what they wanted to do with their lives instead of expecting them to follow him into the foundation, although Will did anyway.

Once Kate had been given the green light, she'd spent weeks planning a year's worth of IVHQ projects. The first began on an island twenty-five miles outside of Belize. The project was to study environmental impact on marine reefs and the aquatic life surrounding them.

I pulled her to me. Her intense ice-gray eyes made my stomach do the same patented Kate Flip it did the very first time she'd come to see me at Joey's Pizzeria. So much had happened since that heart-stopping moment. I loved her fully but cautiously, afraid even after all these years she'd wise up and realize our relationship had been some kind of mistake. She'd grow tired of stepping out of the social strata she was born into, and that would be that.

Those thoughts fell away as I slid my hands up to cradle the sides of her head and gently traced her full lower lip with my thumb. Without breaking eye contact, she caught my thumb between her teeth and ran her tongue around it.

The raw eroticism of it weakened my knees. I needed those lips on mine like I needed life itself.

Our kiss began gently, the dance achingly familiar yet always somehow new and exciting. I wanted to memorize her taste, imprint the way she felt against me, absorb every ounce of the love that radiated from her like a beacon, so when we parted I could remember every glorious detail.

She pulled away. The hunger in her eyes had me shoving the suitcase off the bed, the contents landing in a heap on the floor.

I gazed at the mess for a second, then glanced at Kate. "Oops."

We both burst into laughter and she pulled me onto the sheets.

"This is what I love about you, Flynn." She pushed me onto my back and crawled aboard, hands on my shoulders, hips in just the right spot. She ducked her head and met my lips, pulling back when I strained for more. "We can laugh, and we can love."

She dove in for another lightning peck and reared out of reach, a teasing smile curling the edges of her mouth. "We fit together so well." She slowly ground against me in a breathtaking way.

"Come here, you." My voice dropped as desire pushed hard at the edges of my control. I unseated her, reversed our positions, propping myself above her with my weight on my elbows. Her beauty made my heart ache. I wanted to hold onto this moment forever. "I love you so much."

The hunger in her eyes softened. "Baby, I love you, too." We came together only to come apart, and then after we'd put each other back together, the irresistible inferno of desire beckoned again.

* * *

The next morning dawned drippy and dreary, the sort of melancholy day perfect for a bittersweet parting.

Kate and I dallied in bed as long as we dared, then headed to Tubs' for the gauntlet of goodbyes. Tubs and the entire Art Squad were intent on a send-off with a memorable bang.

When we arrived, Tubs' apartment hummed with chaotic energy. Everyone was full of either advice or demands, ranging from "don't shoot anyone unless they need it," to asking could I take them for a jaunt through the city using newly honed tactical driving skills. Anton offered to pay for any tickets I'd accrue.

Their good-natured comments made me laugh and filled my heart in a way I hadn't known I needed. These people were my family, and I loved each and every one of them.

When the time came, I hugged Tubs hard. She held me tight, pressing lips to my ear. "You give it everything you have, Mikala, and we'll see you in twenty weeks. Be careful."

"I will." I pulled her closer as my throat thickened. I knew my career choice filled Tubs with some incredibly conflicted emotion, but her pride stiffened her spine and she'd never admit it. She'd lived through so much loss in her life. My grandfather, my father, her daughter-in-law. And now, her only granddaughter was heading directly toward another unknown, dangerous life. No matter what, I knew without a doubt she wanted me to follow my own path, regardless of her personal cost, and that did not weigh lightly on me.

On the bright side, once I was done with the academy, I'd have what the NPIU called a "Transition Period," six days to tie up loose ends and prepare to report to my first assignment. Kate planned on flying home so she could come to Quantico with Tubs for graduation. Hopefully she'd be able to stay for at least a few days beyond that.

I finally extricated myself. Kate accompanied me down the elevator and out to the street, leaving the crew to gleefully plan my "You Survived the NPIU Training Academy" party.

No cab sat double parked and waiting. The hollow pit in my stomach grew as I glanced at my watch, but there was still three minutes before they were officially late. I planted the suitcase on the curb, backpack between my feet. Kate burrowed into me, and I rested my forehead against hers.

My heart thumped. Anxious adrenaline raced through my veins, helping to offset the melancholy I felt building like a volcano deep in my chest.

Her shoulders rose as she took a breath. "I know it's the plan, but shit. This sucks."

"I know." I was on that precarious border of either laughing hysterically or bursting into tears myself. Come on, Flynn. Gut it out. "It's going to be okay. You'll be so busy diving and working on that suntan of yours you won't have a minute to miss me."

She sniffled, but then one side of her mouth curved into a half-smile. "Bullshit."

I rubbed my cheek against her temple.

"But hey," she pulled back enough to look me in the eye, "I'll see you in five months. Even if I have to swim back, I'll be there. I love you, Flynn. So much."

I opened my mouth to answer when a horn blared from about three inches away. The taxi had amazing timing.

We loaded my bag and backpack into the trunk and I grabbed Kate while the cabbie slammed the lid and beat it back into the car. My arms already ached without her. "I love you so much." I sealed my declaration quickly but thoroughly and climbed into the back seat before I changed my mind.

Kissing Kate goodbye was hard, but watching her wave with one hand and wipe her tears away with the other was one of the hardest things I'd ever done.

* * *

The movement of the train lulled me into fitful slumber. I dreamed, but the dreams were ephemeral and wispy, indefinable, and unsettling. Change in momentum periodically woke me, and I realized the next stop was mine.

I blearily blinked at my watch. Almost six p.m.

Before I left, Kate had insisted I upgrade to a Blackberry from the old Samsung flip phone I'd been using for years. She was a technology geek, and I was happy to let her take the reins on that decision. She debated and researched for a full week between the Blackberry or the fancy new Apple iPhone but decided a tried and true product was the best option. Over my protestations she even footed the bill.

I pulled the silver device from my pocket and typed out a quick "I arrived fine" text and sent it after following about nine different steps. I wasn't sure if it was easier than multi-tapping on my flip, but it was different and kind of cool.

At the train station, a bus was supposed to be waiting to bring NPIU agent trainees to the academy. I wondered how many of the people onboard the train would be in my class.

Brakes squealed, and the train eventually groaned to a full stop at Quantico Station. I gathered my luggage and joined soldiers in uniform, business people, and regular folk like myself milling near the exit.

After what felt like an eternity but was probably only a minute, the doors hissed open. The view before me wasn't the picture of the Quantico that'd lived in my head since I saw *Silence of the Lambs* as a kid. I wasn't sure what I expected, but the generic, rectangular every-town-has-one mid-twentieth century building was not it. There should have been a flashing neon sign announcing, "Marine Corps Base Quantico" or "Welcome to the FBI Academy." Or something.

The station had an overhang protecting all of about three feet of the platform in front of the building. QUANTICO was spelled out in narrow silver letters just below the overhang, and the structure itself wasn't much longer than an Amtrak locomotive. Teal fencing led to entry doors situated at either end, and between them a span of windows overlooked the railway tracks and the parking lot beyond.

The crowd thinned as we disembarked and made our way through the boxy structure. I followed about a dozen people trudging toward an idling, unmarked bus with the words NPIU Academy lit on the destination sign above the windshield.

The knee-level luggage compartment gaped open like a sideways mouth. The driver stood by and loaded in each of our bags and then one by one we filed aboard. I bypassed open seats and continued all the way to the rear. The back row of four seats was unoccupied. I slid in next to the window and stared through the grimy glass.

"Hey…" A deep voice brought me back to the moment. "Mind if I sit back here?"

I glanced up at the tall, muscular black guy with a friendly smile. "Help yourself."

He wrestled a duffle bag into the overhead and wedged himself into the seats beside from me. "Joe Moseby. But I like Joey better." He thrust a plate-sized hand at me.

"Mikala Flynn, and I like plain old Flynn better myself."

We shook and he settled sideways on the seats with a knee on the cushion and his back against the window. "Duly noted. Where you from, plain ol' Flynn?"

I shifted to face him. "Brooklyn. You?"

"Hunt's Point."

"Bronx?"

"That be the one."

"You gonna miss it?"

"Hell, no. Gangs galore. I got two kid brothers and a sis I'm worried about. But my mom will keep 'em on their toes."

We fell into easy conversation until the bus driver boarded and gave some rapid-fire instructions about what to do once we arrived at the academy.

When the man was done speaking, Joey said, "You ready for this?" His face reflected a tinge of uneasy trepidation and a whole lot of determination.

"About as ready as you look right now."

"Well, then. Let's get this circus on the road. I'm hungry."

He spoke my language. I thought we just might get along okay.

* * *

At ten to seven the next morning, after a solid breakfast of Fruity Pebbles, my roommate, a redheaded accountant from Freeport, Kentucky, named Samantha—not Sam—Harris, and I marched through hallowed academy halls with thirty-three other anxious NPIU special agent trainees. The NPIU contingent was dressed in a uniform of dark brown cargo pants and black polos with the official seal embroidered on the left chest. We were headed to an auditorium for a Welcome to the NPIU Academy session, where we were supposed to get our class schedules and who knew what else.

I was both exhausted and humming with nervous energy. Last night we'd gotten our dorm assignments, talked to counselors and supervisors, gathered uniforms, workout gear, and agency-issued laptops. By the time we hit the bunk it was almost midnight. Before I passed out I managed to shoot Kate a quick "I'm surviving and miss you" text, then fell asleep before she had a chance to reply.

"Flynn, hold up," a familiar voice hollered from somewhere behind me.

I grabbed Samantha's arm and glanced back. "Hey, Joey. "

Joey weaseled his way into line behind us, trailed by a tall, thin man with a headful of short dreads, a neatly trimmed goatee, and rich, caramel-colored skin.

"Howdy." He jerked a thumb at his companion. "Meet Raoul Francesco, but just call him Franko unless he does something to deserve the full name treatment."

I introduced Samantha, and we found seats toward the back of the auditorium and settled in to listen to a litany of agents and support personnel cover a multitude of policies and procedures.

Three hours later we staggered out of the auditorium and made a beeline for the cafeteria and some lunch. Like most everything here, the dining hall was huge. Two volleyball courts could easily fit within its confines. National and international flags hung from the walls. A buffet of hot and cold food, a cereal station, and a beverage station lined one end, and a mix of circular and rectangular tables filled the rest of the space.

Once we loaded up trays we reconvened at a table by glass windows overlooking a dismal hallway.

Joey had chosen the stroganoff, which actually looked good, and jabbed his fork into a hunk of beef. "Hope this is better than the mystery meat they served in high school."

I peered at my plate. Brown gravy covered sliced turkey and puddled against a pile of mashed potatoes. My one nod to health was a single scoop of broccoli. I poked at the meat and wondered if the potatoes were real.

"I don't care what it tastes like. I'm hungry." Samantha had gone the turkey route too, and she took a bite. As she chewed, her expression brightened, and she gave a thumbs up.

I dove in. It was great, solid cooking, and yes, real potatoes. Silence reigned as we plowed through the chow.

Franko finished eating first and pushed his plate away. "I think we shall survive the food," he said in a lilting, Caribbean/Jamaican/something-sounding accent. "So what brings you all to Quantico and the NPIU?"

Samantha paused in the middle of unscrewing her soda bottle cap. "I graduated from college with a degree in accounting. Worked for a branch of the First International Bank in Paducah, Kentucky. It was great for the first four years." She upended her bottle and drained it. "I was working a major international account and something wasn't adding up. Pun intended. Anyway, long story short, I stumbled into a money-laundering scheme run by the Juarez cartel."

"I remember hearing about that." Joey crumpled his napkin and tossed it on the table. "A Mexican branch of First International was being used to filter cartel money into legit businesses, wasn't it? Hold up a sec. Are you that whistleblower they refused to name?"

Samantha was thin and a couple inches shorter than me, with aquiline features and high cheekbones. When she grinned, as she did now, her entire face got its happy on. "Two agents from the FBI showed up and we worked together for over a year putting things together. When the case was turned over to the prosecutors, I was approached and asked if I might be interested in a career with the Feebs." She shrugged. "Law enforcement never, ever crossed my mind. Ultimately I said no, but then someone talked to someone and the NPIU came calling. They were very convincing, and here I am. What about you, Joey?"

"I bleed the Bronx. Joined up with the Marines just after 9/11, did two tours in Iraq and Afghanistan."

"Infantry?" Franko asked.

"Nah, man. Military police. When Homeland established the NPIU and the agency focused on homegrown terror, I was ready to get the hell outta the desert and play stateside. No more camel spiders the size of my head or sand fleas in unmentionable places."

"God, that's nasty." I shuddered. "Scurrying mice and rats big enough to carry small humans down a subway tunnel don't faze me. Spiders? Forget about it. And I have no reference for sand fleas, but I'm sure I could do without that experience too."

Despite my casual words, the ghost of my dad and the military path I'd intended to follow but failed, loomed large and the drumbeat of the hunt-that-could've-been echoed in my veins. Add the terrifying "what ifs" of Kate's mom's last minutes trapped in a doomed tower, and it all squeezed my heart so hard that some days I thought I might die from the pain of it.

Time for temporary deflection. I needed to come up with some kind of simple answer as to why my ass was sitting here, because I sure as hell wasn't ready to talk about my real motivations. "Franko, the question's coming back at you."

He passed a hand over his goatee, and his curiously golden eyes glittered. "The FBI has a small satellite office—a resident agency—not far from where I grew up. The neighborhood kids and I loved to make up crime scenes and play special agents and bad guys." He shrugged. "Always wanted to become a G-man. But the mission of the NPIU, that is what drew me to this agency. St. Thomas is a microcosm of the enormous problem America's law enforcement agencies struggle with in working cooperatively. I want to be a part of the answer."

Samantha said, "The Virgin Islands St. Thomas?"

"That be the one."

Joey flicked a wadded-up straw wrapper at me. "What about you, Flynn?"

"Brooklyn, and my motivation is the same as Franko's without the warm sun and aqua-colored ocean."

No one questioned me further, and convo drifted onto other topics, eventually sticking on where we might be sent upon graduation. Everyone was supposed to turn in their top ten picks by the end of the week. According to the very in-depth schedule we'd been given, Placement Day was scheduled for Week Four.

"I don't care where I go," Joey said as he looked over the page listing NPIU office locations. "Well, I guess I'd rather not land in Montana or Idaho, but whatever."

"Maybe Florida," I said, sort of kneejerk, as I thought about Key West. I hadn't been back to the Conch Republic since Tubs brought me home after my dad's killing. In that light, maybe Florida wasn't such a good idea, after all. "Actually, on second thought, somewhere cooler. Detroit. Chicago. Somewhere in the Pacific Northwest." I wasn't particular about remaining on the East Coast. I'd only be an airplane ride away from Tubs no matter where I went, and Kate would be basically off the grid for the next couple of years anyway.

Samantha pulled the location sheet out of Joey's hands. "Honolulu. But since that's probably not happening," she frowned as she studied the page, "DC maybe. New York. Anywhere other than Kentucky. Somewhere big and busy."

"I'd like to hit Texas or California," Franko said. "Lots of hate groups for this black man to poke at in those two states."

According to Southern Poverty Law Center stats listed after each state's field office location, California currently had eighty-three hate groups and Texas seventy-three.

I ran a finger down the list. "It's mind boggling, the amount of hate in this country. Neo-Nazi and the KKK, anti-LGBT, anti-Muslim. Groups promoting hate music. Holocaust deniers." That one struck close to home. Tubs was living proof, for Christ's sake.

Recruits slowly filtered out of the cafeteria. Franko checked his watch. "Time's up. Back at it, troops."

The rest of the day vanished into a tornado of information. Tomorrow, the real work would begin.

CHAPTER SEVEN

Four weeks flew by both terrifyingly fast and slower than pine sap leaking from a wound in a tree.

I'd managed to talk to Kate three times, but it was tough lining our schedules up. She was under water seven days a week, with most dives occurring at night, and that was when I was usually available. She was having a great time, boating to the mainland once in awhile to do a little sightseeing and a lot of environmental stuff, like helping to clean up the beaches and other public spaces. I wasn't envious, but the unsettling feeling of inadequacy and the "what can I really contribute to this relationship" thoughts had begun creeping in again, as they occasionally did. Kate would usually knock that negative self-talk out of my head, but I didn't say anything to her about it now. She was incredibly busy, and I didn't want to burden her. This span of time apart was the longest we'd been away from one another since we'd gotten together in high school. That's probably why the doubts and insecurities were rearing their ugly little heads.

But it did help to have made some friends. Through those first weeks, Joey, Samantha, Franko, and I had become tight. We did most things together, and tonight we waited, queued up in the hallway, for those ahead of us to file into the auditorium. Placement Day was upon us, and we'd all find out where we'd be assigned, assuming no one else was booted and dropped out.

Our class was made up of one hundred and three recruits, but we'd lost two—one to injury and another who mouthed off to the PT instructor—so we were down to a hundred plus one.

Once everyone settled in, bald and buff NPIU Director Carlos Inquez, flanked by four special agents, stepped up to a wooden podium with a raised FBI seal on the front. I thought they should've covered it up with the NPIU seal, but since we were the FBI's guests, it probably wasn't in good taste to mess with their stuff.

"Welcome to Placement Day 25," Inquez's voice boomed through the microphone. "Yours is the 25th class to go through the National Protection and Investigation Unit Academy. Today you'll find out where you're headed once we're done putting you through the wringer."

Laughter rippled through the room.

Once things quieted, he continued, "You'll be at your assignments for at least two years. If you like your post, you can stay as long as you wish. Hate it, and you'll have a chance to transfer after twenty-four months. We'll read off name and assignment location by division. When your name is called, come up, put a pin in it, and proceed back to your seat." He jerked his thumb at a three-by-five map of the US propped on a table on one side of the stage. "We'll begin with E Division and end with A, moving backward through the alphabet."

Backward? That was kind of weird, but whatever. The NPIU was a bit odd with the way it did stuff, anyway. At the outset, our class had been randomly divided into five divisions. Samantha, Joey, and I wound up in C Division, more commonly called C Div, and Franko was assigned to A Div.

One day during a rare moment of down time I'd chatted with an FBI NAT or new agent trainee. He'd said the Feebs functioned in strict alphabetical order and was aghast when I told him how it went for us. Maybe the NPIU wanted to separate themselves from how other agencies operated or perhaps it was nothing more than crazy management.

Inquez, tapping the sheets of paper he'd been holding against the podium, brought my attention back to the present. "Once you've placed your pin, please return to your seats. Here we go, E Div. Zavier. Chicago, Illinois." He waited for Zavier to walk up, pin his assignment, and return to his seat. Then, "Zalenski. Tecate, California."

Everyone was quiet as names and locations were called. Even though I wasn't married to working a particular place, I didn't want to land in some podunk field office in the Bible Belt either.

As the backward alphabetical countdown droned on, my knee began to bounce and a hangnail I'd been ignoring became irresistible.

Beside me, the muscles in Joey's jaw contracted and relaxed regularly, but otherwise he looked cool as a refrigerated dill. Samantha, who was on Joey's far side, was still except for her fingers, which silently drummed the armrest. Franko, beside her, sat loosely in his seat, knee over ankle, teeth worrying his lower lip. Apparently, regardless of our level of concern—or lack thereof—anticipation caused anxiety anyway.

Finally C Div was up. Inquez called out four names then took a sip of water from a bottle under the podium. "Next up, Moseby. San Antonio, Texas."

Joey stood and made his way up to the map as Inquez droned, "Morrison, St. Louis, Missouri."

A few minutes later he called Samantha's name. She scored Washington, DC, one of her top choices. Then, "Flynn, Minneapolis, Minnesota."

Minneapolis?

For a second I didn't move. That location certainly hadn't been on my radar. I thought Minneapolis was close to Chicago on a map, anyway, so it probably couldn't be all that bad. Although I recalled the Weather Channel making Minnesota out to be either tornado alley or a deep freeze buried under ten feet of snow, depending on the season.

As I made my way to the map I wondered if SUVs outnumbered sedans and if everyone owned a snowmobile and a boat.

It took another fifteen minutes for the director to get to Franko. Mesa, Arizona, for him. At least it was kind of close to California.

Now we all had to figure out how to coordinate across-the-country moves while not washing out of the academy.

CHAPTER EIGHT

Week Twenty.

The end was so close I could feel it in my callused, aching palms. I sat alone at a high top table in the Boardroom—yes, the academy had an actual bar, complete with alcohol, neon booze signs, and bowls of pretzels—nursing an ice water and waiting for Joey, Samantha, and Franko.

Up to now, I hadn't had much time to contemplate all we'd been through in the last one hundred-forty-something days. As I turned it all over in my overwrought mind, I was amazed. And exhausted. From academics to firearms to physical training, defensive tactics, emergency vehicle operations, and live field exercises in Hogan's Alley with a focus on terrorism, life had been a Category 5 hurricane.

This morning I'd passed my last two classes and in a couple of hours came our final challenge: the legendary Yellow Brick Road obstacle course. Anyone could still wash out until that event was recorded in the official NPIU Academy books. The point of the course wasn't simply about making it to the end within the allotted time. We had to show how well we could work together as a group, helping each other through the various obstacles we'd come up against. Assuming nothing went wrong—and plenty still could—the thirty-six-hour countdown to graduation day would commence.

Tubs and Kate, barring any flight delays, would arrive tomorrow evening. I so could not wait. While I talked to Tubs every Sunday, I'd only managed to connect with my girl a few times, and even then the conversations had been painfully short. But each time we spoke, Kate was incredibly excited about what she was doing, and it was a delight to hear the joy in her voice.

I'd done some thinking about the two of us during my time here. She had so much good ahead of her, so much to offer the world. Who was I to tie her to a life of worry and relocation? Loving someone in law enforcement was a bitch. Honestly, what kind of life could I really offer her at all?

But then, time after time, she'd patiently told me, she'd patiently showed me that money didn't matter to her. A person's heart was what counted in her world, was how she judged the good and the bad. Still, no matter how hard I tried to ignore it, my mind flashed back to that bully who hounded me my first year at Stuyvesant, and the little voice he managed to imbed inside me kept whispering that I could never be the person she deserved.

Joey burst into the Boardroom, and with his energy and excitement awhirl, my insecurities faded away once again.

"Done," he said. "We just need to kill the yellow bricks, and we're home free."

We high-fived.

"So glad the sitting parts are over," he said. "I caught Samantha between classes and told her we'd meet in the atrium."

"The atrium?" Not that I really cared one way or another, but it seemed odd to change the plan at the last minute.

Joey's lips curved in a delighted grin. "Girlfriend, didn't you hear they have a dessert buffet set up to celebrate the end of classes?"

"What? No." I hopped off the stool and grabbed my water. "You're speaking my language, baby. Let's go."

* * *

Sunlight dappled the thin layer of dirt and dead leaves scattered over a very rocky forest floor. Quantico's November temperatures—mid-fifties and sunny—were much more moderate than New York's at this time of the year and were about as perfect as you could get.

Instructors were scattered throughout the course, watching the action, listening to the grunts of exertion and shouts of encouragement, assessing us as we progressed through the obstacles.

This was it. One wrong move, one thing they caught they didn't like, and they could still say, "See ya." No one was out of the theoretical woods until we were literally out of the woods.

Each division had been given a staggered start time. A Div actually went first, so Franko was somewhere out there ahead of us. My fellow C Divs and I were in the third wave, and we'd been on the run for about ten minutes. The first challenge was a fifty-foot stretch of waist-high logs worn smooth, set up like monstrous, rustic hurdles. I made it through before either Joey or Samantha and glanced back when I cleared the last log.

Someone had taken a header halfway through and caused a pileup. Joey was helping the fallen to their feet. I didn't see Samantha, but I assumed she was caught in the tangle. I knew they'd catch up sooner or later, so I kept going.

The twisty, uneven path could be treacherous even without any man-made obstacles. I tackled the trail cautiously and wound my way to the top of a steep cliff. Franko had nicknamed this obstacle Break Neck, because it was at least a sixty-foot drop onto various sized boulders. A fall would not have a good outcome.

One of my fellow C Divs prepared to drop off the edge. His white-knuckled hands were wrapped tight around a thick rope that snaked all the way to the ground. He adjusted his footing and disappeared out of sight.

I dropped to my knees a couple feet from the edge so I could get a better view. "Come on, McMillan," I yelled. "You got it. Go, go, go!"

McMillan picked his way to the bottom, taking care not to slip on the loose shale scattered around the boulders, and hauled ass down the path to the next obstacle.

I grabbed the rope and assumed the position. The twine-like fibers were prickly against my palms as I eased over the rocky ledge, concentrating on finding the fastest, safest path down. Despite the crisp air, anxious perspiration trickled down my back. I found a toehold here, a crevice there, and, hand over hand, crept closer and closer to the bottom.

"Flynn!" Joey's voice floated to me. "You're halfway there."

I glanced skyward.

His head was visible, but the rest of his body was as far away from the edge as he could get. One of the more ironic things that'd come out during one liquor-filled weekend was that tough, ripped, imposing Joey was terrified of heights.

A few more long seconds and my feet landed on the rubble at the base of the cliff. I peeled my fingers off the rope and flexed them, then cupped my hands around my mouth. "Come on, Moseby!"

Joey swung himself over the ledge and bounced once against the rocky face. He used the strength of his upper body to control his descent and zoomed down the cliff like Spiderman.

One second he was doing fine. The next he was dangling by one arm forty-five feet in the air. His heels scrabbled against the rock, and his face was frozen in a look of horror.

My heart seized.

Above us, Samantha's head and shoulders popped into view. Her "Oh, shit," echoed through the trees.

"Moseby," I bellowed, "both hands on the rope!"

The muscles and sinew beneath Joey's skin rippled as he fought to regain his grip.

Samantha called, "Small ledge by your left foot."

Joey caught his heel on the protrusion and used the leverage to grab the rope with both hands. He kicked away from the rock, swung himself around. Seconds ticked as he mustered the courage to move again.

From stillness came motion, and then he was again careening toward the ground.

Flynn, I told myself, you may now return to your regular breathing schedule.

Moments later Joey was beside me, hands on knees, chest heaving as he practiced that breathing thing himself. "Jesus," he gasped.

"Good job." I gave his back a thump and turned my attention to Samantha. She dominated the cliff like a mountain goat.

"Damn. That woman is fearless." He straightened, still panting. "Fearless. Oh, shit. Samantha's got herself a new nickname." He elbowed me. "Fearless Harris."

Once Fearless Harris gracefully tossed the rope aside and picked her way over to us, we barreled toward the next challenge.

* * *

I rumbled into a spot at the Quantico train station parking lot to pick up Tubs and Kate in a tricked-out, bright green Dodge Charger. The beast belonged to a fellow recruit who souped up muscle cars as a hobby. This project came complete with an exhaust system so loud the rumble rattled windows of houses and businesses and other cars as I passed by. I fully expected to be pulled over and cited for disturbing the peace.

Tubs had made a reservation for herself and Kate at a Holiday Inn in Stafford, about twenty minutes from Quantico. The plan was to ferry them to the hotel, visit for a bit, and head back. The next day I'd pick them up for the big event.

My Blackberry pinged. *Ten minutes, baby! I can't wait to see you. Tubs says she gets the first hug.* My stomach fluttered as butterflies played a bang-up game of dodgeball. I felt like I was about to go on a date with Kate for the first time all over again—nervous, out of my league—and ecstatic. I imagined her skin tanned to a golden glow thanks to hours in the Caribbean sun, her silky hair bleached lighter by the same, and my hands itched to touch.

Can't wait, I typed back.

One moment giddiness made my breath come fast and my head spin. Then the realization that I'd be in Minneapolis in seven days without either of my loved ones pulled my happy rug right out from under me. I shoved that thought away and the insane joy of our pending reunion flooded back. Nothing but a roller coaster of crazy.

6:59. I rubbed damp palms on my jeans, exited the car, and headed for the depot building.

At twenty-five seconds after 7:05, the Amtrak's triangular set of headlights pierced the distant darkness, dimly at first, and rapidly growing brighter as the train roared in.

The engineer blasted the horn repeatedly into the night. The sound, like the lights, gathered strength as the train approached. Between blasts, the almost shocking quiet was filled with the unmistakable clang of train bells.

As the locomotive whipped past the station, the engineer let the horn rip again, and I had to restrain myself from clapping my hands over my ears. The vibration from metal wheels on metal rails rumbled up my legs through the concrete. Then the sudden, pungent smell of diesel slapped me in the face.

The hiss of pneumatic brakes replaced the screaming horn as car after car whipped by. The gigantic metal caterpillar bled speed almost imperceptibly, then more rapidly until it eventually rocked to a complete stop.

With a synced swish, all the doors slid open. Riders poured onto the concrete apron like ants flooding out of an anthill.

"Flynn!"

The sound of Kate's voice whipped me around, and then she was in my arms, legs wrapped around my back, lips on mine before she buried her face in my neck. Delighted laughter could've been either hers or mine.

Over her shoulder, I saw Tubs dodging through the thinning crowd, rolling both a suitcase that was a smaller mate of the one she'd loaned me, and Kate's carry-on. She brandished a kid-in-the-candy-store grin, and between the two of them, my heart was ready to explode.

"She beat you to the hug, Tubs." I released Kate but kept my arm around her.

"That one," Tubs said, "was so impatient to get to you she couldn't stand it. I thought she was going to rip those doors open herself and hop off before the train," she lowered her voice, "'comes to a full and complete stop.' I finally made her give me her suitcase and told her to find you."

In light of my whirling world, I took comfort in the fact Tubs never seemed to change, from her looks to her no-nonsense, good-humored attitude. The one new thing about her was a bright red fleece coat with a pocket logo for the Museum of Jewish Heritage embroidered on the front.

"Nice jacket," I said.

She glanced down at herself. "The museum decided to keep people warm and advertise at the same time."

"I like it. And you…" I turned to Kate, took in her shining eyes, smooth, tanned face, and sun-bleached hair. Just as I'd imagined. The love I felt for this amazing human sometimes took my breath. "You are a sight for my lonely eyes."

Kate hugged me again. "Oh, my poor baby's got lonely eyes." She planted a kiss on my forehead.

Tubs looked me up and down. "I think you've lost some weight."

"Probably. Food's great, but I think we burn the calories off as fast as we take them in. Or faster. Come on. I'll chauffeur you to your hotel in amazing style."

Tubs raised her eyebrows and peered at me suspiciously. "Oh boy. I know that sarcastic tone all too well. Are there any taxis around here?"

* * *

We arrived safely at the Holiday Inn. I found a parking spot near the lobby and cut the engine. Blessed silence settled over us like a blanket of soft cotton.

Tubs unbuckled her seatbelt. "I swear, if I wasn't already hard of hearing I would be now."

"That's one hell of a muffler." Kate stepped out of the back seat. "But I do kind of like the glowing green paint job."

I popped the trunk and extracted the suitcases. "I'll bring ear plugs tomorrow."

Kate and I trailed Tubs into the lobby. She checked in, and we dumped the luggage in the room and decided to grab a late dinner at a Bob Evans across the road from the hotel.

Once we'd been seated and placed our orders, Tubs and Kate filled me in on what personal belongings they'd packed for shipping to the Twin Cities and what was left behind. Kate planned to hang onto the apartment, so I wasn't too worried about it.

I told them about Cailin McKenna, the Minneapolis agent I'd been paired up with as my probationary mentor. She seemed okay as far as I could tell through the few email conversations we'd exchanged, and she had a friend with a spare room who was willing to rent it to me until I found a place of my own.

Everything was moving at warp speed now, and I was at odds with myself. On the one hand I was ready to move on with it, ready to get to Minneapolis and dive into the terror battle. On the other, my entire life was sitting right here with me.

I didn't want to let either go. All new agents probably went through this, but nonetheless, it was awful. It had been one thing to think about the whole relocation/separation thing in the abstract and something else entirely to experience it.

Catching up while we ate felt like an out-of-body experience. It was as if I was floating above the room, watching myself interacting with Kate and Tubs, laughing at a comment Kate made, listening intently to Tubs talk about some adventure she and the Art Squad had been involved with. I ached to hang onto this ordinary moment as long as I could.

At some point, Kate reached under the table and put a hand on my knee. She always knew when I was not quite me, when I needed help grounding myself. Distance hadn't changed that. She was still as captivating as she'd been when we'd first connected at that long-ago Goldsmith Foundation dinner.

Despite all the reassurance, all the love that I knew—without a doubt—existed between us, that pesky itch in the back of my brain refused to let up. When it reared its ugliness, my happiness was drained from me, as if one of Harry Potter's Dementors had come calling and sucked it all out. The itch skittered through my mind now, repeating in a soul-slashing whisper that I didn't deserve the love, the kindness, the patience Kate sprinkled over me like some kind of magical fairy dust. She was going to wake up and realize how much better off she'd be in someone else's arms. Someone who'd offer her what I never would be able to. I knew I sounded like a record on repeat, but I couldn't find the off button.

The arrival of dessert ended my internal anguish. Kate shoved a bite of apple crisp in my mouth, laughing in delight when melted ice cream dribbled down my chin. I forced those stupid thoughts back into the dark recesses from which they'd crept. I needed to live in the moment.

In the right here.

In the right now.

* * *

The next evening I tugged up my sleeve to check the time. I stood backstage, in a line of fellow almost-agents waiting impatiently to be called out for credential presentation.

Still ten minutes to go.

Franko, positioned alphabetically directly behind me, poked my shoulder. "And the time is?"

"A minute since we last checked."

"How is it possible for time to stop?"

"I don't know. Maybe we're in some kind of vortex."

"This vortex better end with a badge in my hand."

"You're not kidding, my man."

Impatient excitement permeated the packed FBI Auditorium and was echoed backstage.

I wondered how Kate and Tubs were holding up. Probably just fine. During the pre-graduation cocktail hour, I'd introduced them to quite a crew: Joey's mom and sister, Franko's best friend from St. Thomas, and Samantha's parents. Everyone hit it off, and we learned that they—to a person—were all good-natured rabble-rousers who loved to laugh.

That spelled trouble with a capital T for Joey, Franko, Samantha, and me.

Now, through a gap in black velvet curtains separating us from the front of house, I spotted Tubs, Kate, and the rest of them all seated in the very front row.

Yikes.

I huffed an anxious breath. It felt so strange and all together too dressed up to be wearing black twill pants, a tank, and a blazer after all the time we'd spent in polos, cargoes, and workout gear. The tag on the back of the tank irritated my neck every time I moved. Should have cut the fucker out.

Franko leaned forward again. "Why do I feel like until my creds are in my hands, they still might bounce me?"

"Because," I whispered, "they've made us paranoid. Don't worry. It's all good from here. Unless you draw down on the NPIU Director or something."

"They haven't issued us our official NPIU weapon and ammo yet, so I should be safe."

I reached up and squeezed the icy fingers gripping my shoulder. Franko was a freeze baby. Hopefully Mesa's heat would thaw him out a little.

Samantha broke rank and snuck up to us. "You guys, I can't believe it's almost over."

"I know," I said. "I've been literally dreaming about what the leather on the badge and ID wallet is going to feel like, and every time I reach out to touch it someone yanks it away."

"Harris!" one of our instructors barked. "You're outta line." How he knew who was who in the shadowy murk was beyond me.

Samantha made a face and slunk back to her assigned spot.

Out on the stage, the deputy director took the podium and made her opening remarks, which led to the director calling us out one by one to receive a handshake and our official NPIU credentials.

When my name was called, it wasn't hard to hear Tubs' distinctive whistle and Kate's wolf call as I walked onto the stage to accept handshakes and the shiny leather case we'd all worked so hard for. Then I was on my way off the other side of the stage.

The rest of the ceremony was a blur as I fingered the supple leather, the shiny silver badge, and Department of Homeland Security ID displaying my name as a Special Agent of the National Protection and Investigation Unit.

This was really happening.

After my plan to follow my dad's path to West Point and then into the Army fell apart, my dreams and intentions had shifted. I'd made tough decisions, worked harder than I ever had, and I'd nailed it. I knew without a doubt, even with my off-the-rails path, my father would be proud of me. I still intended to do what I could to ferret out the identity of his murderer, but with the passage of time and a much more mature outlook, I understood the chances of success were slim.

Tied to that, of course, was my family's missing puzzle box. At this point in the game recovery was highly unlikely. Whenever I thought about these things, melancholy covered me like a shroud, so I tried not to dwell on either very long. The one potential saving grace was that now I would have enormous resources available, although I didn't know how the NPIU would feel about me pursuing personal objectives. I might be able to get away with it as long as doing so didn't interfere with my job.

While I might not personally bring Bin Laden to justice as I'd originally envisioned, I could now work to stop terror plotted within the boundaries of the United States and its territories. In that way, I felt I could still honor the memory of Kate's mom.

If I'd learned one thing in the days after watching the horror of the World Trade Center disaster with Kate on Tubs' apartment rooftop, it was that flexibility was key. And by God, I was as flexible as they came.

CHAPTER NINE

Forty-eight hours at the Jane Hotel in the West Village with Kate was guaranteed to be a delightfully exhausting experience. In two days I'd be winging my way to the Upper Midwest, but until then, I intended to enjoy every moment I had left with my lover.

The Jane, with its red brick façade and octagon-shaped corner tower, was erected in 1908 as a hotel where seafaring men could affordably crash for the night. Rooms were nautically styled, with lots of wood and brass stuffed in about fifty square feet. Narrow, single bunks for ordinary seamen cost a quarter a pop. Bathrooms were communal. Larger rooms were fifty cents and intended for officers, stewards, cooks, and engineers. The two major pros of the somewhat more spacious quarters, other than an additional two hundred square feet, was the attached bath and the option of a king bed.

A lot of fun can be had in a king bed.

The taxi dumped us in front of a run-of-the-mill hotel entrance. A generic black awning extended from the building to the edge of the curb to shield prospective patrons from the weather.

I rounded up our luggage and tipped the dreadlocked cabbie through the passenger window.

"Tanks, mon," he said with a cheeky smile. "'Ave a great time and don' do anyting I wouldn't. Leaves it wide open." With a wave he merged into traffic and disappeared around the corner.

"Come on, Flynn." The excitement in Kate's voice made my insides sing. "This is gonna be great." I followed her into the lobby, almost mowing her over when she came to an abrupt stop. "Holy 1920s."

She wasn't kidding. We'd stepped from the early twenty-first century into the Jazz Age.

A chandelier high in the ceiling cast soft yellow light, bringing out the dark, rich paneling on the walls. Various patterns, carvings, and a stylized eagle were woven into the paneling, which extended three-quarters of the way to the ceiling. The top quarter of the wall was covered in vintage dusty-rose, fleur-de-lis-stenciled wallpaper.

Two-toned mint and Kelly green tiles in a checkerboard pattern rose from the floor and extended four feet up marble pillars like ceramic wainscoting. Above the tiles, full-length mirrors reflected the honey-colored glow of French sconces.

I elbowed Kate. "Are those real?" I pointed at four objects mounted on the wall just below ceiling height. Two of the strangest deer heads I'd ever seen hung alongside two stuffed peacocks with colorful three-foot trains.

"I'd like to say no, but…" She trailed off, her face scrunched. "I hope this wasn't a mistake."

"Reminds me of something you might see at a *Ripley's Believe It or Not* museum. Come on. It'll be fine."

We continued into the lobby, and once again the magic of the Roaring Twenties erased any thoughts of odd wall décor. More polished wood panels with interesting carvings created a frame around the front desk.

The hotel clerk was all retro in a maroon bellhop outfit with epaulets, brass buttons, and a round, brimless three-inch high hat. I felt bad for him, but a buck was a buck, especially in this town.

Behind him stood a massive bank of old-fashioned mail slots, its shelves worn shiny from decades of use.

At our approach, he politely smiled. "Welcome to the Jane Hotel. Reservations?"

I mentally checked out while Kate checked in. This place was a perfect distraction from our imminent parting. Jay Gatsby was going to walk in at any moment, and he'd no doubt get the party started.

Three hours later, after a little love and a lot of snuggling, we investigated the rooftop bar appropriately located, I thought, at the top of the octagon tower.

Inside, Persian carpets covered a circular, black-and-white-checked floor. Vintage blue and red velvet couches offered a place to take a load off. A bartender, dressed in a white, round-collared shirt and a maroon vest with matching arm garters, poured libations behind a lustrous teak bar.

We slid into a line of guests waiting to place their orders. I killed time studying the faux crumbling brick that had been painted on the bar's interior walls. Kate would, I was sure, know how the designers crafted it to look so realistic.

Kate's hand on my cheek startled me out of my inner interior decorator interval. "Hey, baby, I'm gonna wait out on the patio because if I look at that thing any longer I'll have nightmares."

I followed her discretely pointing finger.

A window at the center of the bar framed a four-foot, mounted monkey. He was perched on a red leather stool, wearing a child-sized tux, holding a silver serving platter in his spindly, spidery fingers. Kate hadn't been kidding about potential nightmares. What was it with the taxidermy here?

"Scoot." I kissed her forehead and shooed her out onto the patio. My turn arrived and I ordered two West Street Sunsets— the bar's signature cocktail—and asked for a double shot of alcohol in both. In three shakes I had our drinks in hand and wandered outside to find Kate.

They'd done a nice job making the rooftop cozy. White wicker furniture with overstuffed red cushions lined a wall at the building's edge. Shabby-chic coffee tables between the chairs were constructed from weathered wood. A striped awning covered half the patio, which was hung with Edison-style string lights in multiple colors.

Kate stood behind one of the unoccupied love seats. Her elbows were propped on the chest-high wall, the sleeves of her hoodie pulled over her hands to keep them warm. She gazed pensively across the Hudson at Hoboken's skyline. Light sparkled through high-rise windows, creating rectangular stars on the black canvas of night.

I set the glasses on the low table, skirted the love seat, and wrapped my arms around her. Silky hair hung loose instead of in its usual ponytail and tickled my cheek. I tucked the strands behind one small, perfectly shaped ear. "Penny."

She leaned against me with a sigh. "Penny?"

"For your thoughts."

A long second stretched into five. Then, "I was remembering another roof."

She didn't have to say another word.

"Oh, honey." I tightened my hold and pressed my cheek against hers.

"My mom would be so proud of you." Kate's voice was uncharacteristically low.

I studied the opposite shore for a moment. "I think she would be. But more importantly, she'd be proud of you, baby."

"I don't—I hope so."

"You know she wanted you to follow your heart. You talked with her about where you wanted to go and what you wanted to do."

"I do know. You're right. She would be. And Will too. Even though he did the cookie-cutter son thing."

"Made your dad happy."

"True."

"I don't want tomorrow to come. Or the next day. Especially the next day." Her voice thickened. "I know I shouldn't be all sentimental, but…" She trailed off and blew out another deep breath.

There it was. I knew it was coming and didn't want to face the emotion of it. I didn't know how to respond. I felt the same way, yet I didn't. I had the luxury of realizing something I'd been anticipating for so long, while Kate would go back to what she had been doing. Her volunteer experience was certainly life-changing, but the newness of it had faded.

The fact of the matter was that we were going to have distance between us. Even if I stayed, she'd be over a thousand air miles away, for who knew how long. When the going became next to impossible at the academy, I admit I did fantasize about hopping the next flight to Belize and diving into Kate's arms. Then I thought about the bills I wouldn't be able to pay and dug deep in order to get over, around, or through whatever I was having issues with.

What mattered most to me was that Kate was living her life, living her dreams. She'd had so much taken from her, and somehow, from somewhere, she'd found the strength to keep at it. We'd both managed to not only move forward, but to succeed. It just sucked that succeeding meant a certain degree of guaranteed heartbreak.

That little voice in the back of my head picked that moment to return. Here I was, again, getting in the way of Kate's happiness. Fuck.

I pulled in her scent. It settled me, helped shush the whisper. "Baby, come on. Let's take this back to the room."

Kate pivoted to face me. She pulled my head down until my lips met hers. What started gently quickly escalated into a hunger that would only be satiated in one way. She pulled away with an impish look, leaving me gasping, and ducked under my arm to grab our drinks. "Come on, baby, I got places to take us."

"No need to ask twice." I hustled after her, my blood rushing in my ears. Loving Kate was like the Foreigner song, "Feels Like the First Time," every time.

We spent hours delighting in each other's bodies. My evil inner critic had been banished, at least temporarily, and my heart was so goddamn full. Eventually exhaustion caught up to us both, and we fell asleep wrapped around each other.

Kate woke me sometime past three in the morning and we made love again, slow and sweet. Part of me felt like I was on the brink of losing everything, and another part felt newly born, on a track I'd not expected, but fully embraced anyway. So many contradictions. I showered her with my love not only in words but with my entire body. She responded in kind. Eventually she fell asleep, her head buried in my shoulder. I stared into the darkness, desperately wanting to believe that, in the end, all our plans would come together.

Somehow. Some way.

CHAPTER TEN

Summer 2016

Junie Lajoie's Spirits and More was a well-worn hole-in-the-wall, blending in with countless other shops in Manhattan's South Street Seaport district. With only three name changes in its past, the establishment had seen close to a century's worth of business. The clientele ranged from Financial District suits to the occasional vagrant on the hunt for some cheap wine. As long as the money was green, the deal was good.

Business was slow before noon on a steamy Tuesday in mid-July. The Haitian storekeeper, Junie Lajoie herself, restocked cigarettes behind the counter and kept a wary eye on two shoppers: a twitchy, unkempt man of indeterminate age whose khaki combat jacket looked like it could stand up on its own and a rangy woman about tall enough to look her in the eye. At a little over six feet, that was saying something.

The woman's dark hair was raggedly cropped, as if she'd taken a pair of shears to it herself. A burn, vivid red against the olive brown of her skin, ran from the back of her left hand and up her arm to disappear beneath a black T-shirt. If the nervous tapping of fingers on her thigh was any indication, she was jonesing for a pre-afternoon cocktail.

Junie's sixth sense of impending trouble had been honed by years of dealing with every type of customer under the fiery New York sun. At the moment, her personal "oh, shit" meter was creeping toward the red zone. She slid three packs of Marlboros into the plexi holder above the counter while keeping her eyes on the sales floor.

Three rows of gondola shelving units created four aisles running the length of the store. Each shelf was loaded with numerous varieties of liquor and wine. Silver coolers with clear glass doors covered the entire back wall and showcased various brands of beer.

Junie glanced at the security mirrors mounted near the ceiling in each corner.

The twitchy man approached the checkout with a 40-ounce Bud in one hand. His other was buried in a jacket pocket. He glanced at the entrance and dropped the can of beer on the countertop. It banged against the scuffed laminate, and the sharp sound reverberated like a gunshot through the narrow space.

The tweaker lurched forward, as if in the throes of a seizure. He slammed one hand on the glassed-in display of lottery tickets and yanked the other out of his pocket.

The muzzle of a silver handgun became Junie's focal point as the junkie screamed, "Open the till!"

Junie froze, then raised one hand and inched the other toward a silent alarm beneath the counter.

One moment the barrel of the gun wobbled at Junie's nose. The next the gun was gone.

The woman who'd been playing "Chopsticks" on her leg had grabbed the back of the robber's filthy jacket and flung him into a rack of mini liquor nips. The rack tipped over and dozens of miniature single-serve bottles sailed through the air.

He landed hard, half atop the fallen rack. The impact jarred the gun from his hand. It skittered across the tiled floor.

Junie, eyes wide, watched the woman's fists work the robber over as she pushed the silent alarm.

Blood spattered the floor, most of it the would-be thief's.

The fight was short but vicious. When the woman disengaged, the man lay immobile. She zeroed in on the gun, scooped it up, and scuttled toward the rear of the store.

Through the reflection of one of the surveillance mirrors Junie saw the woman huddle in the corner between the cooler and the wall. She held the gun rock steady in both hands, pointed protectively in front of her.

In an impressive six minutes, NYPD arrived on scene. Junie worked to explain in heavily accented English that the chick in the corner with the weapon wasn't the one who'd held her up, but the cops were too concerned about getting the firearm away from her to listen.

Both miscreants were removed in handcuffs, one under her own steam and the other on a stretcher.

* * *

Coming back to myself was a little like waking up, except I wasn't in bed and the images that raced through my mind weren't from a dream.

Goddamn.

It happened again.

In the five months since I'd returned to the States after a disastrous overseas HAVOC mission, this weird blackout thing had happened two other times. My NPIU case manager, Stanley, a well-meaning pain in my ass, would've termed the blackout a "disassociation."

I called it bat-shit crazy.

Every night, sleep was elusive. My mind dragged me into a hellish hurricane, forced me ever deeper into my own personal purgatory. I couldn't shut down the shitstorm replay of my fucked-up life as it rolled across the movie screen of my mind. Liquor and physical movement were the only things to give me a little relief.

The first time the crazy happened, I was on the A train headed home to Tubs' apartment late one night after another lost day aimlessly wandering the city. A young man wearing gang colors boarded my subway car and attempted to relieve an elderly woman of her handbag with the encouragement of a five-inch switchblade.

When I "awoke," I was tucked between two dumpsters three blocks from the subway. My heart was pounding so hard I thought I was in the midst of a coronary. It took forever to slow my breathing. When I finally calmed enough to realize I wasn't dying, I emerged from the alley to find everything quiet. No foot traffic and only a few cars moving down the vacant streets. I'd totally lost track of time. What the hell had happened?

Eventually some of the events from the train came back, flickering across the back of my closed eyelids like so many of my nightmares. I floated above the fray, watching myself disarm and beat the crap out of the kid.

Was I on candid camera and recognizable? The city had cameras everywhere. Would someone come looking for me? My intent was to help the old woman, of that I was certain. Defending another person wasn't against the law. At least I didn't cut the kid with his own knife. Or did I? I never did manage to recall what happened to the switchblade once I disarmed him.

The second crazy hit sometime past three in the morning while I roamed the streets of Brooklyn. Some bastard had an inebriated girl—who could not have been more than eighteen—pinned against a rough cinder block wall behind a neighborhood bar. He had one hand wrapped around her throat and the other either groping her or working to unbutton his pants. Didn't matter.

I lost my shit. What I remembered most clearly was the girl's frightened eyes as she staggered away to safety. Guilt sliced through me at the memory, not from the beating I gave the guy, but from the fear I saw reflected on her face.

Sometimes I wondered what bits and pieces I was missing from the narratives my brain gave me. I wasn't sure I wanted to know. Always I tried not to think about what kind of person I'd become. Broken, disfigured, and mostly good for nothing.

Now, perched in a hard metal chair with my wrists shackled to a battered tabletop, my ears unexpectedly cleared. Sound rushed in to fill the void. Indistinct voices, the banging of file drawers, and occasional laughter rumbled through the metal door.

I let the muted din wash over me. My left brow was swollen. I moved to feel my face with my fingers, only to have my hands jerked to a stop by the metal bracelets. A growl of frustration echoed through the room. A couple seconds passed before I realized it was coming from me.

Calm. I needed to calm down. One thing at a time. Take a physical inventory, Flynn. From the top down.

So I concentrated on sorting myself out. My head ached dully. A coppery taste filled my mouth. I pushed my tongue against my teeth, and three felt a bit loose. In a few places, the skin inside my mouth was either cut or felt like hamburger. My bottom lip was cut, and my throat clicked when I tried to swallow.

A wave of nausea rolled through me. Breathing slow and deep, I ignored it and turned my attention to my hands. My left looked like I'd shoved it into a meat grinder, new wounds atop new scars. My right was unscathed. At least I'd be able to wipe my ass.

After that I sat for an indeterminate amount of time wondering when someone was going to come in. How long had I been here, anyway?

As if a magician pointed his magic wand at my memory bank, the image of a man in a camo jacket popped into my head.

Holding a silver handgun.

I squeezed my eyes shut, wincing as the movement tugged at taut skin. The harder I chased the recollection, the faster it floated out of my grasp. I stopped trying and eventually the memory teased again. This time he was on the ground. I was on top of him.

We were grappling.

For the gun? Where was the gun? The sense that my life depended on making sure he didn't rise again was palpable.

Where did this go down?

Shelves. Lots of liquor bottles.

Okay, that's right. I'd been hunting my next blackout.

The squeal of the door opening startled me out of the liquor store. A woman sauntered in. Her brown hair was pulled up in a ponytail, and she wore a gray V-neck T-shirt and black pants. An NYPD shield was clipped to her belt.

In one hand she held two paper cups and in the other a manila file folder. She tossed the folder on the tabletop, set one of the cups near my right hand, and settled into the chair across from me with an aggrieved sigh.

"Detective Aubrey Hamilton, Central Robbery Division." She paused, dark blue eyes drilling me. "Jesus, Agent Flynn. This isn't Aleppo. We appreciate you taking down a stickup artist, but seriously. You didn't have to beat him to within an inch of his life."

My eyebrows bounced upward and my stomach dropped. "Within an inch?" My voice sounded dusty, unused.

Detective Hamilton downed some of whatever was in her cup, made a face. "Why doesn't anyone ever clean that goddamn coffeepot?"

If I hadn't been in such misery I might've laughed at the shitty cop house cliché.

"Maybe the beat-down wasn't that bad," she said. "But he's in the hospital with his jaw wired shut for the foreseeable future."

It was all I could do not to puke. I could've killed him and not even known it. I tried and failed to repress a shudder.

Hamilton stuck her hand in a pocket and came up with a cuff key. "You think you're back under control, Agent?"

I nodded.

She shucked my cuffs and sat back down, nudged the coffee toward me with a pointed look.

I hesitated, wondered if any beverage was a good idea but took a sip anyway. The hot liquid stung my cut lip. She was right. The coffee was terrible.

"So," Detective Hamilton said, "back to the scene of the crime. We thought you were the bad guy. In the corner with the gun and all. You were ready to take us out."

What the fuck did I do?

She let the silence settle. "Have you thought about talking to someone to help you deal?"

"I've heard the suggestion before." Stanley loved to yap therapist at me. One of the many reasons I avoided him like an IED in a diaper bag on a barely passable road. While I recovered from my injuries at George Washington University Hospital and then rehabbed at the Rush Rehab center in New York City, the NPIU required a mandatory twice-weekly visit with a shrink. I considered the whole production a waste of my time and his, but I played it like a good patient. When I was discharged, I ignored his directive to find a civilian psychologist. I might be crazy, but I wasn't crazy like that.

"Your NPIU file's sketchy when it comes to specifics, but I understand you and your…HAVOC?…team were involved in quite a battle in Aleppo."

"Please don't go there" ran like a mantra through my mind. "It was. The Feds love their acronyms. HAVOC stands for Hostages and Victims Out Of Country."

Like a good detective, Hamilton nodded once and patiently waited, wanting me, I figured, to spell it out further.

"We partner with the military and FBI and work abroad to free American hostages. We also attempt to locate and rescue or retrieve US victims of crime in foreign countries."

"What happened in Aleppo?"

Like it was any of her business. Of course, considering the circumstances, I suppose it was. Regardless, it was hard enough to replay the worst day of my life in my head, much less verbalize it.

I huffed a resigned breath. "My team was on a case involving a kidnapped American scientist and his wife. We had good intel from a confidential informant that the couple were being held by Abu Habab al-Shiba, a senior ISIL operative. It was confirmed he was in an apartment building filled with civilian families, using them as a shield. Long story short, a firefight ensued. A stash of fuel stored in one of the first floor apartments was hit. Blew three-quarters of the building and its occupants to kingdom come."

She blinked a couple of times. "Ouch. Go on."

I nodded at my left arm. "I was lucky with second and third degree burns from the back of my hand up to my neck."

So many people had been injured or killed, including the scientist and his wife, who al-Shiba was indeed holding on the third floor. Civilian casualties and the loss of four of our six-member team completely negated the victory of taking down al-Shiba. It haunted the everloving shit out of me.

I also didn't tell her I'd used my own body to shield a toddler who'd followed her dad out of the apartment, a sweet-faced little girl with big smile and a mop of black, curly hair, dressed in a SpongeBob T-shirt and jeans. I hadn't yet entered the building when the first blast hit, and a split second after the initial explosion, I tackled her to the ground and curled myself around her. Another blast made the ground shudder. Debris fell on top of us like gray chunks of cement hail. I thought I'd taken the brunt of it. Before I could move, a third fuel tank blew. We were deluged with more rubble.

My ears rang. That high-pitched ringing was all I could hear. I hugged that little girl to me, realized I needed to get us out of there ASAP. I struggled to my knees, fragments falling off my back like a waterfall.

For a lost second I thought saving her would be the bright spot in the middle of utter hell.

Moments later someone tried but failed to pull her from my arms. We hadn't realized she'd been pinned to me by a piece of rebar that had gone through the sleeve of my uniform jacket, nicked my arm, and extended out directly through her chest. She was no longer a squirming, laughing little kid. She was just…no longer.

I grabbed my knees and squeezed, forced myself back to the present, forced myself to breathe.

Hamilton said, softly, "I'm sorry," and picked up the file folder. "Says here you're an exceptional marksman. Or markswoman."

I opened my mouth to answer, but the interrogation door swung open. A bald-headed black man in a rumpled suit walked in. "Come on, Hambone. We have another shooting in Tribeca." He exited, leaving the door open.

Hambone? That was almost funny.

She pushed back from the table. "Agent Flynn...Mikala, if I may, I'd suggest finding someone to talk to. And think about laying off the sauce."

"Not your call, Detective. But for the record, it's Flynn. Drop the agent and the Mikala."

"Flynn it is. You're a spitfire. I like that." She produced a business card. "Here's my number. I belong to a group. Some vets. Some cops. Some Feds. We meet second Monday, every month. Each of us is dealing with what you are, to one degree or another. PTSD, depression, alcohol, drugs. You name it, we probably got it." Her eyes burned into me. "Can't hurt. Might help."

I inhaled to decline, but she said before I could get it out, "Think about it. You're free to go."

Just like that? Yes, I guess so. I stood, made sure I could stand before I let go of the table. "You got a bathroom I can use?"

"Down the hall on the left. Be safe and stay out of trouble."

In the dim restroom I washed up as best I could. With regret I chucked my throwback Goose Gossage Yankee tee in the trash—it was blood-spattered and the neck had been ripped—leaving me in a black tank top and jeans. I scrubbed blood-spattered, uninjured skin almost raw and then did it again.

With much more care I cleaned my wounded hand. The first two knuckles were raw, and three parallel gouges ran from the top of my wrist toward those knuckles, crossing over my still healing burn scar. The scar ran a ropy path from my hand over my forearm, past my elbow and triceps, stopping just below my shoulder. It was a more bitter than sweet reminder of what I'd survived and what my team had lost. In time, I knew, the painful redness would fade but not ever the memory of what had happened. By the time I hit the street, all I cared about was scoring some vodka, preferably a triple, and then following it up with another.

CHAPTER ELEVEN

The evening was oppressive. Every breath I took felt like I was sucking hot air through a wet washcloth. Wasn't sure if it was the aftereffects of stress or the need for alcohol that caused my body to break into goose bumps.

At the intersection of Madison and Pearl, I stopped in front of a Rite Aid and debated the wisdom of dodging inside for some ibuprofen and Band-Aids. I stuck my hand in my pocket. My cash was still there. Rite Aid won.

Ten minutes later I stood in front of a City of New York garbage bin and applied bandages to various wounds as Manhattanites and tourists alike swept past me like waves of human lava. I unscrewed the top of a bottle of water and guzzled half of it before popping four Advil and finishing off the bottle.

These days my memory was spotty, but I was pretty sure a nightclub catering to those with an affinity for the same sex was located somewhere nearby. I needed a safe space to pull myself together and come up with a half-assed excuse for Tubs as to why I looked like I'd gone three rounds with Floyd Mayweather.

After a couple detours, I found the bar and carefully lowered myself onto a stool. At the sight of my face, the bartender did a double take. It was almost comical. From the varied emotions flickering across her face, I could tell she wasn't sure if she should call the cops, throw me out, or summon an ambulance. I waved off her concern, placed my order, and laid a twenty on the bar top. My drink appeared in record time. Down the hatch it went. I signaled for another. Damn lucky thing I'd stashed some cash over the years. With temporary disability, I was financially afloat for the moment, if nothing else. The NPIU had left my position open-ended, but I wasn't sure I'd ever be ready to return. But sooner or later, I was going to have to get back to work or get the hell out, and sometimes exiting this life entirely felt like the only solution.

I pushed those jagged, complicated thoughts out of my head and focused on the present, which included a tipsy, middle-aged blonde with overdone makeup jabbering the ear off the bartender and a guy two stools to my right throwing them back faster than I was.

An hour later, a lot buzzier and a little less tense, I headed toward the Brooklyn Bridge. The setting sun glinted through crisscrossed guide wires, painting the bridge's wooden slats with diamond-shaped shadows. As my own shadow obliterated the diamonds, I struggled to put together a timeline of my incredibly shitty day.

I'd left the apartment before five a.m., as I often did when I couldn't sleep. The sun had risen as I wandered the streets. I crossed into Manhattan, grabbed a croissant from a food cart, and contemplated where I might find my first dose of joy juice.

I killed time in Battery Park, watching early-bird tourists line up for the boat ride over to the Statue of Liberty and Ellis Island.

Life went on no matter what. I wondered when I'd feel like a bouncing ball instead of a flatliner, when I'd be able ride the ups and downs of life like a normal human being. All I did these days was fight to keep my nose above the water. Some Federal agent I was. If I kept on this path, my career choice would be decided for me.

What time did I wind up in the liquor store?

Sweat trickled down the small of my back. I upped the pace, making it off the bridge onto the streets of Brooklyn in record time. I should've called Tubs, could've texted to let her know I was okay, but I didn't have a cell phone. She was all over technology now, with her iPad, iPhone, and an Apple laptop. The woman even had a Kindle, for Pete's sake.

The fact was, I'd seen so many cell phones used to blow up roadside bombs while I was on HAVOC duty that I'd become wary of cell phones in general. It was irrational. More than ninety-nine percent of the population wasn't out to murder anyone, and I knew it on a logical level. If only I could live in a completely logical world.

It didn't take long before I closed in on Tubs' red brick apartment building. Over the years the color of the awnings had changed from cream to black, but other than that it still looked as it did when I was a kid. Her ninth-floor apartment was accessible via two dodgy elevators (even dodgier than they were back when I'd left Manhattan for Minneapolis), eighteen flights of stairs, or a black metal fire escape that zigzagged the side of the building like a lightning bolt.

In the last few weeks, I'd taken to using a dumpster to launch myself at the bottom of the escape ladder. I'd swing myself onto the landing and climb up to the ninth floor. In the fewer-than-thirty seconds it took, I actually felt alive. I spent hours sitting on the metal grid platform right below Tubs' living room window, drunk and contemplating my existence.

No fire escape today, though. Eventually the elevator regurgitated me into a drab hallway with drab carpet, all in shades of drab beige. That had not changed a bit, either.

The apartment was halfway down the hall, and, of course, the door was unlocked. The lectures I'd given Tubs about personal safety fell on deaf ears. I'd resigned myself to walking in one day to find her dead, just like I'd found my father so long ago. That would be a real treat.

I limped across the threshold and locked the door behind me.

Tubs sat at the table with her head in the newspaper. "Mikala, where have you been?"

"Sorry, Tubs. Long story."

"I'll bet it is." She glanced up at me, eyes narrowed, and pushed reading glasses to the top of her head. "What on earth happened to you?" She rose, circled me as if I were an exotic animal. "Black eye, fat lip. You're leaning sideways. Something wrong with your ribs?"

My grandmother had an uncanny ability to sum up my maladies as if they were her own.

"Yes, yes, and I don't know. Everything hurts."

Ten minutes, more bandages, and an ice pack later, she settled me at the table. "Tell me what happened while I heat you some supper."

She gave my shoulder a brisk pat and made for the refrigerator. The braid she'd always worn now hung nearly to her mid-back and had become more salt than pepper. As she moved, it swayed against her white "I'm With Her" T-shirt.

While the microwave did its thing to my food, she leaned against the sink and peered at me through the kitchen and dining room pass-through. "You look like you're about to keel over." Because of our dusky coloring, it was obvious when either of us paled. I knew she was dying to ask what'd gone down but was doing her best to wait it out and let me explain when I was ready.

"I'm okay." I popped a peanut M&M from the bowl that still had a home on the table and avoided her searching eyes. Better to lose myself in flashes of memory I couldn't quite flesh out.

The thunk of the plate on the table jolted me. I blinked at two fat, potato-filled pierogies covered in tomato sauce, with a buttered roll on the side.

"Thank you, Tubs." I ripped off a chunk of bread, soaked it in the sauce. As soon as the acidic liquid hit my cut lip I winced.

Tubs sat down across from me while I ate. I was aware of her watching my every move, still assessing injuries.

When I finished, she asked, "More?"

My stomach was full, and the aftereffects of my day hit hard. Gravity pulled at my eyelids. "No, I'm good."

"Come on then. Up you go." Tubs hoisted me out of the chair and guided me to my room. "We can talk tomorrow. Right now you might be able to sleep."

I'd never complained to Tubs about my insomnia, but she knew. I allowed her to help me change into a clean T-shirt and shorts. Then she tucked me in. "*Ov yilo isi*, my child."

When I was a kid, every night without fail, she'd whisper that Romani phrase when she put me to bed. It loosely translated to "everything is okay," and before my dad was murdered, I believed her. Now, I held the words close to my heart and wished I could believe again as I drifted into a fitful slumber.

CHAPTER TWELVE

Four days later, the metal grid of the fire escape imprinted itself on my ass. I ignored the pain as I tipped a bottle of booze up for another swallow. I knew for a fact I'd forget all about physical aches and pains once I got enough liquor in me.

If only I had a switch to shut down my mind and stop my head from going where I didn't want it to go. Every sober moment was tainted with the nightmare of that terrible day in Aleppo, and it seemed no distraction was strong enough to stop it.

I forced myself to relax, to concentrate on the moment. Darkness had fallen while I sat and swigged. Even on the blackest of nights, the city was never completely shut down unless a power outage hit. Even then, automated generators chased most of the shadows away.

Sodium vapor lamps lined the boulevard below, casting pools of soft yellow-orange against the uneven sidewalk. Our street had not yet been updated with garish, blue-toned LEDs, so the mix of bar neon, business signs, and vehicle lights held the night at bay in a comforting way.

I assessed what was left of my libation. Three-quarters full. Plenty enough to tamp despair.

The trail it seared down my throat and into my chest made me wince. I leaned against the brick wall with a yawn and stretched my legs out in front of me, allowing my feet to dangle over the rusty edge of the platform. Exhaustion felt so heavy it took almost all my attention. I'd been wandering around since three the previous morning. No wonder the suicide rate was so high for those in law enforcement. One bullet could create blissful nothingness instead of living in torture. If Tubs weren't around, I'd much more seriously consider that final option. Sometimes, even though she was, the thought of creating nothingness was almost irresistible.

Voices in various languages mixed with occasional bursts of laughter floated to me through open apartment windows. I closed my eyes and listened, absently running my fingertips over the pitted metal I sat upon. Through the screen above my head, I half paid attention to the sounds of Tubs and the Art Squad gossiping about the latest on the New York arts scene. Since I'd come back home, I'd only seen the Squad once. I loved them, but I wasn't ready for their life-filled enthusiasm. I had to admit, though, it was comforting to lose myself in their chatter.

I zoned out for a while, floating on my buzz, when a loud voice came through Tubs' window and startled me.

Elizabet Baryshnikov, the special effects makeup artist who sounded like television comedy actress Fran Drescher and was no relation to ballet superstar Mikhail, was on a tear.

"—know you switched out the real Helen Keller Nazi book burning letter for a fake."

A gravelly voice I didn't recognize responded, "Elizabet, I did nothing of the sort. You left to take care of whatever it was you needed to do, and I was gentleman enough to wait for the end of the auction and secure your purchase."

I perked up. The Squad never squabbled. Nazis and fake documents? It took some effort for my liquor-soaked brain to catch up.

"No one else could've done it. When I brought Helen's letter to my insurance appraiser, they caught the forgery. It's well-done, but it's a forgery all the same."

Damn, Elizabet was shrill when she was upset.

"Are you accusing *me* of forging that letter?" The man's gruff tone took on an edge. "Seriously?"

"Scandon Auctions always guarantees their documents." That rich, resonate, accented voice belonged to Sahl, the estate appraiser. "Items that leave the auction have been thoroughly vetted."

Gravel Man said, "You weren't even there. Besides, the auction house guarantees every piece they sell, so take it up with them."

"Pascal," Sahl said, "Scandon's reputation is spotless. They verify the authenticity of all their goods, not only through archival research but also via various independent experts. I've worked with them numerous times when an estate has papers, documents, or manuscripts of value. They do not sell falsified items. Which means Elizabet's letter was switched after it left the building."

"That's right," Elizabet said, "and the letter left with you."

The conversation lulled. This was better than a soap opera.

"Stop." Tubs now. "Pascal, your reputation as a rare documents dealer is already on shaky ground. Last month weren't there three Ethics in Arts complaints lodged against you for selling documents of questionable origin? And on top of that, I know you've dealt in stolen merchandise in the past. You've managed to pay the right people the right amount of money to keep their lips zipped."

How did she know that?

"*Oy vey*, Tubs, why didn't you tell me this news? Pascal, you shmuck!" A very momentary pause was followed by a pained grunt. I imagined Elizabet skewering Pascal's sternum with one of her long, claw-like fingernails.

"I didn't say anything because I knew you wouldn't listen," Tubs said.

Elizabet huffed. "Ugh. I hate when you're right." Noisy sigh. "Instead, I happily wore blinders because this…this shyster is a horizontal mambo master between twelve-hundred thread count sheets." If she were a dragon her words would've scorched.

"I thought you, Pascal, of all people, would understand why I wanted Helen's letter after I told you all about my meeting with her as a child."

I was stuck on "horizontal mambo master." Oh my God. And she actually met Helen Keller? I sat up straighter and tilted an ear toward the window screen.

"Yes, I remem—"

"Oh, shut your piehole, you schmuck. I get a once-in-a-lifetime chance to own that very letter and you insult me by playing Freddy Fast Fingers?"

"That's it. I've had enough," Pascal said. "I don't have anything to prove to you lot. And Elizabet, I have nothing to do with the problems you're having with your letter. I was nothing but a perfect gentleman. I did you a favor, and this is the thanks I get?"

Five seconds of silence passed before the front door slammed. I felt the reverberation against my back.

For a moment it was as if the entire apartment building went silent. Then conversations resumed. Familiar and unfamiliar voices once more blended together into a jumbled mélange. I took another hit and tried to relax into my self-made haze.

Beni's voice floated through the screen. "I told you Pascal Teufel was a rascal from the moment I laid eyes on him, Elizabet." She'd retired from police sketching and painted landscapes as a hobby. Tubs said her latest work had been exhibited at a small gallery in Chelsea. Pretty cool.

Tubs laughed. "Pascal the Rascal. Gotta love that. Elizabet, maybe it's time to give up the dating scene. Or at least let me run your next beau through Interpol."

Interpol? What? I had to have misheard. Then that thought floated away.

"Oh shush. What fun would that be? I have one life to live, and you better believe your matzo ball soup I'm living it." In my mind's eye I could vividly see Elizabet's arms flailing as she spoke. Now five-times divorced and in her late sixties, she was a serial dater who spent a lot of time on eHarmony consorting with various fish in the semi-senior dating sea.

"When we first met," Elizabet continued, "I told Pascal about my undying esteem for Helen Keller, and how we talked about books Hitler had banned. He told me he was into Helen too, which was, my oh my, a big turn-on."

Ugh.

Her voice softened, her tone reminiscing. "She spoke to me as if I wasn't ten years old, as if I were someone important, about the absolute necessity of maintaining freedom of speech round the globe. How she tried to convince the Nazis that lighting tomes afire, literature filled with unimaginably bright ideas, with hopes and dreams for the world was nothing but a catastrophe. She told me she wrote an open letter to the newspaper, but she lost her fight with the Reich. Regardless, she never surrendered sharing her belief in the good of humanity."

Barely missing a breath, she said, "I was browsing art and document auctions online and saw four lots come up with some of Helen's rare personal writings. Her writings! And no, before you ask, I did not stop to wonder why they were not in her archives. Slap my wrist. Anyway, I could not believe my very eyes! One of them was yes, oh yes, that infamous book burning letter. Oh, my dears! I just could *not* believe it. And now. That Pascal…I knew he wasn't always Mr. Goodie Pants, well, he was good in the pants but—"

"Elizabet," Tubs said, "here's some water. Take a drink and calm yourself. You're speaking in exclamation marks."

She stopped yapping long enough to guzzle noisily.

"Ah. Thank you, Tubs. Where was I? Oh yes. We went to the auction, I bid, and I won. Then, disaster! I had to leave before I was able to pay because the JTNY sent me a 911. The latest schlumpette they hired was too hung over to come in. Where's the guilt, I ask? I swear, kids these days. But the show must go on at the Jewish Theater of New York, and, of course, I rose to the challenge. I whipped out my checkbook, wrote one for $13,550, and left the check with that rascal Pascal. He told me he'd tend to business. I thought he was honorable, well, at least with me. I was a…nothing but a silly doofus."

The stamping of a hard-soled shoe echoed off the hardwood floor. I wondered if we all returned to our child selves when we were cut out of something we really wanted. I didn't think I reverted, but then again I was drunk as a monk holding a skunk so I wasn't the best judge.

"E-easy, Elizabet. I-I-I can see how much this letter means to y-you. We all can," Rich said. "W-why don't we steal it back? Serve the fink right."

"No. No, no, no. We don't want to do that," Anton droned. "We're done with that life. Take it to the proper authorities."

"Come on, Anton," said Char Wozniak, the last member of the Art Squad. "You know the fuzz will only blow it off. Add some drugs or murder to the deal and that might interest 'em, otherwise not so much. Come on, you old farts. We might be retired but we're still kicking. Let's do it. Let's get that letter back for Elizabet. Then I'll bring it to Stazio's and have Frank do a workup." She lived with Frank Stazio of Stazio Art Research, Inc. Both bleeding heart liberals, they thumbed their nose at the institution of marriage but had been together for twenty-five years.

"That was years ago. We're old now." Anton sounded like a sloth.

"Come on, Anton," Tubs said, "it's all about muscle memory."

What was she talking about? Muscle memory? If my brain wasn't so hazy, maybe I could focus enough to think coherently about…what? My attention was distracted by Elizabet's rising voice. "I'll throw a couple steaks to the Dobermans. That'll keep them busy."

"Dobermans?" Anton's voice hit his own high note. "No, I don't think this is a good idea. Not a good idea at all."

"H-h-how many dogs?" Rich asked.

For once I wished I had a cell phone to record them. No one would believe me if I told them this crew was contemplating breaking and entering for the purpose of relieving a thief of an item he'd already stolen. It was so strange. It almost seemed as if…what? They'd stolen stuff before? Tubs would never, ever steal anything. Would she? How well did I really know my grandmother? Oh my God. Now I was getting paranoid.

I leaned my head against the rough brick and tossed back some more alcohol. Who needed TV when reality was this good? For the first time in a long time my own woes faded.

Elizabet said, "Only two mutts. Or maybe three. Three. Yes, it's three. I'm pretty sure. Anyway, don't worry, Rich. They respond to a dog whistle. Once they come to us, we feed them the steaks. Easy as lemon peasy pie. Hey! I could throw in some Ambien. Knock 'em right out."

Dog doping? Holy moly.

"Is his property fenced?" Tubs asked.

"Yes, and gated," Elizabeth said.

"How tall is the fence?" I could hear Tubs' impatience leaking out.

"Like I ever had time to measure. Whaddya think I am, a yardstick?" Elizabet had left exclamation marks behind and moved on to verbal swordswomanship. "I'd guess maybe seven or eight feet. It's stone, and topped with metal spikes."

I could see the headline on the *New York Post*. "Geezers Attempt Break-in and Get Crotched."

"I c-could boost you guys over," Rich said. "Not sure how you'll get down on the other side, though." Whippet-thin Rich stood about six-foot-six in his socks and was a lot stronger than he looked. However, I couldn't envision most of these scallywags scaling a fence of any kind, much less one seven feet tall. They were all able-bodied, but each had their own age-related battles. As well as hearts bigger than the Big Apple.

At this point I couldn't stand it anymore. I had to see them, not just hear their conversation. I set my bottle on the metal grating and pivoted to a crouch, eyes just above the sill, like a kid looking through a department store window at a Macy's holiday toy display.

Beni, Char, and Sahl were on the couch.

Tubs stood beside them. Rich kicked back in one of the La-Z-Boys while Anton overflowed the other recliner, which had appeared sometime after I'd moved out.

All eyes were glued to statuesque, platinum-haired Elizabet pacing back and forth across the living room floor like a caged polar bear with flair.

Beni asked, "What kind of security does Pascal's place have?" Leave it to the one with the police background to bring that up.

Elizabet stopped, propped her fists on ample hips. Her back was to me, and her beehive tilted precariously to the side as she cocked her head. "He's got one of those newfangled systems. Front something." She flung a hand in the air. "Front Air? Front Stoop?"

"Elizabet, you never were good at the tech part. Front Door." Sahl picked up his cell phone. "That's the system going into most homes these days. Let me check the specs."

Char rubbed her hands together like a giddy adolescent. "What kind of system is it? One we can bypass?"

Sahl held the phone at arm's length. "If Pascal has the top-of-the-line plan—"

"Of course the man has a top-of-the-line plan to go with his top-of-the-line system," Elizabet said. "Aside from the excellent whoopee, his sense of style and taste for the finer things is what drew me into his world like those poor geese sucked through the engines of Sully's A320."

Tubs made a noise that sounded like a half-gag, half-laugh.

Sahl pulled out a pair of reading glasses and settled them on his nose. "As I was saying, assuming Pascal has the cream of the security crop, here's what we're in for. Twenty-four/seven monitoring. Everyone has that these days. The system runs automatic checks on itself and has a crash-and-smash protection plan. That's standard."

"W-what's smash-and-crash?"

"Crash-and-smash." Sahl shot Rich a bemused look. "When someone breaks in, the idea is to storm the front door and take a hammer to the alarm panel, thereby disabling it for a certain period of time."

"How long?" Rich asked.

"Of that I am not sure. Maybe a minute? Maybe more. Moving on. Next, mobile alerts. Used to be that when a call center was alerted by a triggered alarm, the information was sent to police dispatch. Now, the alert goes right to the owner via a cell phone or other device and then to the cops. Workarounds to the notification system exist, but it would take a fair amount of effort to achieve. Live video streaming is another challenge. Cameras can be anywhere, and often they are hidden."

Anton, who looked like he'd fallen asleep, muttered, "Maybe we should have ourselves implanted with GoPros and call it good."

Tubs shot him a look. "Some help you are." Oh ho. She was warming to the idea.

"Please," Sahl said. "Only if we all work together can we coordinate this plot. Let me finish." He adjusted his glasses and squinted at the phone. "If motion is detected while it is dark, a night vision program kicks in, triggering a notification to authorities and the owner."

Elizabet's explosive "Aha!" made me jump. "I've got it. The costuming department has those black ski masks you always see hold-up artists wearing in the movies. I can talk to the costumer and—"

"Hold on a minute, Elizabet," Beni said. "You ask your costume person to use the masks and you don't think they'll get suspicious?"

"Good point," Elizabet said. "This was easier when we had equipment at our fingertips. But," she swooshed a hand through the air, "I know where they're stored. I'll borrow and return them when we're done." She resumed pacing. "They're not used in the current production anyway."

Char said, "We should get some of those black body suits like Tom Cruise wore in *Mission Impossible*. Maybe Elizabet can get a hold of some of those too."

Anton snorted. "Char, why don't you have some more Kool-Aid?"

She raised an eyebrow. "Maybe you should try some, Anton."

"Thanks, but I'll stick to water."

"Sometimes you're a real stick in the street, Largess."

"And you, Char, are destined to become somebody's jailhouse bitch."

Aside from comments I didn't understand and frankly figured I was conjuring up in my inebriated state, I knew my crazy crew would never be able to pull this off. I'd done plenty far more complex assignments. If I stepped in with a couple support people, we could make things right for Elizabet.

Holy crap. Was I actually thinking about breaking and entering and swiping a decades-old letter? I ran a hand over my face and zoned back in.

"—should check out the collection of puzzle boxes Pascal has," Anton said.

Puzzle boxes? They'd been arguing about jailhouse bitches. I squeezed my eyes shut. How long had I blanked this time?

"That man must have fifty boxes in all shapes and sizes," Elizabet said, "organized on an entire wall. I meant to mention that to you, Tubs, but things happened."

Beni said, "What if he put the Keller letter in one of those boxes? We'd never be able to find it."

Elizabet waved off the notion. "No, he wouldn't do that. He has three very nice display cases filled with rare documents. The most valuable pieces he keeps in his office in a walk-in safe. It's all on the second floor. So are the puzzle boxes."

Tubs walked over to the hutch and picked up our puzzle box. "I'd love to take a look at his collection."

Elizabet shimmied over to Tubs and put an arm around her. "Maybe we can make this a dual purpose heist."

My head began to pound. The desire to get my hands on those boxes, the need to find out if our family heirloom was within reach vacuumed the oxygen from my lungs. For long moments, I struggled to breathe.

"Back to plotting, people." Sahl clapped his hands. "We need steak. I think two of us should climb the fence and enter the premises. We still have the problem of how to descend the other side of the fence. And then how do we get back out?"

"Hell, once we have the letter, what's to stop us from exiting right out the front door?" From the enthusiastic tone of Tubs' voice, she was now fully on board.

Come on, Tubs, I thought, think this through before you get into some serious shenanigans and wind up in Central Booking. I could see it now. The cops would arrive on scene, and one of these geriatric maniacs would be impaled on a spike while drooling, wobbly Dobermans pinned down the other. This was lunacy.

"I'm with you, Tubs," Beni said. "If we get caught I might be able to pull a few strings." She rubbed her hands together. "Just like old times."

Old times? Whatever. Come on, you guys, I thought. Tubs would wind up in jail and get nailed with an extended sentence for attempting to bribe her way out. Beni…what would they do to Beni? I could see the headline now. "Retired NYPD Sketch Artist and Gypsy Sidekick Arrested in B&E."

I downed two more glugs, hissed as the burn flared. Without taking the time to think about why I shouldn't do it, I slid the screen up and hoisted a leg over the sill, arched my back beneath the bottom of the open window, and slithered in.

The problem with my grand entrance was twofold. I should've thought before I acted that I was surprising people of a certain age, and secondly, should have remembered that the fire escape was about a foot higher than the living room floor. Where I'd expected solid ground was nothing but air. Then my hands hit the hardwood and I automatically tucked and rolled.

Right into the coffee table.

Once the panicked screeching stopped, Tubs said, "Mikala! What on earth are you doing?"

I blinked up at her, half on the floor, half on the coffee table, one foot on Char's lap. The bright lights made me squint, and my head felt sloshy.

"Help her up," Anton said from the La-Z-Boy.

Elizabet and Tubs each extended a hand and I sorted my limbs out. Took a moment and a couple long breaths as I waited for the room to stop spinning like a life-sized top. Tubs kept a hand on my shoulder. I knew she was giving me *that* look.

"Quite the entrance, Mikala," Tubs said, her tone back to Sahara. "What were you doing out on the fire escape?"

I ignored that. "You honestly think you can break into a security-alarmed, Doberman-protected compound?" What better way to deflect than go on the offensive?

"Were you spying on us?"

The offensive tactic was a no-go. Tubs could still make me squirm like a damn nine-year-old. "Okay, okay. I wasn't exactly spying—"

"If you weren't spying, then what exactly were you doing out on the fire escape?" Tubs drew her shoulders back and crossed her arms, pinning me in place with piercing dark eyes.

Char said, "Leave her alone and get her something to sit on before she falls over."

Guess I wasn't doing a very good job of holding myself upright. Thought I'd minimized the swaying once the room stopped spinning.

Elizabet flounced to the table, grabbed a chair, and dragged it over. She placed it next to Rich, and Tubs pushed me into it. Once my ass hit the seat Rich reached over and patted my knee. "N-n-nice e-e-entrance, Flynn."

"I aim to entertain. Now, about this strategic plan to retrieve Elizabet's property, assuming Mister—what's his name again?"

"Pascal. Pascal Teufel," Elizabet said.

Beni smirked. "Pascal the Rascal."

"I told you this crazy scheme wouldn't work," Anton said.

I held up a hand. "Never said it wouldn't work. But half a plan and Ambien-laced steak?"

Elizabet looked abashed. "And what would you suggest instead, Hotshot?"

"Thanks for the new nickname. Look, you guys. Someone who has turned his house into a fortress is expecting problems."

"Yes, ma'am. He's a problem all right." Elizabet's scowl pulled the corners of her mouth down.

I could almost hear her grinding her teeth from where I sat. "What you need is an extraction team." As I spoke, a picture above the television caught my eye, a snapshot of my father and mother not long before she died. They'd been swimming and were standing arm in arm in the surf on a beach somewhere in Italy, beaming at the camera with not a care in the world.

Mom was trim, her skin dark from genetics and the sun, and while not beautiful in the classical sense, she was perfect in my eyes. Her long black hair glistened, as if she'd just surfaced. My dad was tall and muscular, his arms ruddy with a farmer's tan, red hair in a neat crew cut. Their smiles radiated youthful love and a giddiness I could only imagine came from enjoying a glorious day off in the sun and sand.

The picture had been hanging in the same place as long as I could remember, and I wondered, not for the first time, what my father would've thought of all that had transpired since he passed.

Shit. I'd gone and done it again. Faded out at a critical moment. Jesus Christ. I wrenched my gaze from the photo. Thinking clearly for any length of time was hard enough since I'd been back home, but add liquor to the mix and herding those drunken neurons into order was worse than rounding up a slew of frisky kittens.

My lids sank shut and I hung my head. What had I been talking about? Lost letters. A pissed off Elizabet. I opened my eyes and everyone was staring, waiting for me to return from wherever I'd gone.

"So, a letter extraction team." Anton broke the proverbial ice, his tone skeptical.

Oh, yeah. Thank you, Anton, for cluing me in. "Yeah, someone to coordinate the op, someone to execute, and somebody with IT knowledge to hack the security system and make sure communications between everyone stay up. Once we have the pieces in place, we can go after the letter."

"My goodness," Sahl said. "That's nice coordination."

I raised an eyebrow. "You need it if you want to be successful."

"I think," Beni sized me up, "you need to do this."

Anton said, "That's a fine idea."

Beni ignored Anton and stared at me with a look I'd not seen before. "Flynn really could do it. She's got enough sneaky experience."

"Wait a minute," I said. "You're really serious."

"Hell, yes," Char said.

Their belief in me was out of place—at this moment in time anyway.

I took a deep, woozy breath, blew my bluster out. "I sure could, but right now I can't—"

"Hush, you," Tubs jabbed me. "You can do anything. It's all a matter of whether or not you want to."

Rich said, "A matter of c-confidence, don't you think?"

Thus began a discussion of various concepts of mind over matter and the powers of will.

I repressed the desire to slap my hands over the mouth of the loudest of the bunch, who, of course, was Elizabet. Instead I twisted my fingers together to keep from covering up my ears. The noise made me crazy. This was a mistake. All I wanted to do was slide back out that open window into the relative quiet of the night.

"One moment," Sahl barked and waved his arms, reminiscent of a fury-driven Elizabet. Things quieted in a hurry. "Tubs is right. Flynn can accomplish anything she puts her mind to. It would be a good idea, no?"

How could I not help these people who were so dear, especially poor Elizabet? Aside from the fact I had no backup, what did I have to lose? Not a whole lot. So why not? What were the chances I might get caught? If I was on my game, not much. The thought of planning and executing something covert and, to be honest—illegal—made my heart thud.

A pounding on the front door interrupted my brain. "Got it," I said. My legs were remarkably steady as I peered through the peephole into the hall to the distorted vision of a bald, bright-eyed man smiling and waving his fingers, as if he knew I was eyeballing him, which he did.

"Fucking A. You've got to be kidding." I banged my forehead once against the wood below the peephole.

"Who is it, Mikala?" I felt Tubs hand on my arm.

"Stan." I straightened, turned toward her. Fuck, fuck, fuck. Stanley Dabrowski, my five-foot-six, perpetually tanned case manager who had become a self-appointed pain-in-my ass. Somewhere along the line, probably when he found out I liked the chicks like he liked the guys, he'd taken a shine and decided to keep prodding me in the direction he felt was right. He showed up at the most inopportune times, and this visit didn't break that tradition.

I spun around, put a finger to my lips, and hissed a quick, "Shh." With a deep breath, I unlocked the door, flung it open, and took a step into the dimly lit hall, my attention locked on Stanley. "Look, Stan, this isn't—"

Fixated on him, I didn't see the wheelchair in front of him. I pulled up a split second before disaster. My forward momentum wasn't so easily stopped, and I almost landed in the occupant's lap. I grabbed the arms of the chair and steadied myself. "I'm sor..."

The eyes that met mine shocked the words right out of my head and choked off anything else I might have said. I was a hairsbreadth from the person who, for months, had a starring role in my nightmares. Someone I'd refused to see even when he'd reached out to me once I'd been transferred stateside. Someone I thought I'd never, ever, come in contact with again.

"Joey," I whispered.

His midnight black eyes glittered with familiar humor, and he gave me that goddamn crooked grin, the one that always allowed him to get away with far too much. He rumbled, voice still as deep and raspy as ever, "Hey, Flynn. Long time no visual."

For once it was a good thing my blood alcohol was above the legal limit. If I hadn't been half tanked, I might've passed out right in the middle of the hallway.

Joey put his large hands over mine, his black skin contrasting against my whiteness, and pried my fingers off the arms of his wheelchair. He gave them a squeeze and pushed me vertical. "'Sup, baby?"

All I could do was blink. The last time I saw the man sitting before me, we were knee-deep in the rubble of what had been the apartment building in Aleppo. He'd been pinned under a boulder-sized chunk of concrete. One moment he'd been standing right beside me watching the little girl run out of the building, and the next the world blew up.

They sent us both to Landstuhl, Germany, and then he took a long flight stateside. By the time I hit the DC hospital a week later I heard he'd been paralyzed from the waist down.

A month after that he'd called while I was in physical therapy and left a message and his number. I didn't return his call. I did not call my best friend back. What the fuck had I been thinking?

The fact of the matter was I could not handle the guilt that shredded me every time I thought about him. So I didn't lift a finger to find him, to see how he was doing. I did nothing at all to contact the one person I knew better than I knew anyone. Who knew *me* better than I knew myself. Then in a millisecond I mentally kicked my own ass. Liar. Kate still held both those spots and I doubted anything could ever change that.

Tubs stuck her head into the hall. "What's up?" Pause. "Joey? What are you doing here?" Then, as if she remembered her manners, she wiggled around me and awkwardly hugged him. "It's wonderful seeing you, but this is...unexpected."

"I know, ma'am," Joey said.

"Stanley," she dragged her gaze from Joey to Stan. "Good to see you. However, I hate to say this is a bad time, but it's a bad time."

Sometimes it was easier to sit back and let Tubs have at it.

"My apologies, Mrs. Flynn. This will only take a moment. I'm glad you're here because this concerns you as well as Agent

Flynn." His semi-smug expression was tempered by an I-got-you-now smirk.

Stanley put his hand on Joey's shoulder. "Agent Moseby has been released from rehab and is in need of transitional housing, temporarily, of course. We were hoping you," he gestured at Tubs, "would be willing to host him until a more suitable situation can be worked out. I know this is a bit fast, but we weren't expecting Agent Moseby to be released for another week."

I loved Joey, but sure as hell wasn't ready to spend twenty-four/seven with the very person I'd failed. Besides, the apartment had only two bedrooms, and we had a burglary to plan. I did a quick calculation in my head. I had enough in savings to put him up in a hotel for at least a week if we found one…I glanced at his ride.

That was wheelchair accessible.

"It's okay." Tubs pursed her lips. "We'll hook Joey up." She knew I felt it was my fault he was in a wheelchair in the first place. She knew he starred in many of my nightmares. She so had to know I wasn't ready for this.

"Bu—" I began, only to be halted by a sharp "don't you even" glare from Tubs.

Faster than I could keep up, Tubs dragged Joey's duffle bag into the apartment, dispatched Stanley, and sent me to my room to arrange things to accommodate a wheelchair. As I cleared my floor of dirty clothes, I caught snatches of conversation as Tubs introduced Joey to the Art Squad.

At the sound of his laughter, I could no longer hold back the tears.

CHAPTER THIRTEEN

The scent of bacon wormed its way into my dream, but the sound of the sizzle was what woke me. Where was I? I remembered sitting on the fire escape, working my way through a bottle.

My eyes felt crusty. I pried them open, blinked. Pebbled, cream-colored paint came into focus.

Something on the ceiling was missing. What was it? My ability to think was missing too. The top of my head felt like it was about to pop off.

Then it came to me. My bedroom ceiling had a Texas-shaped water stain.

I looked again. No water stain. The sizzling meat sounded really close. How much booze had I guzzled last night?

It felt like someone had fitted my eyelids with mini-dumbbells during the night. I allowed them to slide shut and rode a wave of random, nonsensical thoughts. If only the thumping in my head would stop I could think better.

The nonsensical thoughts led to art, which led me to the Art Squad. The geezers were planning to heist something?

Right.

I would have laughed if I dared.

My mind wandered again. Then something came to me about a wheelchair. And Stanley, my caseworker.

Next, Joey showed up on my big brain movie screen. Where the hell did that come from? I fondly recalled Joey's glittering eyes, his huge smile, the glint of his teeth against the rich brown of his skin. He felt so close I could almost reach out and touch him.

I sat up fast and realized I was on the couch in Tubs' living room.

With a curse I steadied myself, one hand on the sofa, the other on my forehead. Took a couple deep breaths.

"Good afternoon, Mikala." Tubs raised her voice above the bacon's spitting sizzle. "Welcome back to the land of the undead."

"You're right, Ms. Flynn," an achingly familiar voice said. "Bacon's a great alarm clock."

Holy mother of all that was purple.

Joey was here. Right fucking here. In Tubs' tiny apartment.

I slapped a hand over my mouth, hauled ass around the couch, and raced past Joey, who was parked at the dining room table. I swerved to avoid Tubs holding a platter of bacon, bounced off the wall, regained my balance, shot down the hall and into the bathroom.

Ten minutes later, teeth scrubbed, body showered, and somewhat steadier, I opened the bathroom door, hoping the previous half hour had been a hallucination. Then I heard Joey's voice and Tubs laughing at whatever he said.

No hallucination here, folks.

I peeked around the edge of the hallway wall. Joey was still at the table with Tubs beside him.

The word "wheelchair" spun around my mind like a literary tornado. In a split second, oxygen vanished. My lungs screamed. I backed up into my bedroom.

Bent over, hands on my thighs.

I forced myself to take deep breaths. Or, really, suck up any breath at all.

Darkness prodded the edges of my vision.

Pain in my head exploded.

A gasp-filled minute passed, maybe two.

What the fuck?

I clenched my hands to stop their shaking. Took a few more breaths.

The ferocious pain in my head receded to a dull throb.

Voices floated into the room. The star of my night terrors was in the middle of telling Tubs about the time we'd swiped some flooring from an Army warehouse and installed it in a dilapidated one-room school in a miniscule village somewhere in Afghanistan.

Gritting my teeth, I forced myself to march out to the table and sit my ass down. "I still can't believe we got away with it."

Tubs assessed me with a raised brow. "I can."

Joey used the last of his toast to clean his plate and stuffed the dripping mess into his mouth. "I'd say," he paused to chew and then swallow, "Flynn was the instigator in ninety percent of the antics we pulled."

"No way. Well, maybe seventy-five."

"I don't doubt that." Tubs took Joey's plate. "Still hungry?"

"No, ma'am. Thank you. It was delicious."

Tubs cleared the rest of the table and busied herself with dishes.

Joey looked me up and down. "Feeling better?"

"Debatable."

"Mikala," Tubs asked through the pass-through, "you want anything to eat? "

My stomach had settled, but not to the degree that the idea of food sounded at all appealing. "No, thanks."

"I appreciate the two of you allowing me to crash," Joey said. "I've got some feelers out. I just don't want to go back to Hunt's Point. Gotta stay away from that shit—" He glanced at Tubs. "Sorry, ma'am."

"Nothing I haven't heard before," she said over the sound of water filling the sink. "Hunt's Point? The Bronx?"

"Yep. My sister and her two kids still live in our mother's place—she passed a couple years back—but the neighborhood's even worse now than it was when I left. Drugs, gangs, drive-bys. I've been telling LaKeisha she needs to get out with Damien and James. James'll be fourteen in a couple months. I don't want him caught up with dope-dealing thugs and their turf wars. Besides, her apartment's on the fourth floor. No elevators. So I need a place we can all move into, in a better neighborhood."

Tubs said, "I understand. I'm sorry about your mom. She was good people. How's your sister holding up?"

"It's been rough, but LaKeisha and the kids are okay."

Tubs wiped her hands on a white dish towel and regarded him for a couple long seconds. "You're welcome to stay here as long as you need, young man." With the flick of her wrist, she folded and hung the towel up.

"Thank you, ma'am."

"All right already. Enough of the ma'ams. Call me Tubs. Anyway, I'm running to the market to pick up a couple things. Any requests?"

"One," I said. "See if you can find chocolate-covered Twinkies. They're Joey's favorite."

He reached across the table and slammed his fist into my shoulder. "Aw, shucks. You remembered."

I smiled at the familiar pain and rubbed my arm. "Some things don't change."

"Okay," Tubs said. "I'll do my best. See you kids in an hour or so. Don't kill each other while I'm gone."

She disappeared out the front door.

Now I was alone with my own personal savior and demon all wrapped in one dented package.

"Hey," Joey's deep baritone scraped bottom. Kindness and affection radiated from him like heat lightning. Kindness and affection I did not deserve.

"Come on, Flynn. Listen to me, okay?"

I crossed my arms, forced my eyes to meet his.

"That cluster in Aleppo, you kept me alive. You did everything you could."

Joey's rough hand caught my cheek. I closed my eyes and felt myself shrink, like a drying leaf that curls in on itself as it clings to the last hope of life. With that thought an incredible roaring in my head blocked out Joey's words. Cold sweat covered my skin. The room closed in, forcing out the air.

I felt strangled.

"Hey." His voice was so far away. "Take it easy."

My eyesight pinpointed. I was a breath, maybe two from passing out.

"Flynn." Joey's voice was abrupt, stern.

I peered at him. My heart pounded so hard I was sure it would splinter apart.

"Look at me, Flynn. How's Tubs doing?"

I opened and closed my mouth, too busy trying not to die to answer. For the life of me I could not breathe.

"What did you do yesterday?"

Yesterday? I squeezed my eyes shut, clenched my fists. "Couldn't. Sleep." I attempted to regulate my breathing. It was second nature when I worked out, when I went running. Why not now?

"Okay." Joey kept his voice even. "When did you wake up?"

The struggle for oxygen took precedence over speech.

"Flynn. Open your eyes."

I forced my lids open again and locked on his for a few seconds. Managed half a lung of sweet air.

"Doing great. So what time you get up?"

Everything was so muddy. Days bled into each other. Impossible to tell where one ended and another began. "Three?" Another half a breath. "Not sure."

"What's Ursula up to these days?"

Ursula, my high school friend? Part of my brain knew he was trying to jar me out of myself, and the other part didn't give two shits.

"How about this?" he said after a yearlong silence. "Let's try a different tack. Listen." He launched into my favorite long-winded joke he loved to tell. It was a ten-minute jobbie and changed a little every time.

I followed his voice, although his words didn't make much sense. But somehow, little by little, he managed to calm the raging crazy inside me. My vision began to clear. The blur of his shirt resolved into its blue and black plaid pattern. I drew a full breath and then another.

Joey slid his hand up and down my arm. "Okay?"

"Uh…"

"Heads up. Come on now."

I forced myself to meet his gaze again.

"This happen before?"

I swallowed a couple times, trying to work up enough spit to speak. "Once. Twenty minutes ago."

"Shit." Joey looked away. "We didn't think my presence here would affect you like this."

We? Great. He and Sassy Pants Stan probably plotted this whole…whatever it was. Some kind of freak-ass intervention?

I studied his hand on me. The long fingers wrapped around my arm held multiple scars, the cuts and gouges lighter than the surrounding skin. Some of the damage was new, but many of those wounds were familiar.

We'd been through so much together. I'd walked away from a bond born at the academy and nurtured through years of intense, hard work with HAVOC. How could he forgive me? I sure as hell couldn't forgive myself. And with that thought the rabbit hole threatened to swallow me up once more.

"Flynn! Stop it. Whatever you're thinking, just stop."

My chest caught with the effort. No matter how hard I tried, I couldn't translate my thoughts into speech or stop them from spinning around in my mind like a mental cyclone.

"Easy, girl. Breathe. Nod for a yes or shake if no. Okay?"

I managed a nod.

"Was today really the first…" He gestured his free hand at me.

I nodded again, concentrating on the flow of air in through my nose and out my mouth.

His fingers tightened. "You're okay. You hear me?"

"Yes." My shoulders dropped a fraction. A few more breaths and I uttered, "I'm good."

"You sure are. How long you been burying your head in the bottle?"

I twitched.

"C'mon. Truth."

He waited for an answer I didn't give.

"Flynn, you don't have to say a word. Just listen." He paused long enough for me to shoot a couple eye daggers his way. "I woke up at the hospital in Germany. Doped up. No memory."

All I wanted was to slam my hands over my ears. I shifted, forced my eyes to lock on his chin, on the damn dimple that made all the straight chicks swoon.

He ignored my restlessness. "The day they told me I'd most likely never walk again, all I wanted to do was get myself to the edge of the motherfucking hospital roof and jump off. I was so pissed. I had shit to do, plans for my life that didn't include a chair with goddamn wheels. It wasn't fair. So I threw myself a hell of a private pity party and checked out. I mean, my body was still there, but I wasn't. Refused to do the damn physical therapy. Wouldn't talk to Stan. Stopped eating. Found a source to hook me up with some Patrón, and after that they were ready to throw my ass out."

Yikes. Patrón was Joey's juice of choice, but when he crossed his tequila threshold, everyone better look out.

"This guy…he lost both legs and his right hand. Poor one-armed fucker. But every morning he showed up in PT, worked his ass off. Mister Fucking Positivity. I wanted to punch his teeth in. One day he rolled up in his electric chair, called me out, right there in front of everyone. Told me I had two working arms and a brain and a beating heart. Best pull my head out of my ass and get to it."

"How'd that go?"

"Told him to fuck off. Went back to my room, finished off the rest of the bottle." He closed his eyes, a dreamy expression on his face. "Damn good tequila."

All this talk of booze made me want to find my own stash and blot out the last twelve hours or so.

"Anyway," Joey said, "I got shit-faced. So shit-faced I slit both wrists. To this day I have no recollection." He held out his arms, palms up. Jagged pink scars I hadn't noticed ran from the base of his palm to his elbow. Must've taken a hundred stitches on either side to sew up the wounds.

An involuntary shudder shook me and my guilt seared my soul. I should've been there for him.

"Listen." Joey froze me with his gaze. "Here's the kicker. Nick, the one-armed wiz, found me in the bathroom. On the floor, in a pool of my own blood. Bastard saved my life."

"Jesus, Joey." Thank the sky and clouds above, but goddamn, it should've been me doing the saving. I should've been present, talked him down as I'd done a hundred times before. Life in Special Ops wasn't for the faint of heart, and everyone hit the dumps sometimes. The military had Battle Buddies. Joey and I had been that for each other—minus the official title—the moment we found each other on the bus headed to the NPIU Academy and then again when we'd both made the NPIU HAVOC Team and some kind of crazy-ass karma landed us in the same six-person unit.

Shame fried me.

"Enough, Flynn." His face shone with kindness. I wanted to smack him for that kindness. What was wrong with him? "Girl, cool down. Hear me out."

"Joey—"

"Shut it. What I'm trying to tell you is someone reached out to me when I was wallowing in purgatory. True, my situation sucked. But I had reasons to live. Plenty of them. My sis. My nephews. You. It just took someone to slap me up a few times to realize it."

I shoved the chair back, a split second from bolting for the door. His benevolence slayed me.

Fast as a snakebite, Joey grabbed my wrist.

"Let go." I attempted to twist away, but his grasp was stronger than my will.

"Knock it off, Flynn!" he bellowed and grabbed my shirt, dragging me over the tabletop until my face was two inches from his nose. "I'm here because I want to be. I'm here because I need a place to crash. I'm here because I goddamn care about you. I've been there. I've got your back."

"Fuck you." My voice was hoarse. "I was the one who should've been there for you. I wasn't. Our team is dead. You're…" I waved my hand in his general direction. "It's my fault. I was the one who gave the go order that day. I was the one who acted on the intel we received. That op was on me. And I failed." I heaved myself up from the chair, bent at the waist because Joey's grip on my shirt kept us face-to-face.

"Sit your ass down." With a shove, he thrust me backward. The back of my legs hit the chair and I landed hard.

For a stunned second I didn't move. Then cold fury drowned out everything.

I kicked the chair away and charged around the table.

* * *

Two voices in the background rumbled like low thunder. Both were familiar, but the incredible throbbing in my skull took precedence. I let their conversation wash over me.

A while later I tried to open my eyes. Only one responded. Hello again, ceiling.

Maybe I was stuck in my own personal version of *Groundhog Day*.

I ran my tongue around my mouth. The inside of my cheek felt like hamburger. Again. The coppery tang of blood lingered in the back of my throat. I reached up toward my face, wincing when I bent the fingers on my right hand to touch my skin. My knuckles felt swollen and thick.

What the hell happened?

I explored my face with my fingertips, felt crusted blood where my once-split lip had been re-split.

What had I done now? Better question, who had I hurt this time?

"Looks like she's awake." Tubs.

"I swear I didn't hit her that hard," a very familiar voice said. Joey? Joey was here?

Then it was as if a vacuum reversed its suction and redeposited my memory into my brain.

Stanley.

The wheelchair.

In my bedroom, freaking out.

At the table. With Joey.

Oh. My. God.

I went after him.

I jolted as if I'd been tasered and struggled to sit up.

"Easy." Tubs' hand on my shoulder steadied me. "You're fine. More or less."

"She still packs a punch," Joey said. He rolled into view, sporting three butterfly bandages on his cheekbone.

Horror replaced confusion. "What have I done?" I whispered.

Tubs stepped away and crossed her arms, peering from me to Joey and back as if she were waiting for another round of fireworks to go off.

"Flynn." Joey rolled closer.

I braced my hands on the cushion, fingers wrapped around its edge in case they took on a life of their own again. I couldn't look at the damage I'd inflicted. I was horrible. Hadn't I already done enough? My first instinct was to run. To fill myself with enough liquor to wipe out the last twenty-four hours.

"Hey." His voice was low, soothing. In that moment I hated him. No, I didn't hate him. I loved him. I detested me. Friendship and fury, responsibility and blame flowed through my veins like million-degree lava. I wanted him to pummel me, to pay me back for the injustices I'd shown him. Maybe he could beat the shame out of me.

I tensed, ready to run before I could do any more harm. Joey knew me, knew my penchant for fleeing situations that caused me to look too closely at my emotions. He maneuvered his chair in front of me, my knees pinned between his.

"Come on." He ducked his head, caught my eye. "It's me. I get it. Alcohol has you by the throat. And, like it or not, you're suffering from post-traumatic stress."

Jesus. Stanley, then that detective. Now Joey.

"Flynn." Joey's voice sharpened.

I blinked my blinkable eye without responding.

"Where did you go just now?"

"No the fuck where, okay?" What was I supposed to do? I needed to move, to walk, to clear my head. Outside. Away from him. "Joey, I'm sorry I went after you. That's inexcusable. And I know it. But I can deal. I don't need you, or Tubs, or anyone else to pull some kind of intervention on me."

Joey leaned back in his chair and scanned me from head to toe. "Bullshit. Tubs said you've been having blackouts, and shit's gone down when they happen. You hardly have any memory of what you're doing. The cops dragged you in and questioned you after you administered a beatdown in a liquor store. You're fucking lucky they didn't charge you with assault. And then here. Right here, right now. Look at yourself. You're not even healed from one fight and now your bruises have bruises. I know people. People who can help—"

What fucking desk jockey sent Joey my way anyway? Stanley, that's who. My brain felt like it might pop out the top of my head. I was so sick and tired of people telling me what I should do. What I shouldn't do. "I don't need any goddamn help, Joe." I lifted my legs from between his wheelchair footrests, pivoted to the side, and stood.

"I'm done. You're welcome to stay here as long as you need, but leave me alone about this, okay? I'm fucking sorry I hit you." I jerked a thumb at my own battered face. "I deserved this. Don't think I didn't."

With that, I limped out the front door.

CHAPTER FOURTEEN

Battery Park City was almost silent at half past four in the morning as I slogged down Murray Street. My destination was Rockefeller Park, which ran along the west side of Manhattan along the Hudson River. The park wasn't large but gave the illusion of nature and solitude.

I left the street and crossed the grass. The air smelled a little dirty, a lot fishy—and full of secrets hidden in the dark.

Benches lined the waterfront walkway, and I settled on one. The sun had not yet risen, but plenty of ambient light cast a soft glow on the world. Across the river, the Goldman Sachs Tower, the tallest building in New Jersey, dominated the skyline. Close by, the Colgate Clock, glowing red and white, continued to mark time, as it had since 1924.

I still had a little while before the residents of New York City hit the ground running. I closed my eyes and tilted my head back. Joey's earlier comments slid through my mind like a swarm of eels, twisting and turning, entangled and slippery.

"Alcohol has you by the throat. And, like it or not, you're suffering from post-traumatic stress."

I could stop any time I wanted to.

I didn't want to.

Then this PTSD bullshit. It didn't pertain to me. I had too much control for that.

What about the two meltdowns I had this past morning? Were they panic attacks? It would make sense that Joey's appearance might be a shock to the system. But it should be done now that I was somewhat more comfortable with the idea of his presence.

But what about those moments where I erupted into violence with no memory of it afterward?

I needed to think about something else. Elizabet's Helen Keller letter and the opportunity to snitch a peek at the puzzle boxes Pascal the Rascal had squirreled away. Nothing like planning an invasion to keep the mind off things one would much rather ignore.

Okay, what did I need to make this happen? A support team. Tubs and the Art Squad were a great group, and between them, no doubt they had a multitude of talents that would come in handy. Something about their talents itched the back of my mind. What was it? I rubbed my temples in hopes it would help bring back the ghost of memory that wouldn't coalesce. Forget it, Flynn. Look forward, not back into a past you can't even remember.

To the future then. I needed people with mad skills.

Joey'd be perfect.

I sat there awhile, feeling the weight of the night press down on me like a living thing as my mind churned. Joey had mentioned Ursula during the fiasco, and I let my brain wander in her direction.

We'd lost touch after I'd been transferred to Minneapolis, another thing that was my fault. Once in a while I Googled her to see what she was up to. According to one article, she'd started a business to subsidize her real passion, which was still hockey.

Something about her business pinged me. What did she do? Detecting? Investigations? I chewed on that wisp of memory as I watched the reflection of lights shimmer on the water.

PI Tech, that was it. I wasn't sure what her work encompassed, but Ursula always used to be up for adventure, the more physical the better. Maybe she'd worked adventure into her job.

I drummed my fingers on the worn bench slats. The sky was beginning to lighten, and I felt the energy of the city rev up as it rumbled to life.

My thoughts wandered back to Joey. In HAVOC, he became a specialist in electronics and communications and an expert in demolitions. He could build a comm device out of two rocks and duct tape and defuse a roadside IED in two minutes flat. His record was pretty good—he hadn't blown himself up yet.

Someone else had.

I dropped my head into my hands. Stop it. Think about Urs and Joey, Flynn. Focus. If Joey could keep his trap shut and stop psychoanalyzing me and if Ursula was interested in playing, we might be in business.

The biggest problem with Ursula was the fact I hadn't spoken to her in, well, forever. Of course, entirely my fault. Then I had to shove that thought out of my mind because guilt made my insides tremble.

Fatigue felt like a thousand pounds on the top of my head. Time to see if I could lose myself in slumber. I dragged my ass off the bench and began the long trek home. But I surprised myself with a bounce in my step and a sense of direction I hadn't felt since Joey and I had been blown up.

* * *

Later that day, Tubs sat down at the table with Joey and me. "I have a proposition."

Joey glanced up from the book he'd been reading, and I paused with a banana halfway to my mouth.

"The Fourth of July's Friday," she said. "How'd you two like to accompany an old lady to the South Street Seaport festivities? There's always entertainment of some sort and food, of course. We leave before the fireworks start. I don't know if they'd bother you, but no need to take any chances."

Tubs blew on her coffee as she watched our reactions.

Joey slurped down a swallow of his own. "I'll never turn down an opportunity to stuff my face. Thanks for the caution with the fireworks. Hadn't thought of them as an issue, but I guess that was before."

They weren't on my radar, either. I loved fireworks, or at least I used to. The city put on an amazing show. Some of my fondest memories, mostly involving Kate, had happened on the Fourth.

Kate. Oh God, Kate. I missed her so much the ache of it immobilized me. I'd hurt her so badly I was sure no way would she ever…get your mind off that track, Flynn. You did it to yourself. I tucked her back into the place in my mind where she was safe. Or maybe where I was safe from her.

Fireworks, Flynn. Think about the fireworks. Big booms, lots of sparks. I didn't figure they'd affect me, but I respected Joey's wariness. Sometimes he was maybe a tiny bit smarter than me. And spending some time with Tubs doing something fun sounded really appealing.

"Okay," I said, "let's do it."

This was the first real preplanning I'd done since I'd come home. Maybe there was something to be said about what I was beginning to think of as the Joey Effect.

* * *

Next on my team-building agenda was to rope Joey into Operation Retrieve Helen. My plan was to take him to lunch and stuff him so full of pizza he couldn't say no. And I knew just the place to do it.

When I was a kid working at Joey's Pizzeria, it had been a busy, boxcar-sized, year-round sauna. Takeout only. Somewhere along the line Joey had expanded into the space next door.

He could now seat about thirty people and the building was blessedly air-conditioned.

It took all of ten minutes for Joey and me to roll/walk to the pizzeria. Once inside, the familiar scents of yeasty dough, melting cheese, and the tang of homemade tomato sauce slapped me right back to my teenage years.

"Hey, Joey," I called to the flour-and-red-stained, apron-wearing man behind the counter. Pizza Joey, now in his sixties, looked as he had sixteen years ago. He was the same smiley, maybe a little more rotund guy I loved, and he still had the same—no, it couldn't be the same, just similar—white cap perched on top of his salt and pepper buzz cut.

He wiped his hands on a bar rag and tossed it into a red bucket. "If it ain't Flynn. Long time no see, kid."

"All of six days, Joe. Find any decent help yet?"

"Nah." He waved frankfurter fingers through the air. "Kids these days. Ya ready to come back to work?"

"Nope. But if I change my mind, you'll be the first to know."

A laugh rumbled. "Sure ya will. Who's your friend?"

"Joey, this is Joey. We were in the same NPIU Academy class, and then both went on to HAVOC."

Recognition dawned on Pizza Joey's face and he came around the counter. "So you're Flynn's other Joey. Let me tell ya. I heard plenty aboutcha outta the kid. Good ta make your acquaintance. Have to come up with a nickname for ya or I'm gonna confuse myself." He stuck his hand out and they shook.

Pizza Joey stepped back, crossed his arms above his beer belly, and eyed my Joey. Instead of asking how he wound up in a rolling chair, he said, "How 'bout JJ. For Joey Junior."

Joey smiled. "Right on."

"Fair enough. Okay then. Whatcha two hooligans want?"

Ten minutes later Joey, or rather, JJ, and I, sat at a table with a pitcher of Coke between us, waiting on two pies, one with anchovies and another loaded with pepperoni and black olives. I'd wanted beer, but Joey talked me into soda instead, and I'd grudgingly agreed.

My earlier buzz had worn off, and I was ready to replace it with some food. I assessed my anxiety levels and was happy to realize I was feeling steady.

I downed half my soda and set the glass down. "I have a proposition."

JJ arched one of his curvy brows.

"So Elizabet, you remember Elizabet from the night you landed on Tubs' doorstep?"

He nodded.

"She got involved with this dude—"

Joey held up two fingers and did air quotes. "Involved? As in romantically?"

"You got it."

"How old is she?"

"Don't you think the senior set still might have oats to sow?"

"Guess I haven't ever thought about it either way. And I think I'd rather not think about it." He grimaced and waved me on.

"For clarity's sake, the bad boy's name is Pascal. According to Tubs, he's a thief and swindler, and apparently an art scene Casanova. Don't ask me how she found out, but she's always got her ear to the creative pulse around town. Elizabet either didn't know or didn't care. I dunno. Her hormones were probably in charge."

I shredded my napkin as I tried to figure out how to proceed. "When she was little, Elizabet met Helen Keller—"

"*The Miracle Worker* Helen Keller? She had face time with her?"

"Yup, she did. As a kid. Unreal, isn't it?"

"Seriously. Seems like Keller's ancient history. To have a connection reaching from the here and now to way back then, it's kind of amazing."

"I completely agree it is. So however they came to it, Keller told Elizabet about Hitler's 1933 decision to hold a book burning party—called the Action Against the Un-German Spirit—on the campuses of universities across Germany. And yes, before you ask, I researched it. The bastard wanted to destroy literature that contradicted the Reich's view of the world, and they added Keller's essay collection to the pile."

"Why?"

"The collection was titled *How I Became a Socialist*."

"Ah," Joey said as he absently wiped condensation from his glass with a finger. "That would do it."

"Keller responded by writing an open letter to students at those schools and the *New York Times* published it. Seriously, Joey, I can't get the first line out of my head."

"What was it?"

"'History has taught you nothing if you think you can kill ideas.'"

"Go Ms. Keller."

"Right? Fast forward to present day. Apparently a trove of Keller writings showed up in someone's attic, and with it was the original letter."

"You're shitting me."

"No, I am not. The letter went up for auction, and Elizabet bought it. For a cool thirteen grand."

Pizza Joey appeared with our pies and plunked them on the table. I glanced up at him. "Thanks, Joe."

He grunted and disappeared into his kitchen.

I handed ol' JJ a paper plate and slid two slices from my pie onto another and took a bite.

"Here's where the trouble starts. Elizabet had to leave the auction before she had a chance to pay for the document. She wrote a check and left it with Pascal, who agreed to make payment and bring the letter home. Elizabet then took it to her insurance company. They, in turn, had to verify for themselves the letter's authenticity before insuring it. It came back as a forgery."

Joey bit off half his pizza crust and shoved it to one side of his mouth. "Could it have been switched at the auction house?"

"According to Sahl, who knows about these things, Scandon Auctions are tight when it comes to authenticating whatever passes through their hands. So the natural suspect is Pascal. Elizabet's really upset about this, and I can't blame her. It's a lot of money, but, maybe more importantly, it truly meant something to her."

I paused with a frown. "Huh. I started out thinking about this as a lark. But after sitting with it for a few days and learning more, it's so much more than that. It's about righting a wrong, one way or another."

"Flynn, you sound more like yourself than you have since I crashed your party."

He was right.

"Want to help me get Elizabet's letter back? For once I'm thinking about someone other than myself." Hold the phones. Did I just say that out loud?

Joey licked grease off his thumb. "You kidding? The Terrible Twosome together again? We'll be totally legendary. And do a good deed in the process. Plus, you of all people know when I'm pissed and when I'm kidding. The docs and physical therapy people just don't get me. They all thought I wanted to kill them."

"If your experience was anything like mine, you did want to kill them."

"True. But neither one of us would be here without them, so we have to appreciate the torture. Anyway, we'll need more help for this than you and me."

"You mentioned Ursula when I had my meltdown. She'd be perfect. The only glitch is an awkward situation of my own making. I need to make it right, then we'll see."

"Got her number?"

In truth, I'd *had* her phone number. She scrawled it on a piece of notepaper after I refused her visit while I recovered in the hospital. I'd been a complete ass when she'd made considerable effort to come, and after that, I didn't figure there'd be any reason she'd want to see me again.

The day I was discharged, I'd found the number in a drawer as I packed up my stuff. I'd tossed it in the garbage can and walked away.

"Hello? Earth to Flynn. You have Ursula's number or not?"

"No. No, I don't. But I can track it down."

"What are you waiting for? Sooner we hook up, the sooner we find some action."

* * *

When we got back to the apartment, Tubs was at the dining room table nose deep in one of her daily newspapers. She peered at us over her readers. "You're back fast."

I stowed the leftovers in the fridge. "Pizza Man, not to be confused with our JJ here, serves 'em up and boots 'em out."

Tubs leaned back in her chair and pushed her cheaters to the top of her head. "JJ. Reminds me of that actor who always said, 'Dyn-o-mite' on that old sit-com." She tapped her chin and squinted at the wall. "What was the name of that show?"

"*Good Times*," Joey said. "I caught a few episodes. In reruns, of course." He aimed his deadly, disarming grin at her.

She waved a hand. "That's right. When you're as ancient as I am you'll be lucky to remember what reruns are."

I ignored their banter. "Tubs, Joey and I need to get a hold of Ursula. I...don't have her number anymore."

She glanced sharply at me. "Ursula, hockey player extraordinaire and all around true-blue friend? The one you—"

"Yes, her," I cut in. "Did you happen to hang onto that old address book I used to have?"

"That scrappy old thing from high school?"

"Yes."

"Do you really think Ursula would have the same number now?"

"I don't know. Maybe her aunt still lives in the same place. She'd know how to get a hold of her."

Tubs looked uneasy. That was one look Tubs usually didn't wear.

"What?"

"Well, I...um..."

I narrowed my eyes. "What?"

She looked down at her paper, smoothed a hand over it. "The day you were released from the hospital and we cleaned out your room, I saw you throw the paper with her number out. So when you hauled that last load to the car, I took it out of the garbage. Ursula had been such a good friend to you. I thought," she peered at me straight, "maybe you'd need her one day."

Elation overrode the sting of shame. I slung an arm around her shoulders and squeezed. "You are simply the best. You were right. You're always right."

"I know I am. So what's going on?"

"Joey's down to help swipe Elizabet's letter, and we want Ursula's help. If she'll talk to me."

"Mikala, you sometimes underestimate those closest to you. And you, young man, I want you to know we don't typically go to extremes like this. But that Pascal, he's a piece of work."

"So I understand." The devilish expression on Joey's face was gratifying. "This is gonna be fun." He leaned forward in his chair, elbows on the armrests, fingers entwined. "Tell me more about Pascal."

Tubs filled Joey in on the parts of Pascal's story I'd left out. When we were done Joey said, "What a fu—sorry. Dickwad."

Tubs failed to suppress a smile. "Yes, he's certainly both."

Operation Retrieve Helen might be easier than I thought. "So, do you have that number, Tubs?"

"I do." She disappeared down the hall.

"Sometimes," I said to Joey, "things are meant to be."

His grin was feral. It reminded me of the expression he'd get right before we headed out on a mission, and it made me feel alive.

Tubs reappeared with the slip of paper I'd crumpled up months before. She placed it in my palm and muttered something about stubborn asses coming to their senses.

CHAPTER FIFTEEN

Shadows lengthened as the sun slid behind Manhattan's skyscrapers. I paced along the walkway that paralleled the East River, drumming up the courage to call Ursula. Across the water, the city was beginning to light up. The evening was beyond sticky, humidity cranked to the max. Sweat trickled down my neck.

In one hand, nestled in a brown paper bag, was a small bottle of Ciroc. In the other, I held a new iPhone with Ursula's number pulled up on the screen. As much as I didn't want a cell, the times called for me to change my attitude and embrace technology like most of the rest of the world. After Kate had given me that Blackberry years ago, I'd stuck with that brand. When I joined HAVOC and spent a majority of my time overseas, I'd relied on a computer instead of a phone and had canceled my contract.

Joey had come with me to an AT&T store and convinced me to try an iPhone. He'd said, "Even old folks can handle an Apple, Flynn."

I'd given him the finger. "Thanks, applehole."

I unscrewed the Ciroc top and tipped it back, reveling in the afterburn. I could do this.

Seagulls swooped down to land no more than five feet from me on the fence built to stop kids and dumb adults from falling into the river. A distant, hardened part of me wondered if skipping the fence might be a good way to allow for natural selection, but then my somewhat appalling thought slid away as easily as it'd come. I propped my elbows on the top rail and gazed across the murky river at South Street Seaport.

So many memories there. So many memories all over this damn town. In my nightly wanderings, I wound up cruising on at least a weekly basis past the building where Kate and I had lived, even though I never intended to go anywhere near it. I'd wind up at the parks where we'd sneak away to make out while we were in high school. I wondered if first love ever really went away. For me, it never would.

The sound of a heavy engine churning through the water interrupted my musing. A light blue tugboat with yellow trim chugged past, belching diesel fumes. The boat's hard-driving propeller left a trail of whitish bubbles in its wake.

One more hit, then I capped the bottle and made the call.

The phone rang three times. I was about to hang up when I heard a breathless, "Hello?"

"Shit," I swore under my breath.

"What? Hello?"

When I didn't respond, the speaker again said, "Hello? Anyone?"

"Urs?" My voice sounded gruff, almost rusty. I cleared my throat. "Ursula?"

"Yeah. Who's this?"

"It's…" Jeez. Do it, loser. "Flynn. Mikala Flynn." My heart pounded along with the beat of charged silence.

Then, "Flynn? Is that really you?"

"It is."

She sounded exactly like she used to, the smile still so obvious in her voice. What had I expected? Hatred? Urs never hated. She always found something redeeming in almost everyone, no matter how minute those positive qualities might be. Pity? God, I hoped not. I deserved her anger, disgust, revulsion…anything but a false sense of compassion.

"Wow. Flynn, you're the last person I expected…Jesus. Never mind. How are you?"

"Okay. I'm…all right." Get on with it, stupid idiot. "Look," I said in a rush of breath, "I'm sorry I never—"

"Stop," she interrupted. "Stop right now. I knew you'd find me whenever you were ready."

I barked a laugh. "Urs, oh my God, you haven't changed. Not a bit. Thank you for that. But I do owe you an apology. And a proposition. Hear me out, then hang up if you want. It's the least I deserve." I cleared my throat. "I…did appreciate that you reached out while I was in the hospital. I'm really sorry I wouldn't see you and, um, didn't call."

"Apology accepted. Move on, bitch. What's up?" Not a hesitation in sight, and her tone was laced with achingly familiar humor.

With every word she spoke it was as if the years between us rewound, leaving bare the tendrils of friendship we'd nurtured through the years. That friendship might now be dented, but somehow the foundation remained. Time hadn't changed her essence, and I had a sincere, albeit half-inebriated, feeling I could still count on her. What you saw was always what you got with Urs. She'd always been as loyal as they came.

"I have a proposal you might get a kick out of, and I understand it's coming out of the blue. How'd you feel about getting together and I'll explain in person?"

A couple of beats passed. "I'll hear any proposition you want to throw my way, Flynn. You're the Pied Piper of Manhattan. You've always been. Blow your whistle and you know I'll come running."

"That was then. Where you these days?"

"Hamilton Heights."

A hesitant smile tugged at the corners of my mouth. "Close to your aunt's place?" Ursula's aunt, with whom she lived through high school, had an apartment in Harlem. On the heels of that thought I was taken aback to realize I had no idea if one of the most important people in Ursula's life was even still alive.

"She's ten blocks away. I go over for dinner every Tuesday night."

Once in a while things came easier than expected. I wracked my mind for a place in Hamilton Heights where we could get together. "I am so glad to hear that. Where's a good place to meet?"

"How about Favela Cubana, LaGuardia Place and Third? Between SoHo and the West Village. You still like Caribbean?"

Other than *sarmi*, Cuban and Puerto Rican had been two of my favorite ethnic foods since Tubs had introduced me to *ropa vieja*, *tostones*, and *pasteles*. "For sure." My stomach rumbled. "Sunday lunch? Say twelve thirty?"

"Good with me. I look forward to catching up."

I did too. But I felt bad the person she was looking forward to catching up with no longer existed.

* * *

I wandered for a while, lost in thought, paying no real attention to where I was going. Hearing Ursula's voice brought Kate back so vividly that I could, even after all this time, smell her perfume, taste her kiss. Feel her soft skin under my hands.

In talking to Ursula, the Pandora's box I'd filled with all that was Kate shattered. Repressed emotion shot through my synapses, burrowing so far into my core I didn't think I could take another second. Incredible pain, intense longing, acute self-disgust—every emotion was amplified to the extreme.

I tried to shut down the hurricane, to block the oh-so-vivid recollection of the way Kate's gray eyes twinkled when she laughed at something I'd said. I desperately struggled to forget the feeling of perfection in the way her fingers entwined with mine. If I didn't banish the visceral feeling of Kate above me, Kate below me, Kate inside me, Kate all over me, I would die. The straight-outta-hell heartbreak, the unrecoverable rent that I, alone, had caused in our relationship sickened me.

At the time it made perfect sense.

To me, anyway.

HAVOC training had ended, and I'd made it through. I was about to be sent overseas, to a destination the NPIU refused to spell out. Didn't know when I'd be back. Kate so didn't deserve to be left hanging like that. To worry, every single day, about where I was and what I was doing. If I was even alive.

My decision to break things off came after a mandatory lecture. One of the original HAVOC agents gave a pointed talk about how hard it was for families back home to deal with the uncertainties that came with having a loved one in units that delved into black ops, especially when those units operated overseas in a war zone. He talked about fear, stress, and depression, divorce and suicide rates. He talked about families he'd seen ripped apart despite everyone's best intentions, and why he'd chosen to remain single.

It was after that discussion I'd made the decision to end our relationship so she could move on, hopefully avoid the heartbreak my kind of life offered. I thought I was doing what was best for her and didn't think for a second about her wishes, wants, and desires.

Every day, for the last three years, when I allowed myself to consider what I'd actually done, I realized what a huge jackass I'd been. I'd broken her heart without talking to her about any of it, had not allowed her to come to her own conclusions and make her own decisions. Just before the end of us, she'd scored an amazing job at an up-and-coming, green-focused architectural firm in Upper Manhattan. She didn't need me in her way.

The old tapes continued to play through my mind, either as an excuse for my actions or the reason for them. I'd always been "that" kid, the kid with the murdered dad, the one who didn't belong. She was the girl who grew up with glitter, glamor, and penthouse life. Those differences wouldn't stop haunting me our entire relationship. That goddamn high school bully, the one who made sure I knew I'd never fit in, that I was nothing but an outcast, never stopped whispering in my ear.

Kate's absolute insistence that our differing backgrounds did not matter reassured me in the moment. But during long months apart, my brain filled with negative self-talk that completely undid my confidence.

Her life had come to a settling point. Mine had not. My job wasn't a five-day, forty-hour-a-week proposition. It was dangerous. HAVOC only increased the danger factor. There were no guarantees I'd make it back in one piece, if at all. But the job was something I felt I had to do. The need to make a difference, to bring people home, to find a little justice in an unjust world rode me like nothing else.

A week after that fateful lecture, I'd sat Tubs down and told her my decision. I explained my reasoning, asked her to stay as far away from the subject of Kate as she could. She absolutely let me have it. Said I was a *bilacho djolano*, which roughly translated as a stubborn, no-good ass. I'd been so rooted in what I was sure was right that I hadn't listened.

I'd sent Kate an email instead of calling because I was afraid she'd talk me out of myself. In the email, I outlined all the reasons a breakup made sense. I added my apologies, told her I'd forever love her, asked her to put whatever I'd left at the apartment in storage.

My phone rang off the hook for two weeks straight. I didn't respond to a single email or the multiple texts that piled up. A month passed and a sickening blanket of abashed guilt wrapped itself around me. Now, the excruciating, flaming pain of shame and remorse far outpaced any initial guilt I'd felt.

I finished the bottle of Ciroc in the shadow of the Brooklyn Bridge, tossed it in a garbage bin, and headed back to Manhattan. It was late enough the slatted walkway was practically empty. Eventually I wound up at a familiar dance/nightclub, found a table safe in a rear corner where the wall had my back.

The server's gaze lingered on my black-turning-sickly-yellowish-purple eyes as she took my order.

I shook my head and gave her a thumbs-up.

She shrugged, made change for the twenty I handed her, and shifted her attention to the next customer.

Fifteen minutes later, a second double burned the back of my throat, the sting reminding me I was, indeed, still alive. It was safer to concentrate on the physical, the here and now, on my immediate surroundings, instead of getting lost in yesterday's sorrow.

I needed to kick-start the old me, the me who looked forward to the next step, the next goal, the new plan. My survival mantra in the Middle East had been "never look back." But how was I supposed to rebuild shields that had been smashed in Aleppo and battered again today?

The heavy beat of dance music muted, though it didn't drown out, the ache in my gut. The thumping of my heart matched the pounding bass.

I set the empty tumbler down and turned my attention to the seething mass of bodies down on the dance floor. The nightclub pulsed with flashing light, pent-up passion, and whispered promises that, from experience, I knew wouldn't last.

Women didn't come here for the ambiance. They didn't come for the party. They came here on the prowl, hunting for anonymous release to whatever unyielding pressure they held within. What was wrong with that? After my bouts of crazy, maybe I needed to release some pressure too. Something to make me forget Kate and her damned touch, her scent, and her all-encompassing love. Something to help me forget everything that I'd left behind.

Maybe it was time to go for it. Lose myself for a few minutes in something other than booze. My vision sharpened as I homed in on the challenge at hand, shifting from woman to woman, never stopping on anybody for more than a few seconds.

Without warning, the heat of repressed desire flared, then pooled low as I allowed anticipation to ignite the blood that thumped through my veins. Sex was almost as good as liquor at helping me lose myself, although I didn't often seek it out. That proposition could become complicated way too fast. But for tonight, it would help me forget—for a little while—the loathsome, vile person I'd become.

The combination of my ramped-up blood alcohol level and the excitement of finding a pair of willing arms became intoxicating. The only thing better about the sauce over sex was that the afterglow lasted longer. On the downside, so did the hangover.

A lone woman danced by herself on the floor, oblivious to the bodies gyrating around her. Fine strands of shoulder-length, jet-black hair stuck to sweat-dampened skin. Her eyes were closed, arms stretched over her head, moving to the pounding rhythm with the gracefulness of an acrobat and the teasing eroticism of a pole dancer. A tight white tank hugged her torso, highlighting her not-quite-flat stomach, muscular shoulders, and sturdy arms. She worked out, and from the look of it, worked out hard. Baggy cargos rode low on her hips, the cuffs rolled at the ankles. I imagined the feel of her skin to be the perfect mix of silk and steel.

Target acquired, I dropped a ten next to my empty glass and slid into the throng of undulating humanity. As I moved with the beat through the crowd, the desperate pull, the driving need to lose myself overtook my body and mind.

It didn't take long to reach her. She danced as if she were born to move with the music. I approached from behind and slid a hand onto that white-covered abdomen.

She stiffened but for only a moment.

I tucked her against me, pressed the front of my legs against the back of hers, and kept us both moving with the rhythm.

Desire sparked then fired hot as we fell into the beat. We shared a few songs, our movements slowing despite the intensity of the music.

At some point she pivoted to face me. I was half a head taller than she, and I felt her lips brush my neck. I stiffened for a second, wary about my scar, but then realized she was on the opposite side. Then I forgot about everything.

My fingers gripped her hips, thumbs through belt loops, pulling her tighter to me.

The woman's dark eyes flashed as she maintained eye contact, the corners of her mouth curling in seductive suggestion. Her arms wound around my neck, hands fisted in my hair.

Our faces were inches apart, breath warm against damp skin. I felt the flush of triumph roll through me.

Her hands pulled my head down until her lips caressed the shell of my ear. She whispered, "Let's move this in back."

She grasped one of my hands, pulling me toward the rear of the club where plenty of nooks and crannies gave the illusion of privacy. On couches, against black-as-night walls, and on pillars that caught strobes of laser light flashing from the dance floor, women allowed lust and desire to lead.

This particular destination was designed to whip partiers into a frenzy and spin them away to let off steam and line the bar owner's pockets with plenty of alcohol-soaked cash. As one of the few clubs in New York City that catered to women, the bar was as anonymous as I needed it to be.

And right now I needed it bad.

The woman tightened her grip on my hand as we stalked past couples in various phases of build up or release. The smell of sweat, booze, and the faint sounds of sex pounded heavy behind my eyes, almost matching the pounding in my skull. In all honesty, my head had ached for the last four days. In my more sober moments, I'd wondered about a concussion, but I figured not much could be done even if that's what it was.

We entered a black-walled hallway, passed the restroom, and exited through the rear door. The nightclub's back patio was fenced, lit with crisscrossed strands of clear Christmas lights giving the illusion of a thousand tiny stars. The summer night was thick, hot and steamy. For a moment anyway, we were alone in the darkness.

The woman slammed me up against the wall. I grunted as she surged against me, capturing my lips in a kiss that made it clear she meant business.

I slid my palms onto her cheeks, tilted her head back. Our mouths clashed, tongues dueling deliciously. Yes, I needed this.

Needed to feel something that wasn't sorrow, wasn't self-hatred, wasn't anyone's goddamn pity.

I ripped my mouth away and gripped her shoulders, feeling slick, overheated skin beneath my palms. I reversed our positions, pushing her against the unyielding concrete wall. She slid her hands over my butt, forcing a leg between mine. She rested her forehead against my brow, our eyes locked.

"You want?" I whispered, my heart battering my being. I waited long enough to give her time to decline my advances.

"I want." Her voice was low, hoarse, with the hint of an accent I couldn't place. "Call me Dante. And that's a stupid question." She punctuated her words with a thrust.

I slid my hand down the curve of her arm to her waistband, unbuttoned her pants, and slid my hand inside. She was scorching hot.

Her hand mirrored my own, and I couldn't stop my hips from rolling when her fingers found me.

I let myself go. I needed this like I needed oxygen. We were well-matched, neither keeping the lead for long. Our mouths crashed together again and again, tongues tasting, battling but not dominating. I basked in the equality of desire met, of the driving compulsion to give and the desperate need to receive. The music inside shook the walls, seeped through the door beside us in counterpoint to the lust-filled, animalistic sounds we made.

Passion soared, then flared white-hot. For that instant, I simply was. No Agent Mikala Flynn who let everyone down.

I felt no hurt, no guilt, no shame. Only freedom.

The voice in my head screamed as I careened to the edge and blasted over like a human cannonball, hanging in the sweet spot a split second before floating like a leaf toward to the ground.

Long seconds passed.

Dante groaned.

I doubled down. It didn't take long before her hips jerked against my hand as she buried a howl in my shirt. I gave her a couple of moments, then tangled my tongue with hers and slowly drove her up and over again. This time she threw her head back, allowing her shuddering cries to echo through the patio and fade, until all that was left was the sound of our harsh breathing and the insistent, pounding techno tunes leaking out the door.

Dante kissed me fiercely before sliding her hand from my jeans.

I wiped the evidence of her desire on the wisp of cloth that covered her and extracted my own hand. Then I zipped and buttoned Dante's cargos and my own.

Her eyes were hooded as she leaned against the wall, arms crossed, the picture of a smoking hot rebel. That seductive smile was back, the one she'd worn as she led me out of the club. "One day," she said, "I hope we meet again."

I traced a finger along her jawbone. "One day." We both knew it to be a lie, but I allowed a ghost of a smile, pressed my lips to the corner of her mouth, and disappeared back into the club. I didn't plan on a repeat performance. Not now, not ever. But in this moment, for the first time in a long time, I forgot Kate and my pain in a way I hadn't before.

CHAPTER SIXTEEN

I stumbled home from the club as the sun rose out of the ocean, staining the sky varying shades of orange creams, lemon yellows, and neon pinks. I crept into the apartment and dropped onto the couch, asleep before I could get both legs on the cushions.

Dreams chased nightmares across the black slate of my unconscious brain. Few of my dreams were anything less than panic-filled. The hellish memories that lived in the deep, darkest places of my soul came back as terror-riddled shit shows filled with death and destruction.

Somewhere along the line, my subconscious shifted out of night terrors into dreamscape. Dante and her devil fingers, her bewitching mouth, her talented tongue. It was a stunning and welcome change, however temporary it might be. I couldn't remember the last time I hadn't been haunted the night through.

I lost most of Thursday, waking only to eat. Tubs was at first alarmed, then relieved when she realized I was actually sleeping and not just passed out. Apparently sex was what I'd needed all along. I finally dragged myself back into the land of the living Friday morning, the Fourth of July.

Tubs, Joey, and I spent the early afternoon wandering around South Street Seaport. The area was chock-full of people ripe for celebrating Independence Day. At the corner of Fulton and Front, a stage had been set up for various speakers and events. Food vendors dotted the sidewalks, and the mood was light.

We stopped for some coffee, swung by the South Street Seaport Museum and browsed, meandered past the Titanic Memorial, which, of course, threw me straight back in time to one of the first dates Kate and I ever had.

As the years since our parting had passed, I wondered if Kate stayed with the architecture firm or had fallen in line and gone to work for the Goldsmith Foundation as her father had pushed for.

Enough, Flynn, I silently lectured myself. Get your head out of the past. This was now, and I needed to stay in the moment, be fully with Joey and Tubs.

Huh. Stanley would be proud of me for recognizing the need to remain present and accounted for. More progress? Maybe.

So I forced Kate from my mind and breathed in the delectable scent of cinnamony roasted nuts, felt the excitement in the air, reminded myself that this is what it was like to be alive.

Eventually, we stopped to grab a hotdog from a blue-and-yellow, umbrella-covered Sabrett's cart that was parked across the street from the stage. Once we were loaded up with dogs and soda, Tubs said, "Let's check out the next speaker. They usually have some good people here."

I devoured half my hotdog in one bite as I surveyed the crowd gathered in front of the metal stage. At least a couple hundred people milled around, waiting for the next big thing.

The back of my head tingled. The situations Joey and I had run across while on the HAVOC team had ingrained in me a distinct sense of unease at remaining stationary in large groups.

That was then, Flynn, I reminded myself. I shoved the rest of the hotdog in my mouth. "If we stay on the edge of the crowd I'm game."

Joey said, "Agreed."

We found an open space on the sidewalk across the road from the stage with an easy escape onto Front Street and chatted about the upcoming presidential election.

Tubs said, "Clinton's in the lead, but it wouldn't take much to knock her out. How can an improbable, idiotic candidate such as Trump, of all people, be nipping at her heels?"

Joey said, "You ain't kidding. Every time he opens his mouth he sticks his size-five loafer in it."

"Hillary has to win," I said. "Bernie, he's got some good ideas, but I don't think he has the numbers behind him to pull it off. A Trump presidency would be ludicrous. The man's a misogynist, a player for the ultra rich."

"Instead of his slogan, 'Make America Great Again,'" Joey said, "he's turning it into 'Make America Hate Again.'"

"Yes. Deep breath, my boy." Tubs rested a calming hand on Joey's shoulder. She was so good at reading people. Why hadn't I inherited her sensitivity? Speaking of sensitivity, Trump could use a serious dose of it himself. He reminded me of President Snow from *The Hunger Games*. It all came down to what the have-nots could do for those who already had everything.

"I think it all depends on the American public," I said. "If they can see what damage Trump has the potential to do, I'd hope they would make the appropriate choice."

"That's the problem," Joey said. "Man, it's getting warm out here." He rolled backward a couple feet into shadow, and Tubs and I followed. "They don't see it. They don't understand bully speak or his smoke and mirror act. He invented a false lifeline and tossed it to the poor, telling them he'll get their factory jobs back. He's working the middle class, talking about tax breaks and reform. But mark my words—if that man gets into office, we can kiss civil rights, trade agreements, same-sex rights, women's rights, so much more, away."

Tubs opened her mouth to respond, but the crowd began clapping. A woman strode onto the stage and stopped in front of a microphone positioned front and center. We were far enough back it was impossible to make out her features. Blond hair was pulled back in a ponytail and she wore jeans and a green T-shirt with an unreadable, colorful logo on the front.

I crossed my arms and shifted my weight from one leg to the other as we waited for whatever we were waiting for. For all I knew, this was going to be a speech about the history of Abe Lincoln or something. I reflected on the day. I'd remained in control. I chalked it up to sleep and Dante's crazy skills. In fact, I'd only taken a couple of hits from the pint bottle I'd stashed in my pocket. In my book, it was a substantial win.

"Thank you," the woman's voice boomed in tinny reverb through speakers set up around the perimeter. "Thank you for being here. It's great to see everyone. Are we ready to talk environment?"

The crowd roared.

"And…" she shouted over the cacophony, waiting for a reduction in the din. The decibel level dropped and she continued at a lower register. "I'm so excited for the amazing musicians on deck after our climate series. But most of all, I can't wait for the grand finale to another incredible, awesome Fourth of July: the fireworks show sponsored by the Goldsmith Foundation." She thrust her fists into the air and jumped enthusiastically up and down a couple times as the crowd lost their shit.

I remembered that. Although her voice had been rendered almost unrecognizable by the sound system, that arms up, hopping around move belonged to one person.

My ex-lover, Kate Goldsmith.

Oh my God. My heart catapulted straight out of my chest and splintered into a trillion pieces on the cracked asphalt beneath my feet. Joey, oblivious to the drama silently playing out beside him, clapped enthusiastically along with the rest of the frenzied audience.

166   Jessie Chandler

Tubs met my wide eyes with an almost comical look of concern. She'd figured out exactly who was addressing the crowd too.

My animal brain screamed, "Get out! Get out now!" I backpedaled two steps, plowing into someone behind me. With an oath, I whipped around, desperately reaching for anything I could get my hands on to keep the person upright. Last thing I needed was to hurt somebody in my haste to escape demons of my own making.

I caught a handful of flowery cloth covering a man's chest, and thin, bony fingers wrapped around my wrist. "Agent Flynn! What a surprise."

I looked into another familiar face. "Stanley?" What the hell. Was he feeling the need to track me as if I was some delinquent? It was amazing how fast rationality fled. "What the fuck are you doing here?" I dragged him closer, almost lifting him out of his loafers. "Are you following me?"

A part of me wanted to rip him apart while another, somewhat more reasonable piece, realized I'd never seen him out of one of his tailored suits before. Today, he was dressed in an ungodly loud pink and yellow, plumeria-flowered Hawaiian shirt and creased blue jean shorts.

Of course Stan would iron his shorts.

"Flynn!" Joey clamped his arm around my thighs, pinning me tight against the wheel of his chair. "Stand down, Flynn. Let him go."

Tubs wiggled halfway between the little weasel and me. "Mikala, stop it."

"He's following us," I said, my eyes still locked on Stanley's. His were round and wide, as if I'd come up behind him and yelled, "Boo!"

"No," Stan squeaked. "I'm not following you. I swear. Harry's from Staten Island. We come to South Street every Fourth."

It took a second to realize that a towering man—almost a foot taller than me—bounced on the balls of his feet right behind Stan. Curly red hair glinted in the waning sun, and he was decked out in a matching Hawaiian shirt. His hands were on Stan's shoulders, holding him back while I tried to yank him forward.

"Stop!" Stan yelled to be heard over Kate, who'd continued with her speech, oblivious to the scene playing out at the far edge of the crowd. "I'm not a piece of Silly Putty. Both of you, please. Let go. And I'm not following you, Agent." He twisted to look at his own personal Mega-Me. "I'm fine." He spun back to us again. "I'd like you to meet Harry, my husband."

Husband? Holy shit.

I set Stan gingerly on his flip-flops and brushed a hand down his chest in an attempt to smooth out the wrinkles I'd caused. Time to get the hell out of here, right fucking now. Problem was, Joey was still clamped to my legs and Tubs was planted like a statue in front of me.

Easy, I told myself. Don't do anything that'll freak Stanley out any more than he already is. He probably had the capacity to call some sort of intervention, and that was the very last thing I wanted. People nearby had backed away, giving us a small ring of space. Most ignored us—just another dustup in the Big Apple—and remained intent on listening to whatever message Kate was sharing. Oh, boy. I needed to find my chill fast. I could see the headlines now. "Federal Agent Freaks Out on Fourth of July, Beats Up Case Manager, Flees Ex-girlfriend."

I plastered on a smile as fake as Stanley's tan. "Stan. I'm sorry." I peered around Tubs to meet Mega-Me's scowl. "Nice to meet you, Harry. I'm Insane Flynn, as I'm sure Stanley's told you. Sorry about that. Everything's cool."

Harry didn't say a word, just continued to smoke me with piercing, angry eyes.

Kindness. That's what would get me out of this mess if I played it the right way. "Joey." I put my hands on the forearm he had locked around my legs. "It's cool. You can let go."

By now, Tubs had moved to my side, although I knew she was watching me like a lioness eyeing up her cubs.

Joey let his arm fall away.

Stanley muttered, "Well, this has been fun, but time's a-wasting. Come on, honey." He grabbed Harry's Frisbee-sized hand and they marched off.

My brain was a tornado, my heart a whirlwind of fucked up, and I needed to make it all stop.

I don't remember what I told Joey and Tubs, but whatever I said must have convinced them I was at least semi-stable, because they let me leave. I weaved through holiday revelers, unsure of my destination but knowing I had to get as far away as fast as possible.

* * *

From the instant I heard Kate onstage to the moment I slapped my first bill on the scarred, beer-stained bar top, vivid memories I thought I'd put to rest hammered me. Nothing stopped the flashbacks roaring through my head like YouTube videos on fast forward. It was worse than watching a horror flick. I didn't want to look, but it was impossible not to.

Hours later, I stumbled out the door of the seedy dive into rain, drunker than I'd been in weeks. All those poor souls waiting for the big Fourth of July bang were going to be disappointed.

As a kid I loved to stomp through puddles, not caring what got wet. Rain never, ever bothered me. Now, for some inexplicable reason, as fat drops slid down the back of my neck, the rainfall infuriated me. The smell of wet asphalt and the damp in the air made my blood boil.

What was wrong with me?

I stumbled along the uneven sidewalk. I was so lost in myself I paid zero attention to my surroundings. Which was a bummer because some shithead snagged my arm and whipped me into the shadows of a side street.

Then I was driven like a pile driver backward into something with no give at all.

I was stunned immobile long enough for my aggressor to grab my wrists and drag them upward against uneven brickwork.

Hot breath blew into my face, smelling suspiciously like sour gummies. How the fuck old was this…kid?

A hand reached between us. Oh, no. No no no. The fight part of my brain kicked in, and kid or not, it was time to end this.

I launched my knee toward his gonads.

Sour Patch felt it coming and twisted. I still caught his inner thigh, which knocked him off balance.

He let go.

I scrambled sideways.

Jesus, if I'd been sober, this whole mess would be over all ready. I blinked hard to clear my vision and aimed the toe of my boot at the inside of his knee and let him have it. The joint gave, popping outward at an angle no knee should bend.

His scream sounded so young.

Connect Four and the bottom drops out, Bucko.

As I mentally patted myself on the back for averting catastrophe, a hand fisted in my hair, jerked my head backward into a very bony shoulder. As I processed that ouch, a sharp blade was slapped none-too-gently against my windpipe.

Shit. I'd forgotten what my Minnesota NPIU partner always lamented. Bad guys were like deer. Where there was one there were usually more.

Wetness dripped down the side of my neck. Probably blood, most likely mine. The good news was I still breathed without bubbles.

With a steamy exhale came the words, "You gonna pay for that, cunt."

Some names were easier to handle than others, but the use of "cunt" was one I couldn't take in any form.

I locked my fingers around the hand gripping the knife and pulled away from my jugular hard as I could. At the same time I snapped my head backward.

A satisfying crunch jarred my skull.

I spun, bent his hand palm up, and jammed it toward his forearm. I pushed until something snapped. The knife clattered to the ground amid his screech.

"Crazy bitch! You broke my fucking wrist!"

I shoved him. He tripped over his fallen comrade and landed on his ass, cradling his arm against his chest.

My lungs were on fire. My entire body vibrated from the adrenaline hit.

I took a couple steps toward the entrance of the alley, then stopped and turned back around. I recalled the business card I'd stuck in my wallet the day I'd been hauled into the precinct. Fished it out and tilted it toward a distant street lamp.

Detective Aubrey Hamilton, Central Robbery Division.

I dialed her number. Voice mail.

"Hey, Detective, thought you'd like to know there's a couple shakedown artists who might be interested in becoming sex offenders if they aren't diverted." I studied the two young men writhing on the ground. "If you send someone in a hurry, they'll probably still be here." I gave the name of the bar and the location of the alley and walked away.

CHAPTER SEVENTEEN

The next morning I stared at my reflection in the mirror. My face was haggard, eyes so bloodshot they looked possessed. I'd survived an almost-encounter with Kate, battled through the associated guilt and self-hatred, escaped Stan and his man, hopefully before he realized I was a stinking mess. I'd stopped an assault—directed at me—without blacking out. I remembered the entire incident. I hadn't wound up hiding behind a dumpster, half crazed and out of my mind.

For the first time in a long time, I saw a flicker of determination in my eyes. Maybe some of the old me was still in there after all.

Sunday finally arrived, and I was due to meet Ursula soon, so I bid farewell to Joey and Tubs, told them this was something I needed to do alone. At Broadway and Lafayette, I exited the subway to another sunny day, and took it as a good omen.

From the stop it was an easy few-block walk to Favela Cubana. I looked forward to trying the food if the butterflies flitting around my stomach would allow me to eat.

As I closed in on the restaurant, my palms began sweating and my heart lodged in my windpipe. My watch put me eleven minutes early. Instead of going inside, I loitered across the street, watching the front door of the restaurant.

The building itself was pale yellow stucco. The business name was spelled out in bright red block letters, mounted above three large, boxy, floor-to-ceiling picture windows. A fourth window had been turned into a glass door that now served as the entrance. An outdoor patio was situated in front of the plate glass windows.

I realized, as I paced back and forth on the sidewalk, that to anyone watching, it would appear as if I was casing the place. I forced myself to stand still and lean against a tree.

At twenty-five after twelve, a lithe woman with hair down to the middle of her back, wearing a red T-shirt and jeans, veered off the sidewalk and disappeared into the cafe.

I recognized Ursula's ambling gait. I squared my shoulders and marched across the street. The interior was dim so I pushed my sunglasses to the top of my head and hoped my eyes adjusted fast. As the door clanged shut, the woman spun around.

"Flynn!" Ursula shrieked as she put an oh-so-familiar stranglehold on me. I hugged her back, both of us laughing and talking at once. In that moment, it was as if all the years we'd spent apart never passed.

The host waited patiently until we were done with our noisy reunion, sat us outside in a corner of the patio, and took our drink order. I figured a mango mojito fit the ambiance.

Ursula's twinkling black eyes clouded as she looked me over. Inside, it had been dim enough that my scars weren't readily apparent. Outside, in the bright, honest light of day, the damage could not be hidden, especially since I wore short sleeves.

Her eyes followed the burn up my arm. "Flynn, you look like part of you was melted."

I hadn't really been around anyone other than Tubs, the Art Squad, and my two Joeys to really have to think about or care what impression people might have when they saw them. But Urs's response, it was perfect. No pity, just an acknowledgement of the truth. She always had the ability to downplay things in a way that made it better, not worse. She knew how to say the right things at the right time. Something I forever appreciated.

I stared at her, hardly believing I was sitting across from one of my best friends once again. "Melted," I echoed. "Great description."

The waiter arrived with my mojito and Brazilian beer for Ursula. We made some fast entrée choices, and he vanished inside to enter the orders.

I sucked down a third of the mojito in two long swallows. It hit all the right notes between the liquor, mint leaves, mango, and simple syrup, but all I honestly cared about was the rum.

"Look at you," I said and studied the front of Ursula's T-shirt. "Riveters?"

"National Women's Hockey League."

I made a face. "Sorry to admit I haven't been keeping up. But I knew you'd make the big time." I leaned forward. "Is that the big time?"

Urs laughed. "It's as big as it gets for women's hockey. We've partnered with the New Jersey Devils, which is kind of, holy shit, if you know what I mean. League's got four teams. Boston Pride, Connecticut Whale, Buffalo Beauts, and us. There's talk of adding Minnesota, but I don't know if that'll happen." She tilted her bottle. "You know how the NHL has the Stanley Cup? We have the Isobel Cup."

"Isobel?"

"Isobel was Lord Stanley's—"

She narrowed an eye at my blank look. "Come on, Flynn. The Cup. The Stanley Cup. It's the ultimate prize every NHL player covets. Don't you remember all the playoff games we watched as kids?"

"Oh. Yeah, I do." In all honesty I might've been watching Kate instead of the action on the television.

"Anyway, Isobel was Lord Stanley's daughter. She was one of the first Canadian women to play hockey."

Most of what she said went in one ear and dribbled out the other. Regardless of my lack of understanding the particulars, I knew it was big. "You were born for this. I'm proud of you, Urs."

Her cheeks reddened. "So catch me up on you."

I hoovered up another third of my drink, wondered when the waiter was going to come back so I could order a refill. "You probably remember I was with the NPIU in Minneapolis."

"Hard to forget that. " She tempered her words with a warm smile. "What was it like?"

"We investigated national terror tips we received from the public and other channels, assisted the locals when we were requested. I liked what we did okay, but once I heard they were creating a HAVOC unit, I wanted in. Since my oh-so-young-and-naive plans to get myself overseas and hunt down the bad guys who caused 9/11 were hosed, this new unit seemed like a gift."

"HAVOC?"

"Hostages and Victims Out Of Country. FBI, sometimes the DEA, the military, and the NPIU. We rescue kidnapped Americans overseas, among other things."

"Sounds like something out of a thriller novel." She rolled the beer bottle between her palms as she gazed thoughtfully at me.

The server reappeared and we reordered. Once he hustled off for refills, I said, "The days, the situations, the oppressive heat, the goddamn unrelenting boredom all blended together. Toward the end we concentrated on humanitarian missions as well as other deployments. We were in Aleppo when everything went sideways."

"We as in?"

I finished off my mojito. "Four of our team died that day. Two of us survived."

Before I could say more the waiter returned with our second round. I grabbed the double rum shot I'd ordered with the mojito and knocked it back.

Ursula's kind, sympathetic gaze was almost too much to bear. "You wound up in a DC hospital. I came to visit; you weren't having it, you stubborn thing. I left my number. Don't know if they gave it to you."

There it was. "Yeah, I got it. I'm so sorry I didn't see you that day. And that I didn't call."

"I mostly wanted you to know I came. Anyway." She assessed me. "What else?"

"What else what?"

"What injuries aren't visible?"

"My best friend wound up paralyzed from the waist down."

Her inhalation was sharp. "Oh, no. I'm so, so sorry."

Instead of meeting Ursula's eyes, I stared over her shoulder at the tree I'd used as a crutch while waiting for her to arrive. The gentleness and understanding she'd had as a kid was something she'd retained as an adult. With the exception, I thought, of hockey. Then it was all about team and winning, no gentleness necessary except when it was time to finesse the biscuit into the basket.

My smile was more a grimace. "It's over. Tell me about what else is happening with you." I felt the muscles in my lower back release. The rum was working.

"You know about the hockey thing. The pay isn't anything to write home about. I majored in computers, landed an internship with a private investigations firm. Initially handled their IT stuff."

"PI as in detective?"

"Exactly." She downed another swallow. "I was lucky. They were great about dealing with my hockey schedule. After awhile, I realized I liked investigations, and they hired me on. Got my PI license. A few years went by, and I decided I wanted to work for myself. So I left."

"A private eye. Wow. I never would have called that one."

"I know. Wasn't on my radar either. But I liked the hunt, the detail work, putting stuff together to solve problems. So I created PI Tech. I specialize in information, and I do it on my own time. I'm in charge of an employee of one, and I can work it around my hockey schedule. Turns out info can pay big."

She was perfect for Operation Retrieve Helen. I said, "Sometimes the payoff comes in the most surprising ways."

"Isn't that the truth."

Our waiter returned with our orders. He dispensed the grub and scurried off to fetch another round.

We chatted in generalities while we ate. I wanted to laugh at the strange ease of it all. It felt weird, kind of like old times, but so not. Kate should've been there, laughing and catching up. She was a ghost at the table.

I held out as long as I could, until the weight of the unasked questions playing over and over in my head began drowning out rational thought. I had to know if Ursula knew what Kate was up to. How she was doing. If she was with anyone. Good God. If I wasn't careful I had the potential to turn into a real stalker.

Our drinks were replaced, dessert turned down, and the table cleared. I leaned back in my chair and crossed an ankle over a knee. "I have a seven-hundred-pound gorilla hanging around my neck, and I'm sure you're waiting for me to ask, so here you go. Have you kept up with Kate?"

Ursula leaned forward. "Can't say I wasn't expecting the question. I see her every couple weeks. We get together, catch up."

"Is she…" I began but trailed off, not sure what I wanted to ask first and what I didn't want to know. I looked up at a bright blue sky dotted with puffy white cotton candy clouds. "What's she doing, other than giving speeches on the environment? Maybe the better question to ask is how is she?"

Urs smoothed out a napkin and placed her bottle on it. Stalling, probably trying to figure out what she should tell me and what she should leave out.

"She's doing all right, considering. Her dad passed away a few months ago, and she and Will have been working to divide up Goldsmith Foundation responsibilities."

"I'm sorry to hear that." And I was. Her father had taken the loss of his wife hard, and I doubted he ever got over it. Who would? "What happened?"

"He was in Poland returning some recovered Nazi loot that went up for auction. Had a heart attack. Dropped dead on the spot."

"No shit. I always liked the man, except for how he kept trying to force Kate into taking over the foundation. So in the end she's stuck there?"

"Not exactly. You know when she graduated from the Cooper Union, she joined up with that volunteer thing she'd wanted to do so bad—"

"International Volunteer HQ," I said. "After I left for the NPIU and she went overseas...that was the beginning of the end."

She frowned, her gaze unfocused. "It was. We were all, for the most part, out of touch by then, weren't we?"

"Yeah. Things happened so fast."

"Did you know she helped design the Freedom Tower?"

"What?" I knew my girl—rather, my ex-girl—would go on to do big things, but, damn. That was beyond. I never should've told Tubs I didn't want to hear about anything regarding Kate. She had to have known Kate's dad died. And that Kate had been involved in the creation of the Freedom Tower. I never once thought about how hard it had to have been for Tubs to withhold this kind of knowledge from me.

"It's her landmark achievement, but I know she's got a lot more in her."

I studied the mint leaves stuck to the ice in my mojito, trying to process this new information. "You know, somehow it all keeps coming back to the World Trade Center."

"What do you mean?"

"Can't remember if I ever told you this, but Tubs' husband, my grandfather, was killed during the construction of the original Twin Towers."

"No freaking shit. Nope, you never told me."

"Then Kate's mom was killed when the towers fell. And like some kind of lopsided full circle, Kate has a hand in the creation of the new Freedom Tower."

"That is weird synchronicity."

"Where is she living now? At her folks' apartment in the Financial District?"

"No. She bought that place in Brooklyn where you guys lived when half the complex turned into condos. Will's in the Williams Street penthouse now."

"She's in the same apartment?" I was stunned.

"It's officially a condo, but yes, ma'am."

I flashed back to our old place, filled with love, laughter, and so much naive hope. The scent memory of frying burger and onions and homemade spaghetti sauce washed over me like a tsunami, triggering a deep ache.

We'd been neighbors this whole time. Why would she cross the river when she had every creature comfort possible in FiDi?

Then it all came clear. I knew exactly why she was there. She never cared about money or class or high society. She cared about humanity, cared about standing up for what was right. She cared about the environment, about making people's lives easier. She'd loved that apartment—or condo—and the memories we'd made there. Then another thought socked me in the midsection. I spit it out before I chickened. "Is she seeing anyone?"

She paused a moment, head tilting to one side almost imperceptibly. "No. She's not."

How did I feel about that? Relieved and then guilty about the relief.

"Hey." Ursula touched my arm. "You okay?"

"Yeah, sorry. So, Will. He take over the foundation?"

"He did. Then when their dad died, Kate went back, part-time. She's taken on the environmental and sustainability side of the organization along with donation coordination while Will deals with the numbers and all the foundation scholarships."

I opened and closed my mouth a couple times. This was all too much. I should've kept my big trap shut. I needed space, needed to absorb all I'd heard. Except I hadn't yet talked to Urs about the entire point of our visit.

A dull throb began to creep up the back of my neck into the base of my skull. "Okay. Thanks for the catch-up." I tipped my glass to my mouth, but it was empty. "Changing subjects, let me tell you about my proposition."

"Hit me."

Twenty minutes later, after I'd run down the problem and our tentative solution, I sold Ursula on the idea of joining our merry band of aging outlaws. She agreed to come to Tubs' place Wednesday evening to meet Joey and the Art Squad. Mission accomplished and then some.

CHAPTER EIGHTEEN

For hours after my meeting with Ursula, I wallowed in an emotional morass of nostalgia and regret. Pain that long ago had morphed into nothing more than a vague memory bombarded me. Alcohol helped. Frankly, if I had an option to mainline the shit, I would've. But I didn't. Instead of drinking my entire night away, I decided to go home sometime after the witching hour and before dawn.

When I tried to sleep, my dreams were fragmented, confused in time and place. One moment I was in Battery Park feeding pigeons and the next I was in the middle of hell. Thunderous gunfire illuminated a nighttime firefight in some desert town. Joey hollered like a record on repeat, "Take cover, take fucking cover!"

I startled awake, soaked in sweat as the echo of artillery fire faded. I forced my eyes open. I was home. I was safe. No one was in danger.

Then Joey's panicked, hoarse shout shattered the quiet. "Take cover! Status check! NOW!"

My heart resumed its frantic drumming. Had his words burrowed into my nightmare? I thrashed to free myself from the quilt someone had tossed over me and rolled off the couch onto my knees.

Joey yelled something incomprehensible, followed by an inhuman wail. I almost upended the coffee table as I rounded the couch and scrambled down the hall to my room.

Where was Tubs? A racket like this would wake a not-yet-risen zombie. Then I caught sight of the bedside clock.

11:29 a.m. She was obviously not home or she would've already been in here.

Sunlight streamed through the window, spotlighting one side of Joey's face. His eyes were screwed shut, face contorted, hands fisting the comforter.

"Joey!" I grabbed his bare shoulder, shook it hard. The muscles beneath his skin were trembling. "Joey, hey buddy, wake up."

His eyes popped open. "Wha—"

"It's okay. You're home, you're safe."

After a few long breaths, he covered his face with his hands. "That was so incredibly fucking right now." He pushed himself upright.

I didn't say any more, let him reacclimate to the present.

"It's...always so goddamn real," he whispered.

"I know. Liquor helps."

His eyes closed on a long exhale. "That's your first problem."

I ignored the dig. "Sometimes oblivion is preferable to reliving it."

"I thought so too. Already told you that. But marinating my liver wasn't the answer. Not in the long run. You gotta deal, girl."

"Like dealing's helping you? Doesn't seem like it, what with all the yelling. And I'm handling this whole thing fine."

"You really think?" Joey nailed me with the most somber stare I'd ever seen him produce. "Look in the mirror. You're fucking haunted. It's in your eyes, in the way you hold yourself. And as for me? I *am* dealing. One day at a time. Sometimes one second at a time. You should have seen me the first few months after…" He trailed off and waved a hand toward his legs. "It was ugly as sin. I was ugly as sin, worse than a bee-stung bear. But Stanley, he helped me. Got me into AA. Speaking of, I need to find a meeting here in town, once I have a place. You can come with—"

"Stop." I straightened, crossed my arms. "Stop right there. I don't need any of that bullshit."

"Own it, Flynn. You only come home to sleep a few hours, then you disappear again. Tubs is worried sick about you, but she doesn't want to say anything. She's afraid this new you will run and not come back."

That stung. I bit off a snarky comeback and pressed my lips together hard. Oh, Tubs. I'm so sorry. But, come the fuck on. Things could be worse. I could be a meth head, holding up pharmacies for my next prescription high. Besides, I had zero doubt I could quit drinking anytime I wanted. I just didn't want to now. Maybe not ever.

He flopped back onto the pillow, laced his fingers and tucked them under his head with a pissed off sigh. Sighs could be telling, and I'd long ago learned to translate his.

"Okay," he said, "Fine. But seriously, you're killing yourself and you refuse to admit it."

So what? The only difference between killing myself via alcohol or with a bullet was the length of time it would take to die. There had to be something in the fact that at least for now, I was choosing the slower of the two options.

* * *

Wednesday rolled around faster than I'd expected. Tubs did a great job keeping me from losing myself in my own head by sending me to the corner store twice and then both Joey and I out a third time to Joey's Pizzeria to pick up a couple pies.

I'd asked Ursula to come a half hour before the Art Squad was due because I knew Tubs would have a million questions for her, and it would be easiest to get that out of the way right off the bat. At seven thirty on the dot, a knock echoed on the door.

I opened it to Ursula in a Riveters hoodie and faded jeans. She wore a wide smile and held a bottle of wine. For a second I froze. She dragged me into a hug, and then we were laughing and everything was strangely okay.

"Come on now, Mikala." Tubs dragged me away from her. "Share the girl. It's been far too long."

After more hugging, more laughter, and introductions to Joey, we settled around the dining room table.

Joey said, "I've heard so much about you through the years I feel like we're already friends. This one," he tilted his head at me, "loved to rehash the trouble—or maybe I should call them adventures—you guys got yourselves in."

The corners of my mouth curled. "That would be a discussion for another time."

"My dear, yes it will," Tubs said. "I want to hear all about these so-called adventures later. Ursula, how have you been?"

Urs gave the short catch-up version. It was one of those magical moments when, once again, it all felt so easy. Even with Joey in the mix, a certain level of comfort settled over us.

Talk moved onto Ursula's current job status. She brought Tubs up to speed on what she did for a living and how PI Tech came about.

Once she was done, Joey said with undisguised glee, "You totally have a skill set we need. You're right, Flynn, this girl's a keeper."

Our discussion was ended by the arrival of Elizabet, who floated into the apartment on three-inch heels, followed by layers of filmy, colorful wisps of cloth that somehow constituted clothing. She carried a purse the size of Delaware and another bag stuffed with who knew what.

After introductions and air kisses, we huddled in the living room around the now pizza box-laden coffee table.

Elizabet positioned herself on the couch in front of one of the pies. "Only Rich and Char can make it tonight. They should be here any moment. I'm starving, so let's eat." When she was hungry, it was best to feed her ASAP.

Tubs handed Joey a stack of paper plates and thrust some napkins at Ursula, who doled them out. I divvied out soda and popped the top on a can of Coke for myself, with a fleeting thought of how good it would taste with an added splash of Captain Morgan.

"Two slices of pepperoni and mushroom, please," Elizabet said with a couple of arm movements worthy of an orchestra conductor and accepted her plate from Joey.

"Why, thank you, young man." Elizabet sized him up with a raised brow and a lusty glint. From her expression she looked like she wanted to eat her pizza right off his chest.

Joey shot me a semi-alarmed look.

With a one-shouldered I-have-no-idea shrug, I watched in fascination as Elizabet fluttered mascara-laden lashes at him.

Yikes.

The last thing we needed was Elizabet deciding Joey was her next romantic May-December conquest. Neither the wheelchair nor his lack of mobility slowed her down one bit. I loved her a little more for that, but still, we had a theft to plan.

After that, Joey could be all hers.

Tubs busied herself shoveling pizza onto plates, either oblivious to or ignoring Elizabet's flirty shenanigans.

Another knock sounded on the front door. I let Char and Rich in and repeated the necessary intros.

Char, slice in one hand, paper cup of coffee from Dunkin' Donuts in the other, asked, "Elizabet, you bring it?"

We all cast a curious look at Elizabet, who dabbed daintily at the corners of her mouth. "Yes." She waved her grease-stained paper towel at the sack she'd dropped by the entry. "Once Flynn is dressed and I have my way with her, not a soul will recognize her."

Ursula gave me the side-eye. I could only shoot her the same in return. The gang was cooking and we weren't even in the kitchen yet.

"What, exactly," I asked, wary now, "is in that bag?"

"Honey, you just wait." Elizabet looked me up and down. "Some of the most perfect break-in wear ever and a few other accouterments."

Joey almost choked on his soda. He placed the can on the coffee table and cleared his throat. "Break-in wear? Accouterments?"

"For sure." Char slid another slice onto Elizabet's plate and one onto her own. "Elizabet borrowed a few things from her costume and props department for Flynn to use when she retrieves the Keller letter."

"It's okay, Char." Tubs pointed her pizza between Joey and Ursula. "They know Pascal the Rascal stole it and they know we're stealing it back. And they're going to help us."

"A-a-a letter for a l-l-letter, give him back his forgery," Rich said.

"Right!" Elizabet nodded, and I was afraid her beehive would upend itself right into what was left of the Canadian bacon-and-pineapple pizza. I wasn't going to be the one to pick pineapple chunks out of her 'do.

"Back to the bag, Elizabet," I said and stuffed the rest of my pizza in my mouth.

The numerous rings she wore made a metallic tinging as she wagged her fingers in the bag's general direction. "Go get it."

I threw my plate in the garbage and retrieved the heavier-than-expected tote and returned to my chair, not at all ready for whatever was inside.

"Take a look." Elizabet was so excited she bounced in her seat like a five-year-old.

I opened the top of the sack. A bunch of black cloth covered who knew what. "What is this?"

Tubs said, "Pull it out."

I did.

Char gave me a shove. "Hold it up."

This wasn't going to end well. I shook the cloth out and realized it was a body suit.

Elizabet did an excited shimmy in her chair. "There's another piece in the bag, too."

I sat on the edge of the couch with a grumpy sigh. With bright looks of expectation Elizabet and Char watched me rummage through the bag. Tubs, Joey, and Ursula looked as confused as I did.

I pulled out a facemask. It was a balaclava, with eyeholes, a mouth hole, and two sausage-shaped yellow lightning bolts sewn on either side of two additional holes where I assumed the wearers ears would protrude. I couldn't tamp down the look of horror that had taken over my face.

Ursula burst into laughter. "Try it on. You'll look like Flash, the comic book superhero. Or maybe his evil alter ego, Firebolt."

"How do you know so much about superheroes, hockey girl?" I asked.

"Can't tell you all my secrets."

"Go see if it fits, Flynn." If Elizabet's smile grew any bigger, her face would burst like an overripe peach. "I think I picked one that'll work for your height."

Everyone was in such a good mood that I didn't have the heart to be an ass and put up a fight. Even Tubs was laughing, and that made my insides soften immeasurably.

Elizabet did have a good eye for fit, because I was able to pull the skin-tight cloth all the way on and zip it up. Then I tugged the mask over my head, and claustrophobia hit. My heart raced and my chest constricted. I couldn't breathe. Again. This was ridiculous.

I ripped the mask off and threw it on the floor. Hands on knees, measured breaths.

Come on. Stop it.

The mask was crumpled on the bathroom tile in an innocuous pile of black and yellow. Cloth and thread, nothing more.

Another thirty seconds and my hands stopped shaking. I grabbed the damn mask, settled it back over my head. Waited for my mind to whip the rug out from under me again. This time the rug stayed where it belonged.

I exhaled and rearranged it so I could see and breathe, then looked at myself in the mirror. Long, long way from superhero. I fled the bath and hesitated at the door to my bedroom, thinking a couple hits from the bottle that was still stashed in my drawer sounded like salvation. After a few seconds of consideration, I turned away with a sense of newfound control and marched out to the living room.

"Would you look at that," Joey said when I emerged. He high-fived Ursula. "I win."

Tubs walked around me. "In which production was this used, Elizabet?"

"*The Superhero Madhouse*. It's The Zapper costume. Don't you think it's perfect for our little escapade? She just has to be careful not to damage it. Look at the rest of the items I brought, Flynn." Elizabet's eyes shone with excitement.

I sat back down in the chair I'd vacated and angled my head so I could see out the eyeholes while rummaging through the bag. Soon a utility belt, a foot-long flashlight, a grappling hook, a crowbar, and a large pair of binoculars rested on the coffee table in front of me.

"Those were the things The Zapper used in the production," Elizabet said.

A giggle bubbled deep in my chest. The only thing useful might have been the grappling hook, if it hadn't been made of some kind of super light substance that would never hold the weight of anything over twenty-five pounds.

Joey met my eyes, and I could hold back no more. Months of pent-up laughter burst out of me, and Joey caught a ride on the hilarity train. Pretty soon everyone was yukking it up.

"Oh dear," Elizabet said. "She's laughing, Tubs. I knew this would work."

Char wiped her eyes. "We know you can't use any of that, but we thought it might be a funny way to kick off the master plan."

I felt...so goddamn good. These people, my people laughing right along with me, strangely meant so much. And this elation I felt, the unchecked giddiness rising like helium inside me didn't come through the fog of a mood-altering substance. This was true, untainted emotion, nonchemical delight, and it felt—

A knock on the front door rudely interrupted my magical moment. Probably some neighbor ticked off because we were making so much noise. Tubs, still snickering, flung the door open.

Everyone went silent so fast that I spun around in my seat to see what the problem was.

Stanley was standing on the threshold.

Seriously? He was worse than a bad penny. More like a defective fifty-cent piece. In his official-looking suit, he appeared way more himself than he had the other day, especially with a paisley pink and purple tie wrapped around his neck.

It was then I realized I was still dressed as the Zapper. Maybe if I didn't say anything he wouldn't recognize me.

"Stanley," Tubs said, "what a surprise. What brings you out at," she made a show of assessing her watch, "a quarter to nine at night? And wearing such a darling tie?"

The flush that rolled up Stanley's neck was kind of cute. "Sorry about the lateness of my visit, Mrs. Flynn. I happened to be in the area and wanted to swing in and see how things were going with Agent Moseby."

Tubs peered over her shoulder at Joey and back at Stan. "As you can see, Stanley, he's doing fine. We're in the middle of a party here, but you're welcome to come on in and join the festivities."

Oh my God, no. Had Tubs lost her mind?

"You do enjoy your parties, don't you, Mrs. Flynn. Thank you, but no. I simply wanted to touch base and make sure everything was going smoothly."

Good answer, Stan, my man, good answer.

"Smooth as a baby's butt. Thank you for checking in. It's been a nice visit, but I should get back to my guests." Tubs tried to push the door closed.

Stan blocked it with a hand. "Where's your granddaughter, Mrs. Flynn?"

For Pete's sake. I stood up. "Right here, Stan."

The double take he did was so dramatic it could've won an Academy Award. "Agent Flynn? Why are you wearing that, that…" Stan was rarely at a loss, but this time the proverbial cat not only had his tongue but had chewed it up and swallowed it for good measure. He pushed the door farther open.

On the coffee table behind my Zapper-clad ass were the grappling hook and the other various "accouterments" that could appear incriminating even if I hadn't done a thing with them. But if snoopy Stanley caught sight of them, who knew what his devious little mind might conjure up.

Then Elizabet and her 'do were right beside me. She snaked her arm through mine and pulled me tight against her side. "Doesn't our superhero look great as The Zapper?"

Stanley's brows drew together and his eyes darted back and forth between Elizabet in her filmy finery and me in my way-too-hot and entirely-too-tight fantastical getup.

"Agent Flynn, are you going to a…a Halloween party? But it's months until October."

"She's testing out a new costume for my theater." Elizabet was quicker on her feet than I'd expected. "Fabulous, isn't it?"

Tubs grabbed Stanley's arm with one hand and shoved a paper plate with a slice of pizza at him with the other and physically marched him toward the door. "Here's some food to sustain you on the trip home. It's been an enjoyable visit, Stanley. Have a good evening."

She propelled him into the hall and gently shut the door. For once she remembered to engage the locks.

For about ten seconds complete silence blanketed the apartment. Then Rich, of all people, began to laugh. A dam burst and hysteria ensued. Again.

"Tubs," I said as I tugged the face mask off, "I thought you lost your mind. I figured he'd see our burglary tools and haul me away, suit and all."

She smiled benignly. "A little reverse psychology never hurts."

I shed my costume, and for the next half hour, we ate more pizza and drank more soda. Before too long, I reverted from

The Zapper back to plain old Flynn, and we focused on the business at hand.

Elizabet took a noisy sip of tea and set her mug on a coaster. "Pascal's having a huge blowout in a couple of weeks—Friday after next—his annual Summer Splash. It's a three-day, non-stop party. He brings in a live band, fancy food. Pulls out all the stops. It'll be perfect."

Ursula asked, "This art room you mentioned earlier, Elizabet, is it alarmed?"

"I imagine. He has some fancy alarm system. Sahl knows all about it."

"Sahl?" Ursula looked at me.

"He's part of the Art Squad," I said, "but couldn't be here tonight. He already looked it up."

Tubs squeezed Ursula's shoulder. "If you like, I'll put you in contact with him."

"Sounds good. I have someone who knows alarms. Then I'll follow up with Sahl if I need to."

"S-s-she does have some skills, doesn't she," Rich said.

Ursula smiled. "I have a few tricks up my sleeve. We'll have a roadmap of exactly where and what your man, Elizabet—"

"—ex-man, thank you."

"I'm sorry. Ex-man. What your ex-man has for home security. Would you mind shooting me his address?"

"One moment." From her purse, Elizabet withdrew a ghastly pink fold-over cell phone case embedded with gaudy fake rhinestones. At least I thought they were fake. With her you never knew. "What's your number?"

Urs rattled it off.

"Now that we have that settled," I said, "we need a communications center, preferably a van of some sort that would accommodate Joey's ride."

"M-my brother has a Dodge Caravan he's not using," Rich said. "I can ask to borrow it."

"Perfect." Joey's grin was shrewd. I loved it.

I felt a familiar quiver at the base of my skull. The quiver turned into a buzz, and the buzz blossomed. It grounded me. It told me, *Flynn, you're on.* Concentrate on the now. This moment, this minute. This second. This breath.

Holy great balls of shit. Had someone found my long lost activator button? I hadn't felt like this since before we launched into the Aleppo op. I sat in wonder, savoring every second of the feeling.

Then I realized they'd gone right on planning without me.

"...comm equipment," Joey was saying. "Ursula, that something you could wrangle for us?"

"Sure," she said. "What exactly are you thinking?"

"Small," Joey said. "Reliable."

I picked up my Coke. Best pay attention to what was happening before I was accused of being drunk. Especially when for once I wasn't.

Urs said, "A new device will be on the market in a few months. I think it'd be perfect. It's a Bluetooth ear bud that fits into the ear canal. It's essentially invisible."

Char did a seated boogie. "We're back in the saddle again, baby!'"

Back in the saddle of what? A half-formed recollection teased my brain and then slipped away as Ursula spoke. "The device does rely on cell service, but in this instance, I think it'd be more than adequate. Especially since I can get my hands on a tester version and it won't cost a dime."

"Now that's a deal." Elizabet's eyes glittered. I could just imagine the delight she'd take if we managed to pull this off.

"Wait a minute," Joey said. "If this is a prototype, how can we be sure it'll work?"

"Trust me," Urs said, "the developer won't let anything out of her lab unless it's working perfectly."

"Who is this developer?" Tubs asked.

"My cousin. Her IQ is about triple mine and she has a bent for perfection."

"Too Tall Trudy?" I hadn't thought about her since high school.

"The one and only."

"Wow. That's great. And helpful." This was coming together too easily. I wasn't sure if I should be suspicious or grateful.

"She was smart as shit in school, beat out the boys in just about every test she ever took, especially in STEM," Urs said. "Works with some real power players in the creative inventions circuit. Last I heard she was rubbing elbows with Elon Musk."

Holy Hostess Ho Ho. I was glad for her. Then Ho Hos were all I could think about. I liked them. They'd have been great for dessert, plus they went well with vodka.

Stop it. Think about something other than booze or Ho Hos. Think about the non-alcoholic, ready-for-action buzz in my brain.

Joey asked, "When can we test the system?"

"Let me text her."

While Ursula connected with her cousin, Char said, "We have transportation and communication. What else? We need to deal with the dogs and you need to find whatever tools that would help you, Flynn."

Elizabet thrust her hand in the air and wagged her fingers. You could take the woman out of the theater, but you couldn't take the theater out of the woman.

Tubs said dryly, "Elizabet?"

"What if we send Ursula into the party as a guest? She could monitor what's going on from the inside."

"Great idea," Char said. "Pascal hasn't ever seen her."

Rich drummed his fingers on a bouncing leg. "How will we g-g-get her an invite?"

"Honey," Elizabet leaned back and made a show of crossing her long legs, "leave that to me."

"Hang on a second," I said. "How about we ask Ursula if she's even interested before we send her into the jackal's lair?"

All eyes fell on Ursula. "I can do it, no problem."

Good enough. Joey and I were assigned to make a trip to one of the many military surplus stores in town and secure whatever we thought we'd need to bridge the perimeter fence and anything else that might be helpful.

Once we waded our way through the shopping list, I said, "What do I put the Keller letter into once I have it? For safe transport."

Rich said, "All you need to do is w-wear gloves and slip the document into a stiff folder."

"I'll take care of the folder," Tubs said.

"My guy should be able to turn off the alarms on any wired cases for as long as we need." Urs picked up her phone. "I'll make sure he's available."

Joey said, "So this question has been on my mind since Flynn told me about what happened. Helen Keller was blind. How could she possibly write a letter?"

Elizabet said, "When Helen was born, she could both see and hear. At about a year and a half, she became very sick. She survived, but ended up both deaf and blind. Probably either meningitis or scarlet fever. Anyway, at that time, there were different schools of thought on the best way to teach children with those kinds of challenges. She learned to read using Boston Line Type—which differs from Braille. She practiced penmanship, and with the help of a grooved board, was able to print. It was reportedly an exhausting process, poor thing."

"That's...incredible," I said. "I can't begin to imagine how one would communicate if both those senses were taken away. Especially in that era."

A little after ten, the gathering broke up. I swung into my bedroom and knocked back enough for a nice non-action buzz. I'd toed the line, but now I could relax. I hit the bottle once more and stowed it as warmth flooded my veins, pleased I'd guzzled only enough to prime the engines for a nighttime stroll.

In the living room, Joey was parked at the dining room table, head bent over one of Tubs' books. He'd stripped out of his T-shirt, and his white undershirt was vivid against his skin. For a moment I studied him. Really took a good look. He'd always been muscular, but his upper body was now even more ripped, thanks to the fact his arms, chest, and shoulders were his means of propulsion. Regardless of all he'd been through, he was a handsome human. If I were a straight woman, I'd give Elizabet a run for her money.

Said human looked up, caught me eyeing him. "Going out?"

I hesitated. "I'm not tired. Got something good to roll around in my head for once."

"That you do."

"We have some shopping, too, the good kind."

A smile dimpled his cheek. "How about Saturday? I have another couple apartments to check out tomorrow and Friday. Want to tag along?"

"I suppose I can squeeze you into my over-packed agenda. Saturday's good for shopping. What time you looking at potential new digs? Late I hope?"

"You used to be so good about getting up early."

"Hey, things change."

"Tomorrow at eleven, Friday at eight."

"I suppose that's eight in the morning."

"Your genius defies explanation."

"Asshat."

"It's how you like me."

I opened the front door. "Joey, you're right. It's exactly how I like you." Sarcastic, alive, and close by.

CHAPTER NINETEEN

Shitholes.

I hated to admit that was the nicest possible way to describe the two apartments Joey and I checked out.

Initially, we thought the first place had potential. It was a ten-story pre-war, rent-stabilized elevator building. An accessibility ramp led to the front entry, which was locked.

The supervisor, a tall, thin, balding guy, buzzed us into the lobby. The faintest scent of urine competed with the odors of decay, fried burgers, and bacon. A bank of old metal mailboxes looked serviceable. The lighting was sketchy, with a single bulb dimly illuminating the chipped, subway-tiled, ten-by-twelve space. The best feature was the elevator at the far end.

It was the best feature until it got jammed between the fourth and fifth floor. We were stuck in the metal sauna from hell for a grand total of six hours while FDNY worked feverishly—no pun intended—to extract us. After we were freed, we heard from a number of residents that this was the fourth time this week the fire department had to rescue someone from the "vewy skewy awigator," as one kid called it. She refused to even get near the broken beast. I didn't blame her one bit.

The next day, I managed to drag myself off the couch in time to accompany Joey to Disaster Number Two. I'm not sure what number disaster it was for him. I hadn't wanted to write off the joint, because it was a ground-floor apartment and that would've been perfect.

We entered the foyer of the four-story tenement through an unlocked front door that had three panes of glass and one rectangular, ragged chunk of cardboard adhered with pink duct tape.

I held the door for Joey and he maneuvered inside. My gut did an all-too-familiar "look-the-fuck-out" flip-flop as the scent of shit wafted sharply from somewhere nearby.

"Did you fart?" Joey asked.

"Nope."

Joey found the super's name on a set of grimy, ivory-colored buttons. While we waited for him to answer the buzz, I took stock. The boxy vestibule was small, with only enough room for me and Joey and maybe another person. A second, locked metal door blocked entrance to the interior.

I looked up, and two sconces held the jagged shards of broken light bulbs. Once the sun went down, this space would get mighty dark mighty fast. The floor was linoleum or had been at one time. A hint of the design was still visible where the floor met filthy grayish walls, except in one corner where some dickhead had tossed a leaky diaper.

That explained the smell.

Joey leaned on the buzzer again. Five minutes later the super let us in. Three minutes after that we were back out on the sidewalk, making sure neither of us had picked up any hitchhikers.

Goddamn, I hated cockroaches.

* * *

Saturday was our military-surplus shopping trip day. I was in a good mood, and the pull for mind-altering substances was manageable. Stanley and Joey could kiss my ass. I was in complete control.

Tubs was off to meet Rich and figure out vehicle logistics. The city wasn't car friendly, and we needed to find a place to store our getaway ride the day before we needed it.

Joey and I headed for Uncle Sam's Army Navy Outfitters in Manhattan, close to the Village. I'd been there once before, but Joey had never set foot—or wheel—on the premises. It was a crazy place with a crazy manager, and the establishment carried almost everything we'd need, along with a shitload of crap we wouldn't.

A two-foot-wide ribbon of black corrugated metal divided the storefront from the dirty, three-story brick apartments above it. A few battered air conditioners listed precariously from wood-framed apartment windows.

Mounted on the rippled metal was a white Uncle Sam's Army Navy sign lit by a single floodlight. Beside it sat a pink anchor.

Below the sign, a stained, partially rusted metal awning jutted out maybe three feet from the façade. Two red lights encased in safety cages were inexplicably installed above the store's entrance.

Display windows on either side of the entry doors were decorated with the last thing I would have expected. Perhaps it was the store's proximity to Christopher Street and the Village. Or maybe it was something else all together. Whatever the case, a unicorn with rainbow runs had come a-knockin.' The interior of both display windows was filled with rainbow crepe paper and rainbow streamers, a rainbow peace symbol flag—which I had to admit was a little ironic in a shop that sold items related to war— rainbow handbags, rainbow leis, rainbow USA flags, and balloons.

Among the explosion of color, I made out the word PRIDE spelled in rainbow crepe paper taped to one of the windows.

We'd arrived a couple weeks late to the party, but here, anyway, the party was still going strong.

The two front doors were propped open, and dog tags hung from rainbow-crepe-wrapped push bars. A stained green rug led past a mannequin soldier standing sentry.

"Ready?" I asked

"Let's do this." He pushed himself over the threshold. I followed and resisted the urge to salute Private Mannequin.

Then the smell hit. Rainbow pride or not, no doubt this was a military surplus store. The abrasive scent of rubber and the unmistakable tang of treated canvas blended with old, musty who knew what.

The odor was a little repulsive and a lot like coming home. My stomach tensed, my heart sped up, my palms grew damp. Vision blurred, and I was hit with an overwhelming need to bolt.

I took a step back. Then another.

A hand grasped my wrist, broke me out of the moment. In that second, sound returned. I hadn't realized it'd left. The din of cars on the street, the shrill voice of a woman at the counter was shocking.

Joey's eyes were pinned on my face, his own a mask of perturbing calm.

"It's okay," he said. "Breathe. Tell me what's on the list."

I let my shoulders drop.

"It's in your pocket." He nudged my thigh.

"'Scuse me," someone said and jostled past us. I tensed as a musclebound guy with dreads and a gray camo T-shirt emblazoned with the words ARMYNAVY.COM worked his way around us.

"It's in your pocket," Joey repeated, his tone even, patient. "Flynn, the shopping list."

"What?" I dragged my gaze to his.

"The list of shit we need?"

"The list." I dug it out. "Got it."

"All right. Now let's buy shit." He wheeled around and away, leaving me to pull myself together. This entire ordeal would be so much easier with a drink. Why the hell hadn't I brought along a little something to ease a case of the nerves?

I forced myself to look at the list and then actually read it. I brushed a hand over my face. My palm was still damp, my fingers trembled.

We needed gloves, a pack to stash stuff in, maybe some tactical boots, decent paracord or utility rope, a multitool, a quality folding knife, and anything else that we might run across that could be helpful or fun.

My breathing evened out. I crammed the paper back in my pocket.

Two more customers brushed by, and I scanned the store for Joey. He was near the back talking to someone. I took a more deliberate look around.

Three rows of fluorescent lights hung from a red, white, and blue painted ceiling. The ceiling itself was festooned with flags from various countries. Apparel and other items dangled from the rafters highlighting sales and specials.

Racks were loaded with camo clothing in colors I never would've dreamed of. Cargos, shirts, and jackets in combinations like Savage Orange, Sky Blue, Stinger Yellow, Tactical Ultra Violet, and Vintage Fatigue, along with standard military issue battle dress uniforms.

Floor-to-ceiling shelves held boots in various styles and colors, and rows of caps and hats were perched on displays attached to slatted walls. Military jackets and coats, some of which I recognized, were outnumbered by ones I didn't. They all hung on long poles like pancaked soldiers.

Touches of military...whimsy, for lack of a better word, dotted the store, from a stuffed toy dog on a high shelf wearing a white and blue hooded cape, a gas mask, and a white French Foreign Legion hat to a full-size, replica zebra with rainbow stripes and an airman's scarf wound around its neck.

It was the weirdest surplus store ever.

I glanced around for Joey, saw he was talking to a guy with a full head of bushy salt and pepper hair. Reminded me of Richard Simmons.

I wandered over to the boot display. Boots had been thrown into big, tan-colored barrels, and boots were stacked in boxes under the racks. Boots had been tossed in a pile on either side of the shelving unit. I rummaged through the mess and found a decent pair of lightweight black tac boots that fit. I crossed those off the list.

A glass display of multitools and knives came next. I was disappointed not to find the brand I'd used while I'd been in the service, but honestly, I hadn't expected to. One of my academy instructors had given me a Spyderco folding knife, and over the years it had become kind of a talisman. I'd snapped the blade in Aleppo trying to lever rubble off Joey. It was fitting in a sad way. Broken blade, broken human.

I picked out a multitool and a solid replacement knife. A many-pierced woman retrieved my choices and took them to hold up at the register.

What was next on the list? Gloves. I found a pair of soft leather ones that would work for climbing Pascal's fence and not leave behind any incriminating fingerprints.

Joey was still in the back of the store blabbing. He didn't used to be a chatterbox. The new, improved Joey was much more outgoing. Wasn't sure how I felt about that. I caught his eye and he held up a finger.

A minute later the guy he'd been talking to headed toward the front of the store and Joey rolled up to me. "What'd you find?"

"Boots, gloves, a multitool and a passable knife, both of which are up front waiting for us to check out."

Joey leaned back in his chair and studied me. "Feeling better?"

"I think it was the smell."

"Brings you right back. What's left on the list?"

"Small pack, some rope, that's about it."

We grabbed those items along with a pair of night vision binoculars and headed for the checkout counter and dumped our goods. The clerk, the woman who'd brought my knife and multitool up, said, "I've got your stuff right here." From beneath the register she produced the multitool and a white box and placed them on the countertop beside the rest of our goods.

"Wait," I said. "I had a black knife from the case in back, not anything in a box. A Smith & Wesson."

She looked from me to Joey and didn't say anything.

"I specifically picked out—" A sharp elbow to my leg shut me up. I scowled at Joey. "What was—"

"Clap your yap for a second," he said, "and look in the box."

I glanced from him to the clerk.

"Go on." He poked me again.

I swatted his hand away and pulled open the box. The butt end of a knife peeked out. "Look. A knife. Now where's the one I picked out?"

"Come on, you hardheaded ass. Check it."

I shook it into my hand.

And froze.

In my palm was a brand new Spyderco. Nearly identical to the one I'd broken.

The clerk smirked.

"But I asked…they didn't…"

"Turns out the manager is the friend of a friend—from back in the 'hood—and he worked some fast magic. You broke your knife digging me out." He shrugged. "Just replacing it."

A lump lodged itself in my throat. "I, uh…thanks." With my gaze locked on the knife, I pulled out my wallet and then my credit card.

Five minutes later we were on the street. I was back in control and impressed as hell. "I cannot believe you managed to pull that off." My hand strayed to my hip, where my brand-new knife was nestled, tucked inside the pocket of my jeans. One thing in my world was back where it belonged.

"You never know what I have up my sleeve. Enough shopping. I'm starving."

Across the street was a Sabrett's hotdog cart. "How about a dog?"

"You don't even need to ask." Joey peeled out. I followed him onto the crosswalk.

Ten minutes and three hotdogs with the works later, we were on the path to the subway for home. With the exception of my averted meltdown, it wasn't bad for a sober half-day's work.

CHAPTER TWENTY

A few days passed uneventfully, which was actually kind of nice. I needed to do some background research on Pascal's property. Tubs didn't have a computer, so off I went to the library while Joey checked out another apartment.

Years had passed since I'd last set foot in a house of literature, and the moment I stepped inside the New York Public Library, the forgotten, familiar smell of books wound seductively around me. I wandered around for a few minutes, fondly recalling all the hours I'd spent there as a kid poring over magazines and reading R.L. Stein, the Alex Rider spy series, and of course, Harry Potter.

After browsing the stacks for a few minutes, I found the computers, but needed to sign up for a library card to use them. Once that was set up, I reserved a computer and went to work. An hour later I left with what I needed.

Joey, Ursula, and I were scheduled to meet at six at Luke's Lobster in Brooklyn, one of my favorite fast food seafood stands, to finalize plans for the heist.

Before we left, Tubs told us the invites were covered and steak was on the doggie menu. Lots and lots of steak.

Char and Tubs were the only Squad members able to accompany us on our little adventure. Elizabet couldn't get out of makeup-ing the cast of *Mountain Jews*, a romantic comedy involving sex, rugelach, and the Prophet Muhammad. The rest of the crew would gather at Tubs' place waiting for the high sign that indicated all had gone well or pulling bail funds together if it didn't.

As the sun sank behind the Manhattan horizon, long shadows crept across the East River like strands of shimmering ivy. At ten to six, Joey and I arrived at Luke's freestanding, thirty-by-forty-foot concrete and brick building.

Silver café tables filled with patrons stuffing their faces were scattered on either side of the squat structure, and two walk-up windows occupied opposite walls. Giggling kids ran wild, chasing birds and each other. The wind shifted, and I caught the scent of crab and lobster and secret spices that smelled reminiscent of Zatarain's but better. We wandered all the way around the building without sighting Ursula and then perused the black and white menu board.

Joey rubbed his hands together. "I could eat three of everything."

"I'm buying. Have at it." Personally, I was going straight for the lobster roll and poppy seed slaw.

An arm settled on top of my backpack. "You beat me."

I stiffened for an instant until my brain registered the sound of Ursula's voice.

"Hey, Urs," Joey said, leaning forward to look around me at her. "Hope you're hungry. She's buying."

"Nice." She focused her attention on the food list. "I'm starving. Coached a girl's hockey summer camp today, and let me tell you, eight-year-olds with hockey sticks are wicked. They're gonna grow into fierce players. Well, a few of them will, anyway. The rest of the mini-marauders were willing to turn their hockey sticks into weapons of mass destruction. I should've worn shin pads."

"Better you than me. You're a good woman." I jabbed my thumb at the menu. "Call it prepayment for services about to be rendered."

Ursula did a terrible job of tamping down her smirk. "Don't worry, I'll be gentle."

"Whatever."

Joey ordered lobster, crab, and shrimp rolls, lobster mac and cheese, a side salad, and a root beer. Ursula followed that up with a shrimp roll, a lobster grilled cheese sandwich, clam chowder, and a bottle of Maine's Shipyard Export IPA. What the hell was I thinking when I said I'd pay?

We found an open table. Fifteen minutes later only crumbs were left.

Ursula pushed her chair back and groaned. "Thanks for the grub. I'm stuffed." She finished her beer and set the bottle on the table, precisely in the middle of the napkin it'd been resting on.

"Another?" I pointed at the empty bottle.

"Sure."

I cleared the dirty dishes, acquired more beer for Urs and myself, and more soda for Joey. Once the drinks were handed off, I sat back down. "So Strategy Planning 101. I'd like to make our move after sunset for sure."

"Always a good plan. Last night Trudy stopped by with these." Ursula pulled her messenger bag onto her lap and withdrew five jewelry-style boxes and placed them on the table. "Check it out."

I picked a box up and opened it. Nestled inside was one of the smallest hearing devices I'd ever seen. It was so small I wondered if I'd have to get it medically removed.

Beside the bean-sized earpiece was a four-leaf clover pendant attached to a silver box-chain necklace. Joey's box contained a similar chain with a Celtic cross pendent. "What's in the other boxes?" I asked.

Ursula said, "Same things. The extra three are for me, Char, and Tubs."

"How do these work, exactly?" Joey asked.

"Microphones are imbedded in the pendants. As long as you're wearing the necklace and the earpiece and your phone is connected, you're good to go. These wouldn't work in a place where there's no cell service, but for our needs, they'll do."

I withdrew the necklace, which seemed sturdy. "What powers them?"

Ursula took my box and fished out the earpiece, which she set aside on a clean napkin. "See here?" She tilted the box and showed both Joey and me a fingernail-sized cardboard tab connected to a cardboard divider that fit perfectly inside. "Beneath this is a USB charger." With a tug, she pulled the divider out and withdrew a thin, six-inch USB cord connected to a flat, quarter-sized round disc.

"All you have to do is plug in the USB and place either the ear piece or the pendant on this disc. It works like the wireless chargers for the newest cell phones and smart watches."

Joey picked it up for a closer look. "The two pieces have to recharge independently?"

"Yeah. In the final version, there'll be two chargers. For now the prototypes only have one."

"How long does it take for them to fully charge?" I asked.

"About an hour a piece. They last two weeks on standby and about sixteen hours in use."

"Amazing." I picked up the pendant and turned it over. "This is so small. Is there a power switch?" The surface was smooth with the exception of a pinhole on one of the clover's leaves.

"No. Since the standby mode is so long, Trudy decided one wasn't needed. That hole you're looking at, Flynn, is the microphone. You have to download a proprietary app onto your phone that syncs the mic, the earpiece, and the cell itself. It'll also monitor the battery life for both the mic and the ear bud. To transmit, all you have to do is speak. The ability to broadcast independently is still in development. I figure there are few enough of us that shouldn't be a problem."

We spent a few minutes downloading the app and testing everything.

The clarity of the earpiece was stunning.

"That's incredible technology." Joey tucked the pieces back into his box. I handed him mine, and he stowed both of ours and the boxes for Tubs and Char in a pouch attached to his chair.

I swilled the last of my beer. "As we've heard loud and clear from Elizabet, the compound is walled and gated."

"What's the parking situation for these bashes Pascal throws?" Ursula asked.

"Good question. Let me text Elizabet." I rapidly typed out my query and had to admit Apple did make it easy. Once I sent that off, I pulled from my backpack a printout of the real estate information for Pascal's place and a Google Earth image of the area.

The photos had been taken in the dead of winter, which was fortunate. The lack of leafy canopy allowed us a great view of the compound. The density of the trees created a respectably private space for someone who could afford it. I'd looked up the property on a realty website. The last time it'd been sold—to Pascal six years ago—it went for a little under three million bucks. By now its value was probably double that, and developers were almost certainly itching to chunk up the lot and squeeze in as many new homes as they could.

The lawn, a limp, brownish-green, surrounded the house and pool and pushed the tree line back maybe a hundred feet. That area would be my most dangerous challenge, because I'd be completely exposed for the few seconds it would take to cross to the house.

Sculpted shrubbery paralleled paver walkways that meandered through the grounds. One path continued past the pool, through some trees, and passed by a Gothic-style greenhouse with attached garden shed, according to the website's description. The path continued on through another thicket and led to two additional outbuildings. One had once been a servant's quarters and was now converted to a "well-appointed" guesthouse. Beside it was an iconic, gambrel-roofed barn converted into an extremely spacious garage.

MapQuest showed two roads intersecting at one corner outside of the property. Google Earth confirmed that fact and showed a large swath—large for Staten Island anyway—of undeveloped land surrounding the area.

Joey tapped a finger on that spot. "This is a perfect entry. Flynn, we could drop you off here," he pointed at the intersection, "and that would line you up to hit the wall near that barn. If I had to guess, there's twenty or thirty forested yards between the road and the fence."

"Yeah, looks good," I said. "Urs, once you get inside, let us know what's happening and whatever red flags you see."

"Okay," she said. "I'll park myself near wherever you intend to come in. What we need is some floor plans of the joint."

"Ask and ye shall receive." I withdrew a reduced-size blueprint and unrolled it. "Thank Sahl. I'll access the back door, which is right by the kitchen. The rear staircase is a few feet further down the hall and leads to the second floor, the art gallery, and Pascal's art room."

Urs turned the diagram to face her. "Then I'll be somewhere near the back door once I get inside."

I said, "All you have to do is give your name at the door, and you're in like Flynn, as good old Mrs. Flanagan from high school liked to say whenever I was in the vicinity."

"I forgot all about Mrs. Flanagan." Urs laughed. "She and her '60s bob looked like Samantha Stevens on *Bewitched*. Remember her trying to crack us up with her ridiculous one-liners?"

The memory made me smile. "She was a great teacher. Wonder if she's still kicking."

"If she is, she'd be about a century old by now."

Joey watched our exchange with a flicker of sadness, which I would have missed if I hadn't known him so well. His teenage years were tough, and he'd dropped out in eleventh grade. I wished he'd had a Mrs. Flanagan in his life. The vibrating of my phone interrupted that train of thought.

I answered, "Hello, Eliz—" and was cut off by a minute long tirade about what a "perfectly perverted pinhead" Pascal was. She eventually wound down and told me what I wanted to know. She wished me love, sent audible air kisses, and hung up before I could wedge in a goodbye. Classic Elizabet.

"They line cars up and down the drive," I said. "No valet, first come first serve."

"Perfect," Joey said.

Urs stretched her legs out and crossed her ankles. "I've been tossing this thought around for a few days. Will it be weird if I show up alone? I have no qualms about going in on my own, but…"

"No," I said, "I don't think being alone will seem weird. I think it's pretty much a free-for-all, from the sound of it."

"I agree," Joey said. His eyes glittered like they used to as we strategized an op. From his expression I knew we were falling into that space where we could read what the other was thinking without a word passing between us. The joy I felt was almost overwhelming. "If Pascal's like any other red-blooded male with too much money and ego, he won't worry about who's arriving with whom. He'll be too busy schmoozing, scoping out the chicks, acting important."

"All right then," Ursula said. "The dogs."

Joey wadded up his napkin and tossed it to the side. "God, I'm full. Anyway, Char will distract them, hopefully near the entrance to the driveway. It would be away from the barn and as far away as she could get from the house. Thankfully she decided not to drug the mutts since she wouldn't be able to monitor them. Have to admit that makes me feel better." He was a tough guy with a couple soft spots, one of them for anything with fur and four paws.

"You and me both," Ursula said. "How's Char getting inside the compound? And how long will the meat occupy them?"

"Good questions," I said. "She's planning on a lot of steak, but maybe we should send her with some big old beef bones too. Or, hell, maybe Char is a closet dog whisperer. But she claims it's all under control, so we'll go with it. As far as how she's getting in, Elizabet got Char on the list using her middle name. Pascal doesn't know it, and since she won't be anywhere near him, Elizabet figured that would work.

"Once Char is in, she'll park as close to the end of the driveway as she can and slip into the woods. Once the mutts are knee deep in red meat, she'll give us the high sign. On her mark I'll go over the fence." I sighed myself. "They eat too fast, I run like hell."

"I've seen Flynn haul ass," Joey said, "especially when someone's chasing her. And I'll bet you can too, Ursula."

Once again I hurt for Joey. Running was no longer in his wheelhouse, and he'd loved to run. Then I recalled the mantra he'd utter under his breath when things went to shit. "Heads up, eyes on the prize, move forward, never back." I'd completely forgotten that ritual. Those words were a hard lesson, and the correlation hadn't dawned on me until this moment. Progress. It might come slow, but it was coming.

"Earth to Flynn, hello?" Urs poked me in the shoulder. "Hey, Space Case, tell Joey the story about our race down Bleeker after school."

"What?" I blinked myself back to the present.

"Running." Urs laughed. "Never mind."

"She's bragging about how fast she is," Joey said. "Race down Bleeker?"

"That's another story for another time. And, for the record, she cheated." I rubbed my eyes. "She sprints faster than I do. But I've always kicked her ass in distance."

Ursula turned a wide, "I told you so" smile on Joey, her eyes shining.

"Big mouth, I'll take you down," Joey said. "I'm awesome at short sprints these days."

Without a blink, Ursula said, "It's on." She stuck her hand out and Joey shook it. The excited expression on his face brought my smile back. This felt good. Laughing and joking around really was medicine. "Okay, let's talk timing. Ursula, did you manage to find out anything about the alarm system?"

"Pascal does have a high-end system, but nothing that can't be hacked by someone with mad skills. I happen to know somebody whose skills fit that description and have used him a number of times. He lives in Minneapolis, works remotely. His name is Coop. We met a few years ago at a computer conference in the Twin Cities."

"You can vouch for him?" I knew if Urs brought him up, she trusted him, but I figured Joey would like the confirmation.

"I've got some decent hacking skills myself, but he's light years ahead of me. He's become my go-to guy when I need another set of hands. I ran some checks on him after we first met, and except for a brief affair with a Mexican cartel leader, he's clean. I trust him."

Joey's eyes widened. "Seriously? An affair with the head of a Mexican cartel? Is he gay?"

"No," Ursula said, "it wasn't a guy, it was a woman. They broke it off while she was trying to extricate herself from the cartel."

A long-ago recollection swam into focus. "Wait a minute. A few years after I started with the NPIU, we were briefed that a woman who ran one of the deadliest cartels in Mexico also spent a good deal of time in the Twin Cities. She had a real rep for brutality." I trailed off as I tried to put the pieces in order. "I remember being fascinated with the idea of a female drug lord, since most women avoided violence and this one embraced it. My unit wound up helping the locals raid a meeting of cartel leaders in an abandoned hockey arena a few miles north of Minneapolis. We nailed the female leader and a few others. I think she was placed in Witness Protection. It's gotta be the same person."

"Damn." Ursula sized me up. "That'd be a hell of a coincidence."

"Nah." Joey glanced at Urs. "No coincidences. Shit happens for a reason whether we like it or not. Now, back to the alarm."

"Right-o," she said. "We've got the system schematics, and as long as you both are comfortable, I'll have Coop dial in to our comm systems. He'll be able to talk to us and he can hear what we're saying in real time. Makes everything easier that way."

"No problem with me." I looked at Joey.

"Agreed."

I said, "Shouldn't take me long to get from the fence to the house, as long as I'm not mauled to bits by the mutts. Most everyone should be down at the pool or hanging around the kitchen since we all know food and alcohol is where the party starts. Booze reportedly flows like Niagara Falls at Pascal's shindigs."

"Maybe everyone will be too drunk to notice anything," Joey said with a fake hiccup.

"That would make life easier," I said. "So Pascal's art area on the second floor. What's its status?"

Urs said, "Three freestanding cases are separately alarmed, as is a safe in an office adjacent to the gallery. Alarming a safe is a little redundant in my book, but it's a free world. Coop ran a history on the systems. It appears that when Pascal's in residence, he deactivates most of his house with a few exceptions. He leaves the alarms on those three cases and on the safe. A separate keypad on each case activates and deactivates the system, same for the safe."

"Do I need the code?" I asked

"No, Coop'll cut the alarm to whichever case the letter is in."

"I like it." This was coming together better than I ever expected it to. "Specs on the safe?"

Ursula grinned. "Coop ferreted out the company Pascal used to install the safe, which was built with burglary in mind. He can cut out the alarm signal, but you guys would have to figure out how to open it. Hope you're good at safecracking."

"I'd be a great safecracker if I could slap some C4 on it," Joey said. "In all reality, if the letter's in the safe and not in one of the locked cases, we might be doing this for nothing."

"Not much we can do except breach that bridge when we come to it," I said.

"One last thing regarding security," Ursula said. "Cameras are mounted on the fence surrounding Pascal's property."

Of course they were. "Considering the amount of security the man's got, I'm not surprised."

After a moment Joey gave Urs a nod. "Gonna have us a little challenge there. Can Coop do anything with them?"

"Yes, indeed," she said. "All we have to do is let him know where you want to go in, and he'll kill that cam until you're over the fence and far enough away it won't pick you up."

I hoped to hell he lived up to the hype. "I want to meet this Coop. He seems too good to be true."

"He's great at what he does. If you make it back to the Twin Cities, I'll hook you guys up."

"That'd be good." On the blueprint, I absently traced a line from the top of the rear staircase to the gallery, which appeared to take up half the upper level. I'd pushed aside the thought of Pascal's collection of puzzle boxes in light of the business at hand, but now that I was looking at the actual space, I was sure they had to be there somewhere.

What if…oh, for Christ sake, stop it, Flynn. Eyes on the letter, not on a dream. I washed the thought of the boxes away with a swallow of beer. "We nail the timing and we're halfway there. The rest of it will take care of itself." At least I sure hoped it would. "Five minutes tops from the fence to the back door, and then, what…a couple minutes to get inside and upstairs, another five to locate the letter, a couple to retrieve it. Then another five to get back to the fence. Unless I run into a problem, of course."

"There's always a problem." Joey sounded giddy and I loved it. He went on to say, "With luck this will all be done in about twenty minutes."

Ursula glanced at me. "Assuming all goes as planned, once you've swapped the letters, you want me to wait for you?"

"No. Just get the hell out," I said. "If worst comes to worst, we'll link up and fight our way to freedom like badass Amazons from Themyscira."

She laughed. "Xena and Diana. That would be an amazing combination."

"We'd be invincible. I want to be Xena."

"No, I wanna be Xena. My hair is longer than yours."

She had me on that point.

"All right," Joey said, "you two can thumb wrestle it out later. Right now we need a pre-burglary meet location."

Urs tilted her head and squinted in thought. She used to do the exact same thing when she was studying for a test as a kid. It was weird how little things unleashed buried memories. She said, "There's a Sunoco gas station less than a half mile from the property."

"That works," I said. "Let's meet at eight."

"Perfect." Joey finished off his soda and screwed the top back on. "That should cover things. Now I can go back to my useless hunt for apartments."

"In the market for a place?" Ursula asked.

"Yeah," Joey said. "You have no idea how many dives I've checked out. Ask Flynn, she went to a couple with me."

"Don't even get me started." I rolled up the blueprints and tucked them into the backpack. "I'm out. See you at home, Joey, and Urs, Saturday." I gave her a hug and left the two of them to bemoan the state of apartments in Gotham while I found a drink with more kick than beer.

* * *

The evening air was soupy, thick enough to swim through. Sweat rolled as I kept pace with evening foot traffic. Not far ahead, the mass of pedestrians was veering toward the street and then cutting back onto the sidewalk. I wondered what was clogging up the works.

It didn't take long to get close enough to see the reason for the disruption. A homeless woman, curled in the fetal position next to an empty storefront, was either asleep or had passed out on a grimy, tattered chunk of cardboard.

While that unfortunate sight was not uncommon in the city, what was uncommon was a shaggy, cream-colored dog of maybe thirty pounds with huge dark eyes and rusty-colored paws sitting between her and the stream of people marching by. The mutt wore a collar attached to a leash that disappeared beneath the slumbering woman. If anyone got too close, the dog growled, upping his game to a warning snarl if his growl was disregarded.

The woman's salt and pepper hair was matted. She could've been thirty or sixty. She was wearing at least five shirts, and at her ankles, visible beneath a pair of threadbare jeans, were the gathered cuffs of a pair of sweatpants. It was plausible she might've passed out from the stifling heat. Dirty bare toes peeped through a wide gash in one of her sidewalk-colored sneakers.

Two teens, a boy and a girl, loitered in front of the woman and her canine companion. He was skinny and tall, wearing a pink polo with a cringeworthy popped collar, sharply creased boat shorts, and loafers with no socks. His partner in crime was a girl with oversized sunglasses and Daisy Dukes, her butt cheeks on full display. At first I thought they were trying to see if the woman was okay, but then I realized they were taunting the four-legged furball instead. The mutt crouched on its haunches, trembling as it snapped its teeth at them.

The dog's owner didn't so much as twitch.

A snarl turned into a yip as Daisy took a swipe at the dog with her foot. She missed, but only because the pooch was faster than she was. As the girl lashed out a second time, I grabbed her from behind. Her foot sailed harmlessly in front of the mongrel, who lunged in a flurry of wild eyes and gnashing teeth.

"Hey!" Polo shouted, indignation staining his face as I pinned the girl's arm behind her back. "What are you doing?"

I towered over them both by a good six inches, which made it easy to clamp onto the scruff of Polo's neck. I dragged them away fast and headed around the corner of the building before they could gather their wits. Once we were a few yards in, I sent them reeling with a none-too-kind shove.

Polo tripped over his own feet and fell. Daisy caught her balance and spun toward me, holding the wrist I'd used to steer her. "That hurt, you motherfucker!"

The boy regained his footing and his skinny chest puffed up like a raptor's. "The fuck you think you are, bitch?"

I took a step forward, and they took a step back. Then we did the tango again. "Call me the fuckup fairy. You've fucked up and I'm here to correct the problem." I dropped my voice and added a bit of a snarl of my own. "Don't you ever, *ever*, do that to anyone again. That woman is homeless and helpless. And that dog of hers might be the only friend she has."

Three strides behind Polo and Daisy was a crusty-ass garbage dumpster next to the rear door of some restaurant. The outside of the container was covered with what had to be years of slop, creating thick, black molasses-like icicles. The lid was thrown wide open, and it gave me an idea. I took another long step toward them.

"Leave us alone, you fucking bitch!" The girl's bravado was belied by the fact her voice was so high windows would shatter had we been near any.

Daisy's words gave Polo a bit of backbone. "You can't tell us what to do."

"Who says I can't?" I advanced again. They stepped back.

"We do." Daisy's voice shook despite the bravado of her words.

I pressed forward. They backpedaled. We didn't stop until their backs were pressed against the dumpster. "I'm your living nightmare."

Polo screeched, "Fuck you, pussywench."

Pussy what? Kids these days. I shoved Daisy out of the way. Got an arm across Polo boy's chest and grabbed the waistband of his shorts. He thrashed in my grasp, but it didn't matter. I pivoted in a quick circle to get some momentum and heaved the howler into the dumpster.

Then I turned on Daisy in time to see her hauling ass out of the alley. She took a hard right and disappeared. Inside the dumpster, Polo's nice pink shirt was now coated with a multitude of slimy substances as he wallowed in bags of overheated, reeking garbage. I had a feeling those two snot suckers wouldn't bother the homeless, or anyone else for that matter, for a good long time.

Doling out punishment to a couple of entitled brats was fun. As I walked out of the alley I realized I was getting stronger, and that felt damn good too.

A crowd of maybe fifteen had gathered around the homeless woman and her nervous mutt while I'd been gone. The rest of New York continued to scurry by as if nothing out of the ordinary was going on.

I pushed through the throng and caught sight of somebody on their knees doing chest compressions. Oh, shit.

"Anyone call 911?" I bellowed.

"Yeah," a guy with a deep voice answered.

I knelt beside the Good Samaritan. "I'll breathe twice for every thirty compressions."

She yelled over the din, "Thirteen, fourteen, fifteen…"

I tilted the woman's head back and waited. When the Good Samaritan hit thirty, I delivered two breaths. We repeated the cycle over and over and I wondered if the medics were ever going to show up. Finally someone tapped my shoulder. I glanced back into the face of a firefighter in full turnout gear holding a bag-mask. "Paramedic. We got this."

Thank freaking God. I fell back on my butt, panting, and I hadn't even been the one doing the hard work.

Another firefighter nudged my CPR partner away. She staggered to her feet, hands on knees, head bowed.

I scrambled up and pulled her a dozen feet away from the action. "No matter what happens, you were amazing."

She'd returned to her previous hands-on-knees position. At my words she looked up. In that instant, it was as if my past melted like hot wax and filled up my present.

Familiar ice gray eyes bored into mine, eyes my soul knew. My own heart stopped, and for a moment I wondered if the medics had extra oxygen.

Kate.

Her shocked expression had to mirror the one on my own face.

Her mouth opened, then closed.

My ragged breathing grew more ragged as flight or freeze kicked in.

"Flynn?" Her voice was thin, either from lack of air or shock.

I wondered for a brief moment if I should duck the incoming punch I surely deserved.

"Hey, ladies!" someone shouted.

Part of me was thankful for the interruption.

A firefighter approached with the homeless woman's dog in his arms. "We're working on Lizzy and an ambulance is on the way. Problem is, this one can't go along for the ride. I can't leave him here. Either of you able to help?"

The guy spoke so fast that I couldn't sort out his words to answer. Apparently Kate was having the same issue.

He continued, "Name's Vinnie. Lizzy's really sick, needs a place to go, a nursing home, something. She's a neighborhood regular. Real nice lady. Me and the guys at the station have tried to help her out for years, but she's too proud to accept much. Her only concern is this one." He kissed the furball's head. Gotta love a firefighter with a soft side. "Who's a good boy, hey?"

The dog's tail wagged, and he stretched up and touched his nose to Vinnie's.

Vinnie pulled his gaze away from the mongrel. "If Lizzy knows he's being taken care of, I think she'll let us take her in. I'd do it, but I already got three at home and don't dare show up with another or my old lady's gonna boot my ass."

The dog had calmed, but the wary look of fear lingered in his eyes.

Tubs' apartment didn't allow animals—although I knew a few residents who snuck pets in. I didn't know what happened if they got caught.

My brain already felt fried. Trying to process this new problem was one thing more than I could handle.

"I can't," both Kate and I said in tandem.

I looked at Kate in a combination of horror and awe. That's how we used to be, on the same page, finishing each other's sentences. Somehow she always knew what I was thinking before I spoke.

Vinnie held the dog in one arm and ruffled his furry head. "That's a good buddy." Furface squirmed and tried to lay one on Vinnie's chin. "Come on. You sure one of you can't help the little dude out? He's a good boy. His name's Mr. Bones."

"Mr. Bones?" My voice was weak from more than exertion and shock. This was heartbreaking.

Vinnie tipped his head toward Lizzy. "She's seventy-four, has out-of-control diabetes, congestive heart failure. Fourth time this month she's crashed. Like I said, we've been trying to talk her off the street. One joint works with the homeless population not far from here. We could try again to pull a few strings to get her moved up on the wait list. But she's stubborn as a pissed-off mule. Won't go without Mr. Bones, and if he's not a service dog, they won't let her have him there."

"What's the name of the place?" Kate asked.

"Turning Point Nursing Home and Rehab."

"Part of Cobble Hill Health?"

"That's the one. On Henry off Warren."

"I'm familiar. That'd be a great choice." With a resigned sigh, she said, "Hand him over."

The relief I felt in Kate's willingness to take Mr. Bones was acute. Now I wouldn't have to be on the hook or worry about what happened to him. Besides, she had the resources to find a good match for the mutt, and maybe she could find a way to help Lizzy too. That was just the way she operated. I knew that part of her would never change.

"Yes!" Vinnie placed the dog in Kate's arms, draped the leash over her shoulder, then pulled a card out of one of the deep pockets in his turnout jacket. "I knew you two looked like a kind, understanding couple."

Bad timing for relationship assumptions. I opened my mouth to correct things, but he said, "Gimme a call in a day or two, and I'll let you know where Lizzy is."

Reluctantly, I plucked the card from between his fingers and watched Mr. Bones melt into Kate's arms like he was home.

Kate's arms had always been home.

Stop it. For fuck's sake. What was I doing? I had to remember what I went through to pack her away into that box in my brain so I could continue to function. Some days I was sure the pain and guilt would kill me. I had to get that "Kate equals home" business out of my mind straightaway. Damn it. I could lecture myself all day long, but the train had left the station and, like it or not, I was on it.

"Can't believe I'm doing this," Kate muttered.

She really was taking him. She was half angel. No, strike that. She was all angel. Of course she was.

"Fantastic." Vinnie squeezed both our shoulders and hustled off toward Lizzy, who was now on a stretcher. I blinked a couple times at the card in my hand, then looked at Kate, who was nuzzling Mr. Bones.

Had I fallen into a rabbit hole and come out the other end to a world tilted on its side? Here I was, in the middle of Brooklyn, standing in front of Kate, the lost love of my life, for the first time in years.

My Kate.

Not my Kate. My ex-Kate.

Hopes and dreams of the past stood right smack-the-fuck dab in front of me. I should be having a meltdown. Of monstrous proportions. Wait a minute. Why wasn't I having a meltdown of monstrous proportions? Why wasn't I losing my shit? Why hadn't I turned tail and fled like the coward I was?

Maybe my CPR adrenaline had already spiked, and there wasn't any left for a panic attack.

Before I could further examine my curious and somewhat terrifying reactions, Kate distracted me by cooing at the dog, "Hey, Furminator, you want to go home with Flynn, don't you."

"What?"

Mr. Bones licked her cheek. She gave the dog a half-grin. Those dimples seared my heart. They were deeper now, and if possible, even more delightful. My heart gave a dangerous thud and my stomach remembered how to do its Patented Kate Flip.

She looked at me with the same combination of "I told you so" and a hint of the achingly sweet love she used to radiate whenever she saw me. Or was I imagining that? Of course I was imagining that. She had every reason to hate me. But my heart wasn't listening.

With business-like efficiency, she said, "We split custody. I take him one week. You take him the next. Together, we bring Bones to Lizzy and visit every Thursday." I couldn't meet her eyes, but I could feel her gaze burning me as she scrutinized my reaction. "Deal?"

I opened my mouth. And like the doofus I was, nothing came out. Why didn't she at least slap my face? I snapped my mouth shut and watched Mr. Bones gaze lovingly at her. She frowned an achingly familiar frown, and wham! Back in the time warp vortex. This was not the moment for a reality TV episode of *Back to the Future*.

"You're staying with Tubs, right?"

"How did you—"

"Never mind that." She waved the hand that wasn't holding Mr. Bones. "I'll be over next Thursday. We'll go see Lizzy and you take Bones for the next week."

"Bu—you—how can you even look at me?" I could hardly put together two words in her presence. Just like it used to be. A whole lot of "just like it used to be" was going on around here. If I were her, I'd simply kill me and get on with my day.

"Flynn." Before she glanced away, her eyes glinted with a flash I used to recognize as anger. She pulled in a deep, measured breath. "You have *no* idea how furious I am. Don't let this pseudo-calm demeanor fool you. I'm pissed as hell at you."

She peered over my shoulder again for a second, and I could see how hard she was trying to keep it together. "Okay." She pulled a deep breath. "I'll be over next Thursday at four thirty. That should give us enough time to see Lizzy before visiting hours are over, and then we can make the pooch exchange."

All I could do was stare at her like a complete imbecile.

"I'll see you then." She turned on her heel and walked rapidly away, with Mr. Bones staring at me over her shoulder.

My head was going to explode. I was going to see Kate again. I wasn't sure if I was elated or terrified.

CHAPTER TWENTY-ONE

Something hit my temple. The object wasn't hard, wasn't sharp, but carried some mass behind it. I twitched and regretted even the thought of moving. My head weighed at least fifty pounds. It felt like someone had taken batting practice on it. I tried to raise a hand to my face. My arm would not obey. The blood in my veins had been replaced with lead.

Where was I? Inside or out?

My cheek was the next target and I jerked as the missile hit home. My entire body ached from my head to my heels. Now what had I done? I was a living refrain in a country song.

"Flynn," called a singsong voice. "Wake up."

I tried to speak, but my mouth was dryer than the desert during a drought. The inside of my eyelids had permanently adhered themselves to my eyeballs.

Plink! Another direct hit an inch above my ear.

Laughter above me.

Joey.

"Stop." It sounded like "Saaap" because my tongue was stuck to the roof of my mouth.

"Get up. You're going to have permanent grid marks on your face if you don't move."

Wham, right in the ear. Bastard. What the hell was he throwing at me? Then he smacked my cheek again with his unknown ammo. I hated him.

Slowly, ever so slowly, I eased from my belly onto my side. My stomach roiled. I swallowed hard, mouth no longer dry. Inhaled slowly. The roiling settled into a semi-tolerable churn.

What had Joey said? Grid marks? I ran my fingers over the rough metal surface below me. As I did, a light breeze caressed my cheek.

I cracked open an eye. I recognized Tubs' living room window above my head. Check on the where. Now I needed the how.

As I puzzled over this, Joey's head popped through the open window and what looked like a dismembered hand lobbed a dark, round, quarter-sized object toward me. It sailed harmlessly over the edge of the fire escape.

"Hey." His voice floated out the window. "Three hours to get ready. Ass up."

Maybe if I ignored him he'd disappear.

"Come on, Flynn. We can't run this without you."

I searched my memory. Nothing. I swallowed hard again. My last recollection was leaving Joey and Urs at Luke's Lobster. "Three hours?" I needed water.

"Yes. It's five. We're meeting Ursula at eight at the Sunoco, and then you're snatching Elizabet's letter right out from under Pascal's big red nose. Remember?"

"It's Saturday?" I croaked.

"Sure is. I'd ask where you've been the last thirty-six hours, but I have a hunch you have no idea."

He was right. That pissed me off, but I had no energy for a retort.

Tubs' head appeared next to Joey's. "Mikala. Pull yourself together and get your keister in here, pronto."

As she spoke, Joey hurled another bomb at me. What the hell was he using for ammunition?

Tubs disappeared into the apartment.

He lobbed another volley, caught me smack dab between the eyes. My head snapped back and slammed against the steel grating. "Goddamn it, Joey—"

"Get in here."

"Asshat."

He laughed coldly. "Move it before I waste the rest of my grapes on you."

* * *

As I cleaned myself up, I tried desperately to remember what had occurred between leaving Luke's Lobster and right now. Nothing. I hadn't blacked out like that in awhile. What triggered my binge? I'd been doing so well.

In my opinion, anyway.

Twenty minutes later, fully dressed and somewhat less bleary-eyed, with an ache poised to blow a hole out the back of my head, I approached the table.

Joey set aside a book on looted World War II art he'd been paging through. Tubs pushed her reading glasses up and regarded me without expression. Then she unfolded the newspaper she'd been reading and tossed it on the table in front of me.

I did not like the way they both looked at me. "What?"

Tubs nudged the paper closer. "Page two. You should check out the pictures and read the story."

"Come on." I made a face, but picked up the paper.

"Read it," Joey said.

The headline in the upper right corner read, "Kate Goldsmith Walks the Walk."

My heart thumped, echoing painfully from my chest into my head.

Below the headline were two pictures. The first was a shot of a group of people crowded around something. The angle of the photo made me think the photographer stuck his camera up as high as he could reach and hoped for the best when he hit the shutter release.

The other was of a firefighter engaged in what looked like a serious conversation with two women. One had her arms wrapped around a furry dog.

I looked closer.

Kate. Kate was holding the dog.

My heart went from hammering to seized. I blinked once, then again. The image had not changed.

The woman standing beside Kate was me. Oh my fucking God. It was me.

The caption read, "Kate Goldsmith and Good Samaritan Save Woman With No Home."

A flash of recall exploded.

A kid in a dumpster.

An alley.

An alley steeped in the stink of rotting garbage.

A woman passed out on the sidewalk.

But the memory felt like it was in the wrong order.

As I fought to make sense of my thoughts, I saw a photo of a homeless woman on the ground in front of an empty storefront.

With a dog.

The same dog in Kate's arms.

I breathed slow and deep, then read the story below the pictures.

Meet Lizzy. Lizzy is a self-described "woman without a port," often seen wandering Brooklyn Heights with her dog, Mr. Bones. Firefighter Vinnie Vincenzo of FDNY Engine 224 Fire House says she stops in periodically, and in turn, the station has taken a shine to her and her four-legged-friend.

Vincenzo said, "She's a great lady with a stubborn streak as long as Manhattan. She loves that mutt of hers. In fact, she'll go hungry just to make sure the pooch is fed. Once in a while she swings into the firehouse and brings me and the guys a treat. Other times she comes in to take a load off and chat."

According to Vincenzo, Lizzy has diabetes and heart problems. "We've been trying to help her into a safer living situation," he said, "but we haven't been able to find a place that will take Bones. So she refuses to leave the street because she won't leave her dog."

Yesterday evening, Lizzy collapsed on the sidewalk in front of the vacant American Beer Distributing Company building. Eyewitnesses say an unidentified woman confronted and escorted away two teens who were harassing Mr. Bones as he stood guard over Lizzy.

Moments later, Kate Goldsmith, philanthropist and co-head of the Goldsmith Foundation—a beloved New York institution—came across the scene. She assessed the situation and began CPR. Before medics arrived, the woman who removed the two young adults returned and joined Goldsmith in the attempt to resuscitate Lizzy.

Lizzy was transported by ambulance to the ER at NYU Langone Hospital. At the time of publication, she was in serious but stable condition.

Goldsmith refused interview requests, but a source said she indicated she'd "take care of Lizzy and Mr. Bones." This isn't the first time the Goldsmith Foundation has reached out to help the homeless, but this is the first time the face of the company has been caught delivering first aid in a time of crisis. And who is the mystery woman? Is she after the ever-so-eligible Kate Goldsmith? Only time will tell.

I read the story twice. Initially I was amazed they actually inferred Kate was gay like it was no big deal, and then I realized I was the mystery woman. Flickers of memory struck like lightning, illuminating small but visceral recollections. It was like watching a movie someone put together using 30-second clips out of order and context, but rich in emotion.

I raised my eyes. Both Tubs and Joey were staring at me, assessing my reaction. What did they want me to say?

Tubs finally spoke. "You're something of a nameless celebrity, Mikala—the Mysterious Stranger talking to the 'ever-so-eligible' Kate Goldsmith. You hit the *Times* too."

"Are you kidding?"

Joey handed me the paper, folded open to another picture of Kate with Mr. Bones and me, but taken from a different angle. The expression on my face was a combination of surprise and horror. The photo caught Kate mid-sentence, intently staring at me with an excruciating familiar expression that meant she was about to get her way.

The pain of regret ripped through me, shredding me again. Goddamn cell phones and their all-too-handy built-in cameras.

Before the article, I was hungry, but now I felt like throwing up. I tossed the paper on the table and escaped Joey and Tubs' expectant gazes by ducking into the kitchen to pour myself a glass of water. In three seconds flat I'd sucked it down, then did it again. I braced my hands on the edge of the sink and took a deep breath as I attempted to sort out my memories.

Something important about Thursday hovered at the edge of my consciousness. One vivid recollection I had was of a kid wallowing in restaurant castoffs inside a dumpster. I sort of remembered talking to a guy with a thick New York accent, probably the firefighter. I squeezed my eyes shut, but that didn't do much except aggravate the drill burrowing its way into my skull. It was show time and I was a sizzling hot, fucked-up mess. After all my boasting, I wasn't sure I could pull this off. What if I screwed up and someone got hurt? Or I got caught and sent to jail? Well, Smarty Pants Flynn, it's too late to back out now. There was only one way left to go and that was forward. I really needed to get myself under control.

CHAPTER TWENTY-TWO

The evening was balmy, and a few stars twinkled on a canvas of black.

Instead of Elizabet's superhero Flash suit, I went simple and efficient with black T-shirt, black cargos, and the boots I bought at the surplus store. My headache was finally at bay and I was nervous, but it felt like a good nervous. The kind that sharpened all my senses, kept me on the edge, raw and wary and ready to roll.

We picked up the van—white with no side windows, perfect for our purposes—and met up with Char and Ursula at the Sunoco.

Char had a huge cooler in her back seat filled with ice and all kinds of raw beef and huge bones, enough to occupy the dogs for some time. At least I hoped that would be the case. I was worried the cooler would be too heavy for her to carry into the woods, but then she pointed out the wheels mounted on one end that allowed her to pull it.

The comm units worked perfectly. I couldn't wait to tell Trudy how impressed I was.

Urs left first, followed by Char. Then it was time for Tubs, Joey, and me to make our move. They dropped me off on the back side of Pascal's property and continued around the impossibly long block to set up operations as close to his driveway as they could get.

I faded into the woods between the road and Pascal's property fence, feeling keyed and very much alive. Leaves blocked most of the ambient light, bringing a rather eerie twilight to ground dwellers and skulkers alike. I pulled the night vision binoculars out of my backpack and did a fast scan. Other than trees and two squirrels, all was quiet. Thanks to a recent rain, the leaf-strewn ground smelled pungent and earthy. The soggy leaves and pine needles cushioned what could have been crunchy footsteps.

The trees pushed right up to an seven-foot brick fence topped by iron spikes. All we needed now was a moat and medieval knights waiting to slay intruders. As I assessed options for breaching the fortress, a familiar, welcome shiver ran down my spine. The quest was beginning to take over. Adrenaline surged. My body felt on edge, honed and tight, ready for anything.

My mind felt the clearest it had in months. Remnants of my hangover dissipated like smoke in the wind. My senses were everything, muscle memory reawakening. I was in tune with my surroundings in a way I hadn't been for a long, long time.

The end goal was clear. Retrieve the Keller letter and don't get caught. My side-goal, a quick perusal of Pascal's stash of puzzle boxes, would, with luck, come together as well. Easy in, easy out. It would be what happened between the in and the out that would define this particular escapade.

Thirty yards to my left, the gabled roof of the barn loomed large behind the stone enclosure. I skirted the fence, picking my way through the undergrowth until I wound up at the foot of an enormous maple with low-hanging branches that stood almost directly behind the barn. The tree was immense, tailor-made for climbing and spying. I grabbed a low-hanging limb and swung into the tree, then clambered up the trunk, using the branches as a ladder. Rough bark's sharp edges were a welcome reminder that this was reality, not another drunken hallucination.

Camouflaged by leaves, I was able see into the compound without exposing myself. The fence itself was ten feet away. The top was wide enough to stand on, and spaced every couple feet were what looked like wickedly sharp-tipped black finials.

The barn, a well-preserved structure made of stone and wood, was a rock's throw inside the perimeter. Illumination from sash windows running the barn's length cast bright rectangles onto the grass.

The lights were on, but how many people were home? Faint voices carried on the light breeze, but I couldn't pinpoint where they were coming from. The sudden, unexpected hoot of an owl startled me out of my reconnaissance and knocked me head over knickers into the past. To another night, in another part of the world, up another tree. My sights were locked on the front door of a ramshackle hut as I waited for the target to appear. Three American hostages were reportedly inside, according to a confidential informant of Joey's.

My heart thudded hard and I was sure the occupants of that mud hut could hear it. My legs ached from hours hunched in the same position, and the shirt beneath my ballistic vest was stiff with dried sweat. When the blazing sun went down, so did the intense temperature, and I fought to keep an inner chill from becoming a physical shiver.

Our team of four was positioned so any one of us would have a clear shot, regardless which direction our man fled. The alive part of dead or alive wasn't in our operation protocol on this mission.

Seconds melted into minutes, minutes into hours. I didn't know the time because I didn't dare move to look.

The stock of my rifle was cool against my cheek. Come on, asshole, open that goddamn door.

"Flynn," Joey said in my ear. What the hell? He knew better than to break radio silence.

"Flynn? Hey, Flynn. You copy?"

For Pete's sake, Joey, shut up.

"Mikala!" Tubs' semi-panicked voice squawked into my brain, startling me enough I almost fell out of the tree. My first thought as I grabbed a nearby limb was why the hell was Tubs in this godforsaken place, and my second was the realization that I wasn't in a godforsaken place.

I was in Staten Island.

Up Pascal's tree.

On the hunt for an old letter.

Christ almighty, I'd done it again. Pent-up air whistled between my clenched teeth. I pressed my back against the tree trunk and peeled my fingers off the branch I'd been using to balance myself.

"I'm here," I whispered as I tried to reconcile the vision of the fence and the barn in front of me as reality instead of a hut in the middle of Afghanistan.

"Flynn?" Joey's voice was steady but had an edge he used when something was not quite right. "You ready for Coop to cut the cam so you can secure your access rope?"

Another breath. Do not let your voice shake. "Almost." I scrambled to peel the pack off my back and the rope out of the pack. Earlier I'd tied a grappling hook to one end. Now, the damn thing caught on something as I attempted to pull it out. "Shit," I muttered under my breath as I worked to free it.

"Flynn," Ursula said. "You need an assist?"

Finally the hook came free. "It's okay. I'm good. Coop, I'm behind the barn. Go ahead and cut that camera."

"Behind the barn, check. Hang on." A few seconds later he said, "Cam's down, video's looping. If you need a new exit point, let me know. It'll take about ten seconds."

"Got it." Willing my hand to stop trembling, I wound up and slung the hook toward one of the spikes. It missed with a cringeworthy clang. Three tosses later, the hook snagged the metal base of one of the finials.

"Rope's secure," I reported.

As I descended the tree, like a bolt of lightning out of a blue sky, I was struck with the thought of what might happen if we failed.

If we got caught.

Arrested.

Jailed.

Stop it, I ordered myself as I hit the ground. This is child's play. I'd operated with a group of elite specialists performing various ops and rescues for years. This should be easier than a walk in Central Park.

But Flynn, my high school bully whispered in my ear, that elite group was decimated, thanks to you. All that's left now is a half-alive, liquor-loving loser and a talented man who's confined to a wheelchair for the rest of his life thanks to your ineptitude.

I squeezed my temples, willing that voice to shut the fuck up. As I worked to re-cage emotion, the familiar, irritating pull for the blinding comfort of alcohol grew into an almost desperate craving. Come on, I told myself, get your shit together and get on with it.

Usually, once a mission got rolling, I was rock solid. The fact that sudden insecurity exploded into a mushroom cloud of apprehension was not helping my cause here. This was only the beginning of the show. It was imperative I crush whatever doubt I had about failure and fix my sights on the path ahead.

"Hey, Flynn!" someone squawked, startling me again into the present. "That's a ten-four, good buddy! Always wanted to say that on the radio. Figured this was as close as I'd get. Char over and out." I weakly smiled at her attempt to channel Burt Reynolds.

"You got it, Char," I said under my breath.

The levity allowed me a couple seconds to get my brain under control. I picked my way to the fence, found the rope, and gave it a tug. It was securely hooked. Now to finish the waiting game.

Two minutes later, Char whispered with a little less projection, "Ursula and I are parked. We're both near the front gate. I'm in the woods to the left of the house with my box of doggy delights. The first rump roast is unwrapped and I'm working on the second. Let me know when to blow the whistle."

Joey said, "Copy that. Status check, Ursula."

"Here." Urs sounded breathy. "I'm almost to the house. Long-ass driveway. Gotta be sixty cars lining either side."

"I love it when a plan comes together," Tubs said, her voice slightly tinny. "Good job, everyone. Joey and I are idling on a side street about half a block away, with a great view of Pascal's pretentious palace gates."

Ursula asked, "Coop, you reading us okay?"

"I am. Let me know when to cut the alarm." I appreciated Coop's business-like, slice-through-the-bullshit approach. It would be the icing on the cupcake if he could pull off what Ursula said he could.

As I waited, I rolled the rope between my palms. It was real and substantial and helped ground me.

Maybe a minute later, Ursula said, her register low, "I'm inside."

"Okay," Joey acknowledged.

"Oh my," Urs whispered.

I tensed as I imagined her brows mirroring her vocal astonishment.

"Sorry," she hissed. "Pascal has nearly naked waiters and chicks in bikinis strutting around with trays of tropical-themed booze. Lots of partiers inside and out. Looks like they're mostly beating a path between the house and the pool."

I let out a breath, forced my shoulders to relax.

"Toss one back for me," Char said. "A drink, I mean. Not a partier. Unless he's handsome."

I'd be happy to toss back a drink, Char, I thought. I could do some serious damage to Pascal's alcohol supply.

No, no, no.

With a mental face slap, I yanked again on the rope. Still secure. Let's get this show on the road. "Char, whistle up the dogs. If you have a visual on all three of them, let me know and I'll hop the fence. Hopefully there aren't any additions to the pack."

"Whistling now."

Everyone was silent as we waited for Char's report. Thirty seconds stretched to at least a year.

Eventually Char croaked, "Got 'em. I blew and within moments they were streaking toward me like hellhounds nipping the heels of the dead. As soon as their noses got within sniffing distance, it was all over. All three mutts are knee deep in beef. Hurry up because they're chowing butt like starving demons."

Joey said, "Coop, do your thing and let us know when the light's green."

"You got it." Thirty seconds later, "Clear to go. Give me the word when you're ready to bring things back online."

"Here we go." With a running start, I hit the fence and launched myself skyward. With the help of the rope, I scrambled up the stone side like a vertically challenged crab. I grabbed one of the finials and used it to swing myself onto the fence top. I crouched low and held still, waiting to see if any alarm sounded. I felt amazingly alive. My muscles trembled in anticipation, like a racehorse waiting for the starting gate to pop open.

Before me, all remained quiet. From my vantage point, I could see a corner of the guesthouse, which was about twenty-five yards from the barn.

I moved to my left and could see five cars parked between the barn and the house. Three men appeared to be lounging against one of the vehicles.

Good to know.

I let go of the spike I'd been hanging onto for balance and pulled up the rope. Then I dropped it down the inside of the fence, where it disappeared in shadow. Unless someone was purposely walking the perimeter and specifically looking for anything out of the ordinary, no one would notice it.

Time to play for real. I set myself up and rappelled to the ground, which came up faster than I'd expected. My feet hit the turf, followed by my ass. Out of practice much, Flynn? Thank God there was no one here to witness my lack of grace. I scrambled up, pointedly ignoring the tape in my head that said, "See, idiot? What do you think you're doing?"

"I'm in." I kept my voice low. Thick grass cushioned my steps and smelled freshly mowed. I headed around the far side of the barn, keeping it between me and the guest house.

"Copy, Flynn," Joey said. "Urs, update?"

"Floating between the living room, kitchen, and back hall. Lots of drunk partiers coming and going. Someone said Pascal was poolside judging a wet T-shirt contest."

"Figures." Char poured an amazing amount of sarcasm into that one word. "Before you ask, Joey, the dogs are still working on the first roast."

"Good," he said. "Flynn, let us know when you reach the main house."

Silence fell.

I did a fast peek around the front corner of the barn. Three linebacker-sized guys leaned against a car parked near the guesthouse. They were the same men I'd seen from the top of the fence. I hadn't realized they were dressed, or rather, undressed, for the pool. Hairless chests and brightly colored swim trunks glowed in the low light. I watched them for a few seconds. They seemed absorbed in their conversation and that worked for me.

Another thicket of woods encircled the barn and guesthouse. A gravel drive made a wide cut through the tree line, and another, smaller, break was the pathway to the main house.

I backtracked and slid into the trees, paralleling the edge of the clearing. When I came around far enough, I had a clear view into the barn's interior. Double doors were propped open wide, revealing a collection of expensive cars. I recognized two white Porsches, a yellow '80s Corvette, and what looked like a cherry-red Plymouth Barracuda. Damn, those were hard to come by.

I was within a half dozen steps of crossing the driveway when bouncing light reflected off the trees and rapidly got brighter. I backtracked fast and ducked behind a tall oak. A black Humvee raced by and skidded to a stop in front of the barn.

The pulse in my neck thudded.

Two men, maybe in their mid-twenties, climbed out of the Humvee. One disappeared inside the barn while the other headed between the barn and the guesthouse, toward the fence.

Oh, shit. Was Coop's loop compromised? Every muscle in my body contracted, ready to react in a hurry.

The man who'd been headed for the fence stopped at the rear corner of the barn and didn't move for a good twenty seconds. What the hell was he doing?

I considered warning the others but wanted to make sure we really were busted before sounding the alarm. Once I pulled that trigger, there'd be a lot of unsynchronized moving parts. Unsynchronized moving parts were never a good thing.

He bounced on the balls of his feet a couple times, then turned around, fumbling with the zipper on his pants.

His zipper. All he'd done was take a leak. He wasn't looking for evidence of a breach.

Relief made me weak, but I shot across the gravel roadway into the trees on the opposite side before he got any closer.

I murmured, "Thought we had trouble, but we're good. Headed toward the house now."

"Copy," Joey said. "Ursula?"

"I'm here." Her voice crackled strangely. Maybe Trudy had a little more work to do on the system. "Be at the back door in a sec." Silence. Then, "All clear right now. Wait, stop. Pascal just came in from the pool. He's in the living room with a couple of underage teenyboppers hanging all over him like he's Hugh Hefner's younger brother."

Gross. I darted through the trees, following the paver path. The scent of grilled meat floated heavy on the air, competing with the tang of chlorine. The combination reminded me of hot, carefree days growing up in Key West and other, much darker days I did not want to think about.

Keeping inside the cover of the woods, I skirted a vast chain-link fence that enclosed a deck and an L-shaped pool. Floodlights brought virtual day to the entire scene. A sliding glass door between the house and pool was open, and a steady stream of guests wandered in and out. Probably seventy-five people were scattered around the water. Some splashed in it, others danced on the deck. Music and laughter rose over the general cacophony of the poolside din.

"Pascal still inside?" I whispered into my comm.

"I think he's about to... Okay. Yes. He's headed out."

From my position behind a tree, I watched Pascal emerge from the house. Although I hadn't gotten a visual on him that night at Tubs, he was easy to recognize as the leader of the lair. He wore a robe-like cover up and had his arms around two girls who sure did look scandalously young. Wait'll Elizabet hears about that little tidbit, I thought. She'd be spitting venom. The trio wandered over to the grill, and Hef—I mean Pascal—spoke to the grill master.

In the shallow end of the pool, a couple of women in barely there bikinis were perched on the shoulders of two guys, and from their expressions, taking great delight in beating each other senseless with pool noodles. At the deep end, a blue slide arced toward the water and the diving board launched partiers into the air. Both had a line of dripping guests waiting their turn.

I had to admit Pascal knew how to throw a party.

Hugging the shadows, I made for the back door. Then I was inside, standing beside Ursula. A long hallway stretched the length of the house to the front door. A maroon Persian rug runner covered the hall floor, and half-moon sconces mounted on dark wood walls dimly lit the corridor. To the right was the kitchen and on the left was a spiral staircase leading to the second floor.

"Flynn's in," Ursula murmured. "I'm off." She flashed me an okay sign, which I returned, and she disappeared into the kitchen.

"Heading upstairs," I reported, voice low. I stopped at the top of the landing. Hearing nothing but chatter from below, I ventured cautiously into the hall, which was a mirror image of downstairs, except the carpet was a lighter color. Lights were off, probably because no one was supposed to be up here.

The master and another bedroom were situated across from two smaller spare rooms. The main staircase was located dead ahead, about three-quarters of the way down the hall in the middle of Pascal's private art gallery.

"Heads up," Urs said faintly, "I'm trapped by Pascal's girlfriends. I—gotta go."

Uh oh.

I'd taken no more than two steps when I heard voices in the stairwell ahead of me, getting louder by the second. The closest hiding place was one of the bedrooms. I tried the door to the room closest to me and the knob turned in my hand.

I slipped inside, stifling a giddy giggle. This was fun shit. I felt so fucking alive. Blood whooshed through my veins. In the past, I hadn't simply gotten used to taking risks, I'd lived for them. I should've realized that hadn't changed. I rapidly flashed my light around the room. Bed, dresser, closet.

I returned to the door, opened it a crack, and peeked out.

A woman spoke rapidly while the other person, also female, gave one-word responses.

"Hurry," one of the women keened.

"It's here somewhere," the other said, her words punctuated by the bang of a door.

"Not in there."

They were coming closer.

God, I hoped they weren't looking for a place for a quickie. I gently pulled the door closed, darted to the far side of the bed and ducked, waiting for the door to swing open.

Five seconds passed excruciatingly slowly. Then ten.

"Here!" one of them shouted. Then I heard the muffled yet unmistakable sound of someone violently praying to the porcelain god.

Ugh.

Update time. I whispered, "I'm stuck in one of the bedrooms. Someone decided to come up and puke in the bathroom."

"Pleasant," Urs said. "Let me know if you need anything. Everything down here is fine. Pascal is now at a patio table with his arm candy, scarfing hot dogs."

"Char," Joey's voice popped in, "status on the dogs."

Char said, "All's well. Busy on their second rump. Not eating as fast as I expected."

"Copy. Flynn, let us know when you move."

"Will do."

The stomach-clenching sounds of retching stopped.

Another two minutes passed. Then, "Come on, Tara. You can make it down. I've got you."

I gave it to the count of ten and cracked the door in time to see the backs of the women's heads disappear down the stairs.

"On the move," I whispered and slipped out of the room. Hugging the wall, I slunk down the hallway. As I passed the bathroom I made sure to breathe through my mouth. I came to a stop at the threshold where the hall opened into Pascal's gallery. The floor was mahogany hardwood, probably hand cut.

On my left was an open space the size of one of the spare rooms. The dark-painted walls were filled with artwork, mostly paintings. Ceiling-mounted accent lights were on but dimmed, allowing picture spotlights to highlight the pieces. An overstuffed, dark-brown love seat and matching chair occupied the center of the area.

Pascal's office occupied the far corner. The bulk of the gallery was across the way, past the top of the stairs. Two black, moveable art display panels were placed in a rough L-shape about five feet apart, creating corridors on either side. The art was lit by track lights.

I veered to the right and scurried down the aisle between the display panel and the wall. Exactly as the blueprints indicated, three humidity-controlled display cases were lined up in the middle of the room. Built-in bookcases took up the back wall, and recessed lights on each shelf glowed upon the items. I did a double take.

Holy shit.

Pascal's collection of puzzle boxes occupied every single shelf.

"Made the gallery," I whispered and made a beeline for the bookshelves. With my fingers over the lens of my flashlight to reduce the glare, I scanned the shelves and came up with a big fat zero. Familiar disappointment coursed through me.

"Uh oh," Ursula said, startling me out of my puzzle box fixation. "Pascal and another dude are headed upstairs."

I faded into the shadows where I could still see the top of the staircase. Pascal appeared, stopped on the landing, and spoke to someone coming up behind him. "I've got three Maxes. *Profile*, *Better World*, and *Liberty 1986*."

"Very nice." Pascal's companion joined him on the landing. He sounded kind of like Tom Selleck of *Magnum PI* and *Blue Bloods*, but was lacking about a foot-and-a-half of height. "I've been hunting for years for an original Peter Max *Better World*. Might you consider selling?"

"Depending on the offer, maybe. They're right over here." Pascal led his potential buyer to the right, away from me and out of my sight line.

"You can see I'm not kidding about my inventory."

I scuttled forward and ducked behind the waist-high railing that encircled three quarters of the stairway. Now I could see Pascal and his buyer behind the couch, backs to me, surveying the artwork on the wall.

"No," Not Tom Selleck said, "you're not kidding. You've amassed quite a collection."

"Thank you. Over here are the Maxes I have. As you can see, *Better World* is pristine."

Silence.

I imagined the buyer studying the piece.

"It is. I'll give you twenty thousand."

Holy shitballs.

"Twenty grand is a drop in the painter's pallet, my good friend. How about twenty-five?"

"Let's split the difference and call it twenty-two-five?"

"Deal." Pascal answered faster than I'd expected. "Come on, let's toast to your new acquisition."

I wondered about the authenticity of the work. Hopefully Not Tom Selleck wasn't about to get bait-and-switched as Elizabet had, but my expectations were low.

Heavy steps faded as they returned to the party.

"Pascal's back," Urs said. "Sorry about that. Things move fast down here."

"It's okay," I whispered. "Anyone else headed my way?"

"Not at the moment."

"Copy." I pivoted away from the railing and crept to the closest case. All of the cases were lighted from within, so I could easily see the contents. The first item on the top shelf was a Teddy Roosevelt letter to his son, Quentin. Five additional documents weren't letters. I scanned the other shelves, no luck. I flipped around to the other side. All comic books.

I moved on. The next case held a number of handwritten documents. The pulse in my neck thrummed harder.

On to the last case.

The first item on the top shelf? The goddamn Helen Keller letter.

Holy freaking shit.

The keypad on the side of the case glowed red. From the backpack, I withdrew a leather portfolio. From it I removed the forgery. I flipped it over, and something on the back caught my eye. I angled the paper at the lighting within the case. "Love, Elizabet" had been written in pencil.

I stifled a laugh. "I've got the letter. Coop, cut the alarm."

"Hang on," he responded.

Seconds crawled by. The red light blinked once, twice, then went out. A green light popped on. I raised the lid, lifted out the original Keller letter and replaced it with the fake. I slipped the original into the folder and closed the case. "Hit it, Coop."

"Ten seconds."

One long breath and the green light winked out and red glowed steadily.

"Reactivated." Elation colored Coop's tone. When this was over I had no doubt Pascal would be in the market for a better security system. Now all I had to do was get out. I grabbed my backpack, retraced my steps. I was five feet from the rear stairs when a loud whooping stopped me cold.

"The alarm in the office was just triggered." Coop spoke rapidly. "It wasn't you, Flynn. I suggest everyone gets out. Now."

I hit the top of the stairway. The noise of the alarm made it hard to hear.

Urs said, "I'm out."

"Char," Joey said. "Status?"

"Headed to my car."

"Flynn." Joey's voice was growing more strained by the second.

"Almost to the bottom of the—" Two steps away from the hall leading to freedom, something smashed into me from behind. I bounced off the wall, almost fell down the last step, and caught myself on the kitchen doorframe. A figure dressed in black streaked past me out the back door. It took a stunned moment to realize my backpack was no longer in my hand. It wasn't on the hallway floor or on the staircase. It wasn't anywhere.

Oh, hell no.

My stolen letter had just been hijacked. Fuck that.

I burst out of the house, leaped down the steps. Caught sight of the thief in black disappearing into the woods. I charged along the pool fence toward the trees. Not one partier appeared to notice what was happening and didn't care a bit about the shrill whooping of the alarm.

"Flynn. Flynn, do you copy?" Joey's voice was now dead calm. That was his panic mode, but I had no time to explain.

"Hold on," was all I managed as I concentrated on where I'd seen the thief disappear into the woods. I hit the wood line and stopped. The sounds of someone crashing through brush and undergrowth came from dead ahead.

I took off into the forest, playing dodge 'em with branches I couldn't see, leaping over fallen timber if I saw it in time, silently swearing if I didn't. I was going to have very bruised shins when this was over. I gritted my teeth and pushed on.

Even if I couldn't breathe and was likely to break a leg, I felt fucking incredible .

Aware.

In tune.

God, I'd missed this.

My mugger burst into a clearing some twenty feet ahead, silhouetted by moonlight as he dashed across the open space. I flew out of the trees, gaining on him with every step. He was shorter than me and couldn't run worth shit.

I pumped my arms and gritted my teeth, gaining ground fast. I'd be damned if I would let someone rip off my rip-off.

Three more strides and I leaped. We both went down hard, thrashing through long grass. I caught a shoulder strap of my backpack and yanked.

The little bastard had a tight grip, but I had arm length. I pulled him toward me using the strap as leverage. When I got him in range, I clocked him with a solid roundhouse to the face.

He grunted, let go of the pack as he fell.

I scrambled to my feet, tossing the backpack somewhere behind me. My brain told me to get the hell out now, but any good sense I had evaporated in the heat of the melee. I wanted—needed—to kick some ass. It never occurred to me my ass could be the one that was kicked.

He regained his feet and backed up.

I advanced.

He dropped low and lunged, driving his shoulder into my midsection. I twisted, deflected most of the impact. As he sailed past I gave him a hard shove. He stumbled to a knee, then was up and coming at me again.

My breath came in short, hard pants. Everything shifted into slow motion.

I attempted a sidestep but timed it wrong. He barreled into me and down we went. We tumbled across the meadow, both of us grappling for the upper hand.

The bastard was a squirmy little fucker. He managed to get on top of me, wrapped the fingers of one hand around my throat, and tried to hammer my face with the other.

I blocked the flurry of punches with one arm and used the other to seize the cloth on top of his head. If I could catch his hair beneath the facemask I could use it to leverage him away.

Instead of snagging hair, the entire mask slid over his head and came off in my hand.

I froze. He froze.

Staring down at me were the fine-boned features of a woman under a dark mess of hair.

I squinted into the shadows of her face. So damn familiar. Then physiological memory hit me in a rush. My insides clenched. "Dante?"

CHAPTER TWENTY-THREE

She inhaled raggedly. I couldn't see her eyes but I could feel her gaze.

"Yes." Her voice was tight, low, and immediately recognizable.

Thoughts flew through my head faster than a Vegas card dealer dishing cards out to players. She couldn't know about the Keller letter, could she? Did I say something about it during our tryst? I had no memory of doing so, but considering the amount of liquor I'd swilled, who the hell knew.

Her breathing slowed. "I can't believe you, of all people, are after the rock too. Did you get it?"

"Rock?"

"The Hatton Garden emerald. Who's paying you?"

The alarm that had been screeching in the background abruptly stopped. The absence of noise was stunning.

"I'm not after any rock and no one is paying me."

"Right." The disbelief was clear.

Dogs barked in the distance. Fuck. The Dobermans. "I'm not. I'd prove it but we don't have time. We have to get out of here."

She backed off me and I scrambled to my feet. Where was the backpack? After a frantic second I spotted it, scooped it up, and bolted in what I hoped was the direction of the barn.

Behind me I could hear Dante's harsh breathing. "Hey, wait up."

I slowed. "Are you crazy? The dogs are about to tear us apart."

"Dogs?"

If she was a thief, what the hell kind of thief didn't do their homework before a break-in? "Yes. Dobermans." I moved through the trees, trying to avoid getting tangled in anything that might slow me down.

I burst out of the woods, Dante still on my heels. Crossed the driveway to the to the barn, and reentered the shelter of the thicket on the other side. If we could—wait a minute. Why was I thinking in terms of "we"?

Shouts in the distance diverted my attention. The barking was getting louder.

We circled toward the back of the barn and guesthouse. Escape was now only a few hundred feet away.

A grunt from behind made me glance back to see the dark silhouette of Dante's feet sailing through the air. She landed with an audible thud and didn't move.

Crap.

Keep going or backtrack? I didn't owe her anything. And the little shit tried to steal my letter.

Aw, hell. I couldn't leave her like that. I spun around and dashed toward her. Sometimes I'm a sucker for a damsel in distress, even if she tried to mug me.

She looked up with wide eyes. "Goddamn...root."

I held out a hand and pulled her up. Then we were off again. The barking was insanely loud.

My escape route was now only fifty feet away. I gunned it, streaking into the shadows behind the barn. The relief in seeing the rope still dangling where I'd left it made my legs feel rubbery.

I hit the wall and leaped, using the rope as leverage to scrabble my way to the top. I balanced myself in time to see the Dobermans race around the corner of the barn. Their black eyes locked on and their high-pitched yips ricocheted off the fence like an auditory pinball.

Dante was only halfway up.

I reached down and held out a hand. She grabbed it. I jerked her up as the dogs hit the wall. The pack leaped upward, as if their back legs were springs, howling loud enough to wake the undead.

I left Dante crouched on the brick as I leaped to the ground on the other side, rolling with the impact. I scrambled to my feet, wished Dante some mental luck, and took off through the trees like an Olympic triathlete.

* * *

"I can't believe we pulled it off," Char said as we filed into Tubs' apartment.

"But we did." I withdrew the portfolio with the Keller letter and laid it on the coffee table.

Ursula held up a hand and I slapped it. "I thought Flynn was a goner for sure when that alarm went off."

"Me too." I pulled up my pant legs to inspect the damage to my shins. Scraped and bruised.

Joey guzzled his third bottle of water and crushed the plastic container between his palms. "I tell you what. It's harder than I imagined being the communications guy. Was ready to melt down a few times, but damn, that was a good time. Ursula, you were right. Coop is everything you said he was."

"He's a good man," she said. "Bit of an oddball, but has his shit down."

"Wait till Elizabet hears the news," Tubs said. "Too bad she couldn't get out of work tonight. She would have loved it.

Mikala, you are something." Tubs squeezed my shoulder and kissed the top of my head, making me feel like I was eleven again. I didn't even try to pull away.

My mind was still flying, but my body was crashing fast and craving hard. I excused myself to the bathroom and on the way made a pit stop for a couple fast ounces.

I'd finished recapping the bottle and was about to tuck it back in the drawer when Joey rolled through the door. "Flynn. Really?"

I stashed the bottle under some jeans, slid the drawer shut, and turned to face him. "Nothing wrong with a little pick-me-up."

He scowled.

A lecture was the last thing I wanted. I was still edgy and knew it wouldn't take a lot to push me too far. "Don't, okay? Not now."

We held each other's gaze. It was a stalemate until he looked away with a frustrated sigh. "I wanted to talk to you earlier, but we didn't have time."

"About?" The suspicion in my tone was laughable, but I couldn't help it.

"Ursula."

Uh oh. "What's up?"

His scowl faded, replaced by a smile. "She found me a place. Big enough for this thing," he whacked the wheel of his chair, "and my sis and kids."

Totally the last thing I expected to hear, and I tried hard to shift gears. "Joey, that's great. After all the shitholes we looked at, I was beginning to wonder if we shouldn't move everyone in here." The alcohol was burrowing into my veins. It felt so damn good.

"It's a three-bedroom in her building. Happened to come vacant at the right time. We can move in next week."

"That's great. I'm really happy for you." I gave him a hug and stepped back.

"Tubs volunteered you to help with the move." His eyes sparkled.

"Of course I will. But right now I have to use the bathroom, and then I'll fill you guys in about the last five minutes of my escape."

* * *

After I tucked the rest of Char's roasts in the freezer and Tubs secreted the Keller letter safely in her closet, we settled in the living room. Tubs and Char sat on the couch, Ursula claimed the love seat, Joey had his chair, and I sat on the floor with my back up against a cushion next to the fireplace.

Tubs broke out some snacks, and we dug into two family-sized bags of Old Dutch Ripple Chips and her homemade French onion dip while we shared our experiences of the night. I told them about Dante but gave a sanitized version of how we met.

Tubs pinched her chin thoughtfully. "She said she was after the Hatton Garden emerald?"

"Yup," I mumbled, mouth full of chips.

"What is that?" Ursula stifled a yawn. We were all winding down fast.

"One second, Ursula," Char said. "Tubs, you think Pascal has it?"

"Don't know, but I wouldn't put it past him. Tell them the story."

Never would I have expected either Tubs or Char to have any knowledge of this weird emerald business, and I didn't know jack shit about it myself.

Char said, "It was one of Britain's biggest jewelry heists ever."

"Worth millions in jewels, gold and silver, cash, and other items no one knows anything about," Tubs said. "The news called it a crime of 'epic proportions.' And guess what. Four geezers masterminded the whole caper. We should hook up with them."

"Did they catch 'em?" Joey asked.

"All but one," Tubs said. "Two-thirds of the loot is still missing. Part of the missing booty is an emerald that had been mined in Brazil. Three people were killed trying to bring it to market, and it became known as the Emerald of Death. A brave Israeli investment broker bought it. The broker sold it to a London businessman after he was diagnosed with pancreatic cancer."

"That doesn't feel like very good odds to me," I said. "What happened to it then?"

"The London buyer was plagued with mysterious maladies for over a year and decided to take the emerald out of his home and put it in the Hatton Garden Safe Deposit vault." Tubs shivered. "I would want that thing nowhere near me."

Char said, "Speculation about the emerald occasionally pops up, which is why we're aware of it, and, according to Beni, it does in law enforcement circles too. I'd sure like to know where your friend got her information."

"She's not my friend, but after hearing all that, I'd like a crack at asking her a few questions. I doubt I'll ever see her again after tonight's escapades, though. I never would've dreamed she was a burglar."

After more discussion, things wound down and Char and Ursula bid us good night.

With much relief I lay down on the couch. My muscles were sore and I was exhausted, but my mind was still spinning. Old-guy bandits, a cursed emerald, Dante, the Keller letter. Gnarly Dobermans. What an insane day, beginning with my hangover from hell and ending with a successful Operation Retrieve Helen.

I wondered if Dante escaped. If she had been taken down, she could rat me out to cut a deal. But really, she didn't know my name. Did she know anything else that could identify me? Nothing I could think of. Was I missing something?

For an hour I tossed and turned, trying to clear my mind. It was impossible. What I needed was the oblivion liquor could give, but my body was too fried to leave the apartment to get it. The bottle of vodka in my dresser beckoned like a beacon. I threw off the quilt and sat up, head in my hands. Maybe I could sneak into my bedroom and grab it without waking Joey.

The worst that would happen was that he'd catch me and bitch, but then he'd already done that tonight. I found myself slinking down the hall, taking care to avoid the creaky parts of the wood floor. The door to my bedroom was partially closed and the room was dark. Joey wasn't a snorer, so it was a fifty-fifty shot he was asleep.

With a silent sigh, I moved on down the hall and shut myself in the bathroom. I used the facilities, washed and dried my hands, and thought about it. The dresser containing my booze was only few feet inside my room. I could go all ninja and hope I was stealthy enough not to wake Joey. I leaned against the counter and considered what I was considering. What was wrong with me? Could I not make it through one stinking night without a drink? Or more to drink, actually. Okay, so I was using alcohol as a crutch. Did I care? Did it matter? The refrain, "I could cut alcohol out of my life anytime I wanted," swirled around my mind like a vortex.

I could totally quit drinking if I so chose.

Couldn't I?

Really, what was the harm, except to my liver, if it helped keep the monsters in my head at bay? Drinking kept me sane in some twisted way. The phrase "monsters in my head" made me think of Detective Hamilton and her PTSD group. Hell, I didn't need that, either. I didn't have PTSD.

Did I?

Why was all this doubt creeping in? Come on, Flynn, stop analyzing yourself. Get a grip, I told myself. You're fine. March yourself back out to the couch.

I bypassed my bedroom and the contents that were singing my song. I laid back down and stared at the ceiling until sleep eventually won.

CHAPTER TWENTY-FOUR

"That's it." Joey dropped the last box next to his chair. "Thanks, Urs, and have a good practice."

"Later. I'll pop in when I'm done. Text if you need anything." Ursula exited with a wave.

We'd spent the afternoon moving Joey into his new digs three floors above Ursula's garden-level apartment. The place had wide halls and an elevator that functioned and didn't smell like urine.

Joey had accumulated a bit more than he'd had when he arrived at Tubs' door, but it still wasn't much. We cleared out a storage locker he'd rented years ago and carted a dozen boxes, an old full-sized bed, a dresser, and a wobbly card table with two folding chairs sixteen blocks with two hand trucks and a red Radio Flyer wagon borrowed from Joey's nephews.

The apartment itself was more spacious than I expected and had been recently upgraded with new paint and appliances. The counters were still higher than Joey liked, but he could work with it. He was delighted the bathroom was roomy enough he could actually turn around, and all the doorways were wide enough to accommodate his chair.

LaKeisha and the boys wouldn't move in until they'd packed up their old place, which was going to be a challenge since Joey and LaKeisha's mom had lived there for thirty-five years. I figured Joey could use some days of peace and quiet to prepare himself for their arrival anyway.

The hard ball of guilt I'd carried since Aleppo had softened, I realized as I surveyed the mostly empty living room. The hardwood floor was worn, the radiator was painted school bus yellow, and two large windows overlooked the side of another building. The apartment might not have the best view, but it would be filled with a whole lot of love.

I dropped into one of the chairs at the card table we'd set up. "You owe me pizza. Tomorrow."

Joey rolled up to the table. "I can order up a pie right now."

I was hot and tired and the apartment wasn't air-conditioned. What I really wanted was a cold beer or three. "No, tomorrow's good. Give you a chance to get used to the place."

I could feel his eyes on me. I raised my head to meet his gaze, which was surprisingly intense. "What?"

"You want to get out of here and find yourself a bar somewhere, don't you?"

Not much use in lying. "Maybe. One with air."

"Can't fault you for that." He sighed. "Look. Your drinking is a way to combat the crazy spinning in your head. I know that. You know that."

This was the last thing I wanted to discuss and he goddamn well knew it. We'd had a great day. I wanted to keep it that way. I pushed the chair back from the table and stood. "See you tomorrow about noon for that promised pie." I headed for the front door.

"Come on, Flynn."

I whirled on him. "I can take care of myself, Joey. If I need help, I'll let you know, okay?" I pulled a deep breath, let it out slow, and in a more even tone said, "It was an awesome day. I don't want to leave like this."

"You know I care, right?" The earnest expression on his face broke my heart. "I love you like a sister."

"Jesus. Did you have to pull that card? I know, okay? And I love you too."

"But you're still gonna go."

"I'm still gonna go." The pull to run was strong. So strong.

"Fine. Get out of here then, twitchy woman. Tomorrow is the Thursday two for one at the pizzeria down the street." He balled up some newspaper and whipped it at my head, a half-smile creasing his face as I ducked out of the way and it flew out into the hallway.

Like a proper adult, I stuck out my tongue at him. "Tomorrow, then." I pulled the door closed and picked up the wadded newspaper, distracted by Thursday. What was it about Thursday?

As I waited for the elevator, the thought solidified. The memory of the firefighter talking to us rushed in, filled gaps, and shocked the shit out of me.

Kate and the dog. And me. On Thursday. At four? No. Four thirty.

Holy shit.

I was going to see Kate tomorrow. I didn't know if the meeting was going to be good or bad, but I did realize it gave me an opportunity to apologize. Face-to-face. To take her anger and upset as the direct hit I so deserved.

It was then I realized a part of me was excited just to be next to her, breathing the same air. It was terrifying and exhilarating all at the same time.

On the elevator ride down I let the thought of tomorrow slip into the background as Joey's words insistently banged against my brain. His comment about the crazy in my head wouldn't stop. Was I a fool to think I could tame my issues without help? But I had help. Help in a bottle. I knew it was nothing more than a temporary fix, but it was enough. Wasn't it?

I sounded like a broken fucking record and I goddamn well knew it. The elevator crept downward about an inch a minute. I stuck my hands in my pockets, the fingers of my right hand recognizing the feel of Hamilton's card. Why hadn't I tossed it long ago?

The elevator doors finally slid open. I stepped out and aside to let a mom with a stroller in, then exited onto the street. Faceless pedestrians streamed along the steamy sidewalks, and cars passed by, one after another after another. The world kept moving no matter what. No matter the injustices, the tragedies, the hurt. We were all together on this circus ride called life whether we liked it or not.

Across the road, a homeless guy in a pea green army jacket slept huddled in the doorway of a closed storefront. Had the crazy in his head become too much to handle? Did he run out of options to tame the beast?

That man could be me. I could be him. Grudgingly, I acknowledged I was walking a high wire with my life, one misstep away from losing everything.

Then a second realization burned its way into me.

I wanted to live. Really live. Without the false comfort alcohol provided. Tubs and the whole Art Squad were back in my life, so were Joey and Ursula. It blew my mind that Kate was still single. I wondered if—barring her hurt and anger—she missed me as much as I missed her. That was a pompous-ass thought, and I knew it. I knew she was furious, but I also knew her fury would fizzle soon enough, and we could maybe actually talk once we were in close proximity, thanks to Mr. Bones. I wondered if I could fix the biggest mistake of my life. Would she allow herself to trust me again? Did I deserve it? Probably not.

Especially not if I kept on with the sauce, that was certain. In the end, if nothing else, I prayed she'd at least allow me to make amends. And I needed to do the same with Tub and Joey. I'd been a first-class tool for too long, and they both had put up with my shenanigans. Hell, maybe down the road there might be a Hatton Garden emerald to think about. Which reminded me of Dante. She brought up way more questions than answers, and I had enough on my overloaded plate.

Tears threatened and then overflowed. Fucking defective waterworks. I swiped at my eyes and looked again at the homeless guy, so lost and so utterly alone.

I pulled Hamilton's card out of my pocket. It was so worn and creased the information on it was barely visible. This was only a first step, but I had to start somewhere. I took a deep breath and punched the numbers into my phone.

Bella Books, Inc.

Women. Books. Even Better Together.

P.O. Box 10543
Tallahassee, FL 32302

Phone: 800-729-4992
www.bellabooks.com

CPSIA information can be obtained
at www.ICGtesting.com
Printed in the USA
LVHW010822170120
643905LV00002B/2

9 781594 935695